The Devil At Four O'Clock

The
Devil
At
Four O'Clock

By MAX CATTO
Author of *Gold in the Sky*

William Morrow & Company, New York
1959

For Dr. J. E. Naftalin

It is hard for a man to be brave
when he knows he is going to meet
the devil at four o'clock.
—Spanish Proverb

Part
One

1

THE island of Taluha blew itself out of the Pacific one morning in March. It went up with fissionable fury; the tidal wave it started lifted ships in distant Indonesian harbors eighty feet above sea level; there must have been an element of insane comedy (after the dead were counted, for there is never much comedy in death) in the sight of six-hundred-ton freighters stranded on green hillsides like toys washed out of a baby's bath.

It took four months for the dust of the disintegrated island to creep round the stratosphere to Europe, but London and Paris got some remarkably lurid sunsets out of it. It became quite fashionable to dine on the Eiffel Tower in late August to watch those unnaturally molten green-and-crimson skies.

When the survivors were landed at Tahiti I flew out from San Francisco to cover the story for the magazine *Now*. The colonists—for the island had been a French dependency (presumably the jagged stump left of it still is) —had had forty-eight hours' warning of the er·ption; they had all been got off to Tahiti in time. I took with me two photographers and our line-wash artist, David Metzger. The cameras were too late to record the eruption, but I could trust David to re-create the blow-up from the descriptions of the survivors.

Actually, he improved considerably on nature's crudely inartistic attempt.

(He said with easy candor, rather surprisingly, for he was a devout uncynical Jew, "Give me a brush and a few

sticks of charcoal and I'll always go one better than God."
Just the same, I noticed that unconsciously he came to
terms with God: he gave his sketches the Biblically fiery
Sodom-and-Gomorrah touch.)

We interviewed the survivors in Papeete. They were
suffering, most of them, from delayed shock. Maybe it was
the loss of their homes, the dissolution of their community
. . . a lot of them had been born on the island, France was
no more than a tie of blood and administration to them.
They told us about the eruption in flat, starkly realistic
terms: embroidering nothing, plucking absently with their
fingers, the women shivering a little—staring out across the
Pacific as if searching for the pumice fragments of their
shattered island. It was possible to get out of their stories
the authentic stench of burning lava, the cap of the volcano exploding, embers raining out of the sky, the solid
green earth quivering and heaving as if the whole island
were coming to the boil (as indeed it did, boiling over like
scalded milk). They were a solitary community, a blob on
the ocean, six hundred miles from the nearest source of
help—the island's only value was that it was a radio-telephone station linking the chain of French dependencies
from New Caledonia to Papeete.

They were good photographic material, all except the
children. How do you get children—to whom a natural
catastrophe is just an overlarge and momentarily exciting
game—to suffer convincingly for the camera?

Then we came to interview the Governor. And that was
when the story really began: for there was something
hidden under the theatrical froth of the event. Perhaps
David Metzger communicated it to me—he was abnormally
perceptive—but even I began to have the feeling that there
was a peculiar withdrawal about these people, an uneasiness, an evasion, something they didn't care to speak
about. I don't think they were cunning or devious—no

more cunning, no more devious, than ordinarily human Frenchmen you meet in Montmartre or Provence. It was just that they had shut their minds to something painful. A kind of mental renunciation. Maybe it weighed heavily on them.

An iceberg shows only a fraction of its bulk above the surface; I smelled a large amount of submerged iceberg. A reporter develops a psychiatrist's nose.

We photographed the Governor. He didn't object to that. But he did object inexplicably to David's sketching him; David sat in the corner, watching him, silent but for the scratch of his charcoal; the Governor kept swiveling away from him, so that in the end all that was presented to the artist was the back of an implacable head. I gathered that he didn't like David. (Why? Did he scent an inquisitive antagonist?) The Governor was a veteran of the Indo-Chinese and Algerian wars; a small brown colonel with pale blue eyes, cold and desiccated; I think he was ridden fantastically with caste. He said dryly—as if delivering a communiqué after a reasonably successful retreat:

"Everything went well." (The eruption, presumably, went best of all.) "The community behaved magnificently. There was no panic. None at all. There had never been an eruption on the island in recorded history in the Pacific. But there was no doubt in our minds that it was now about to occur. Fortunately there were two freighters and a schooner in the harbor. By a lucky coincidence there was also the seaplane that was to take me on leave. We organized the withdrawal on a strictly military basis: the sick and the children first. Once we were at sea there was great danger from the tidal wave that followed," and for a moment the Governor stared emptily at the Pacific through the window, recollecting the vast racing wall of water: he had achieved another victory.

5

With the economic satisfaction of a staff officer, content with a bloodless triumph, he added, "We survived that, too."

He had said his set piece; he thought he was finished, he stood up waiting for us to go. But David whispered to me, in English, "Ask him if everybody got away."

I asked it. The Governor said colorlessly, "The natives —the Melanesians—had an instinct about it. Some folk-memory of an old eruption. They did not wait for us to remove them. They left in their own canoes."

"And the rest?"

"I have already informed you. The colonists withdrew."

David asked him quietly, "And are we to understand that nobody was left behind?"

The Governor walked to the door, then he turned and gave David a bitter glance. "Did I say that?"

"No, Governor, you didn't. What would you choose to say?"

"Four men remained on the island."

"Why?"

"It was their own decision. It was against my express wishes. They chose to return to the hospital."

"Who were they?" asked David softly.

"An Irish priest named Father Doonan. And three condemned criminals."

And he went out, walking away from the cold spreading ripple of shock, murmuring bleakly as if it absolved him—was that how Pilate washed his hands?—"I was not responsible. They were aware of the danger. A report has been rendered to the proper authorities."

I said to David quickly, "What's all this about?"

"Haven't you felt it? They've all got a guilt-complex like a hang-over. It's a mile wide."

"Well, what's behind it?"

"Why ask me? I'm only the artist. Get them on the

couch and talk to them. Prod them a little, it'll all come spilling out."

"This Father Doonan and the—" I boggled over the word "criminals." The association with a priest was faintly ridiculous—"how did you get wind of them?"

"How did the dog get wind of the fox? By sniffing around." Suddenly David grinned, "You want to see them?" and I stared at him stupidly, visualizing the last boiling flash of the island, melting the four men's bones away to nothing; what was he talking about? "I managed to get rough descriptions of them," said David, taking four sketches out of his pad. "Some of the survivors are getting attacks of conscience. They're beginning to talk. They even helped me to pull things into shape. They say they're not bad likenesses, at that." And he slid the first sketch into my hand.

I found myself looking down at a round humorous face, deftly penciled, snub-nosed, with rapt anxious eyes. David was watching me covertly: he was detaching himself from it already—the baby was mine and he was depositing it gently in my lap. He said, "That's Father Doonan. Part bog-Irish, part mystic. The doctor from the hospital said he was born to be crucified." I was still staring at the sketch; the humorously earnest features didn't seem to be the Calvary type. "We have Jews like that," said David. "Dangerous primitives, always trying to get behind the sham scenery of the religion to see why they can't make the drama come true." He pushed another of the sketches into my hand.

But I still held on to the one of Father Doonan. I don't know why it affected me; it was like watching a man crawl out of the coffin that should decently have held him.

"What happened to him?" I asked.

"I don't know. I didn't get that far."

7

I said obstinately—I was getting involved, I knew it, and David knew it too—"Well, where did he come from?"

"That I can tell you. He used to be a parish priest in a dockside tenement district of New York."

I looked at the second sketch. The brusque pencil lines showed a worried drawn face, a little sly, a little watchful; David had worked, probably intentionally, a kind of derisive quirk into the corners of the mouth. I guessed him to be about thirty; a badly worn thirty. "That's Harry Frobisher," David said. "An Australian, they thought. He never told them. Why should he? With his history, maybe it was safer to let them find out for themselves. He was doing four years with the other two for manslaughter. At least, they thought it was manslaughter. There'd been a brawl in a saloon in New Caledonia, and a Melanesian bartender was killed. I don't think they really knew who'd done it, but they were three troublemakers and it was a chance to get rid of them. They were going to Tahiti in the seaplane to serve their sentence; they'd just stopped off at the island."

David waited for me to absorb it: he said gently, "Rather bad luck on them, wasn't it?" And then he gave me the next sketch.

A plump, impudent face; thickened and wary and middle-aged. The face of a Montparnasse butcher. David had caught him, rather unkindly, with a boozily sexual joke on his lips. Chattily, like the guide in a museum, David said, "And that's Marcel. They never got to know his real name. That kind of Frenchman in a French colony'd be too damned careful to tell them more than it was good for them to know. You couldn't trust a native woman within fifty yards of him, they said."

Then the last sketch came into my hand. A Negro; the lips less spatulate than usual, the nose less compressed, nicely chiseled actually, a lazily composed face: but black,

8

shinily black. "That's Charlie," said David. "Just Charlie. No more to him than that. He said he came from Iowa. Maybe he did—within a thousand miles of it or thereabouts. He was six feet six inches tall, they told me, a black heavyweight showpiece of a man.

"And there you are," David ended up lightly. "The rogues' gallery." He added quickly, seeing my expression, "Not including the priest, of course."

I riffled once more through the sketches. The four faces, slickly penciled, three of them so carefully anonymous, peered at me from behind the equalizing mask of death. I wondered what they had really looked like. What had happened to them? Why had the Governor's face emptied itself of its guilt? Why had they chosen to go back to the hospital? And *what* hospital? David was still watching me shrewdly. He knew that I wouldn't let go of the thing now; one way or another I'd ferret something out.

I said to him, shrugging, "Can I hang on to them for a while?"

"Keep them," he said carelessly. "I've finished with them." He looked satisfied. Something about the business had obviously griped him; he'd purged himself of it smartly, passing the bellyache on to me. "Just to save you time," he said, "if you're interested, talk to the seaplane pilot. He's about ready to open up. There's a fat little truck driver named Aristide. He may cost a few drinks. And there's the doctor I told you about from the hospital. Have a word with the Matron, too."

I found the seaplane pilot in a bar. He was a chunkily muscular, wooden-faced Parisian. He wore a short leather jacket. "My bum-freezer," he smiled conversationally, before he knew what I wanted. The antique seaplane he flew had belonged to the Americans. They'd left it behind in the Pacific. They'd used the island for base-hopping operations during the war. He was the least emotional of

9

them all, and I thought I'd have most trouble with him. In fact, he yielded up his part of the story quite easily.

"So you have begun to ask questions about it, have you? Well, it is a bad business." He let me buy him a beer and he played uneasily with his glass. "It has weighed on me. It reflects no credit on any of us." Suddenly—bluntly and wryly—he faced up to his conscience. He said, "All right, ask your questions. What do you want to know?"

Then Aristide, the fat little truck driver. He had to be tracked down through three bistros. His type you see driving the smelly *essence* trucks along the Boulevard Haussmann, fighting an unending war with traffic signals and shrilling cops, drooping eyes and derisive: *I hate the combustion engine, treat the thing like a woman, the big stick, a little affection, then let her signpost her own way to hell.* Aristide was that kind, except that he'd always take time off to watch a pretty girl cross the road, making a swift sculptural appraisal of her bosom—and not gallantly, either, just feeling it anatomically. He was a greasily pungent man (absinthe and garlic). His part of the story cost three brandies. He was stubborn; at first he wouldn't even discuss it.

What was the sense, he protested sullenly, in dragging up dead men now?

"The priest will have got to heaven by now," he shrugged. "If he has any influence up there he will have smuggled the three roughnecks in with him. If not, you know where to find them. They will be below. I am prepared to gamble a thousand francs that that is where they are." But he didn't really think it very funny; he didn't bother to laugh.

"What did you have against Father Doonan?" I asked him.

Absinthe and brandy don't mix very well. He just

screwed his eyes at me. "Have against him? But that is ridiculous. Nothing at all."

"Then why are you depriving him of his existence? You're wiping him out of life as if he'd never been. You're robbing him of his name." I guessed that he was a Catholic, and he was; when I said, "Isn't that a mortal sin?" it shook him. That was the moment for the last drink.

He muttered, "I didn't think of it like that." By now he was half maudlin. A hard word and he'd have come to tears. "Just tell me what you want to know."

Dr. Wexler, from the hospital, was a wizened elfin Austrian of about sixty. An aloof, cynical man—maybe he had reason to be? Later they told me he'd been hunted out of prewar Vienna. He had the abundant hair of an Einstein and the worn dispassionate profile that looks good on an old coin. He said coolly, once he knew what I was after, "Why not leave them alone? What good can come of digging into the business?" and I thought, 'Oh, no, Doctor, you're not going to get away with that . . .'

"Didn't you like Father Doonan?"

"Very much. Oddly enough, I liked all four of them. The three vagabonds, too."

"And you owed them something, didn't you?"

He crinkled, "As much as a man of my age can value it, yes, I owed them my life. Did they ask you to resurrect them? Why not let them lie? They are dead."

"They're dead," I persisted. "But where is their memorial?" He looked at me sharply. I think for a brief shocked moment he was seeing again the scalding eruption of the island, dissolving the four men away vaporously: nothing left of them, not even a memorial. (Perhaps that'll be the real cruelty of the hydrogen bomb, flushing us all away to nothingness.) "Very well," he said meekly. And he opened up; I couldn't have got more out of him if I'd dug into him with a pick.

There are some people who can reconstruct an animal from its jawbone. David had started by slipping me the jawbone; now I had the whole animal, the guts and the skeleton and the flesh. Dr. Wexler turned out to be the keystone of the story. He was the one who'd come down the burning mountain with the others, smelling lava, running from hot ashes, seeing the obsessive determination of Father Doonan leading the procession of the children, and the frantically confused heroism of—as he fondly called them—the three vagabonds. And when he'd finished he said ironically, "So what are you going to do with them? Let your magazine editor butcher them to make a Roman holiday? Fake some spectacular pictures? Blow them up into heroes? They weren't heroes; three of them weren't even honest. I wouldn't have left a franc on the table while they were about. They were just unnaturally good men."

But he knew by now that I wouldn't do anything with the story; there was the wrong kind of echo about it. It would have haunted me forever from the other side of the brain.

Dr. Wexler said, "They've gone. Utterly. Not even a bone, not a solitary knuckle left of them. The best thing we can do for them is let them have the gift of silence. They deserve a little something from us."

I took the story to David. I knew now why he'd preferred sensitively to stay on the fringe of it. He said gently, "Well, what are you going to do with it?" Keep it for my scrapbook, I shrugged . . . "Never mind," he grinned consolingly. "Think of all the local color you've got. A hundred and six interesting survivors. Snatched straight from the jaws of death. And ten dramatic photographs of the Governor. All right, let's forget it. I'll give you some damned good drawings that'll do the Metropolitan Museum of Art proud."

And he did.

So the story had pieced itself together: and to what purpose? What a strange, troubling story it was. For a long time it wouldn't crawl out of my mind. Then one day I looked at it and I thought: 'Well, at least, there's my private memorial to Father Doonan and the three forgotten bums, Harry Frobisher and Marcel and Charlie.' And not a bad memorial, at that. Here it is.

Part
Two

Part

Two

2

WE came in with the dusk (began the pilot), flying low, searching for the island. And very nearly we didn't make it. We had a new navigator, a boy with a Sorbonne education. He was as delicate as a surgeon with his sextant, he could plot you a course like Picasso on the chart, and he couldn't find his own way to the toilet in the dark. Me—I point my nose crudely across the Pacific and smell my way from island to island. I haven't lost an aircraft yet.

You know how dusk comes to the Pacific? One moment the sun is hanging on the horizon like a fireball and the sea is shimmering like hot milk; the next the sun has toppled over the edge of the world and there is nothing but empty ocean and cold gray stain below. When you are running low on gas the outlook for an aircraft is equally gray. I said to the navigator rather coldly, "What do we do now? Swim to China?" but the co-pilot suddenly saw the island and pointed. "Don't curdle your insides. There it is."

I saw a thin humped shadow rippling on the sea. It looked like the half-shell of a walnut. Twenty minutes later and you could have lost it on a dinner plate.

We went peeling round in a wide circuit, our engines growling like a dog that has seen a bone, flattening out, preparing to touch down in the lagoon.

It was a very old seaplane—as seaplanes go, almost as old as Methuselah. Most civilized people, as an act of charity, would have written it off as junk. We French have no charity toward old mechanical contrivances. We make

17

them work best of all. We were *en route* to Tahiti. We were breaking our journey at the island to pick up the Governor, who was going on leave. He would have some pretty unusual and discomfiting passengers: the three prisoners who were going to serve their no doubt deserved four-year sentence in a filthy Tahiti jail. They were probably not very dangerous, but the cramped fuselage of an aircraft is no place for taking chances with men in close custody.

They were linked together, wrist to wrist, clamped to the bulkhead by a thin steel chain.

A buck Melanesian constable with naked blue-black legs and a vast frizzy mop of hair sat guard over them. He had an old carbine on his lap. He slept magnificently all the way.

Then the prisoner named Harry Frobisher—the Australian? I never found out—twisted suddenly to the porthole and said, "Here, what's all this? Why're we going down?"

The co-pilot told him shortly, "We're stopping."

"What for?"

Our educated navigator was from the Sorbonne, I told you. He had the excellent manners of a college boy. "To pick up the Governor," he said.

Harry Frobisher said lazily, "Do we have to? Aren't we happy together? Who the hell wants company?" I heard him yawn widely. He said to the navigator indulgently, like a good-natured professor reprimanding a class, "All right then, for this time. But just remember, next time I'd like to be told."

The co-pilot caught my eye. He wasn't a man with much sense of humor; he didn't know whether to be tickled or annoyed. In the end he decided to let it annoy him. He gave a sour kind of grunt.

Then Harry Frobisher twisted again to peer below. The

steel chain that linked him to his companions tinkled softly and the sound of that chain grated uglily on me. They were bums, they were no good to anybody, they were a menace to any community, they carried trouble about with them the way a mongrel carries fleas; but you had to be sorry for them. "Where is it? I don't see anything," he said.

"Look. There, to starboard," said the navigator, pointing. "The island."

"I still don't see it."

I looked over my shoulder and said, a little touchily, "You don't have to see it."

"And you be bloody careful you don't miss it. You're carrying privileged passengers. You see that you take good care of us." Now he saw the island and he said, "Christ, is that all there is of it? I wouldn't have bothered with it."

Suddenly I felt like the co-pilot: acid. 'A comic,' I thought. 'Well, just wait until you've done a year in a louse-ridden Tahiti cell and let's see how comical you feel then.' He wasn't very old, this man Frobisher, but he looked as though he'd given himself an extra thirty or forty years of bad living in which to be kicked around. A debased, buccaneering character out of a waxworks show. He hadn't shaved for five days. (Nobody provides a barber in our New Caledonia jails.) He had one of those thin, sad, hollow faces that belie the sly mischief in the eyes—it's all right to laugh with such men providing you take care to lock up the silver first. I saw him lean over to the friend next to him, the fat one, the Montparnasse butcher, Marcel, and kick him gently awake.

"Sleeping beauty," he said softly. "Get up."

Marcel didn't open his eyes; he made the thick wet sound a fat man makes when he is licking his lips.

"What did you do that for? I was having a wonderful dream," he said. "There was a plump native woman with

19

no clothes on tickling my belly with a feather and I was just going to make an indecent proposal to her when you woke me up."

"I woke you up just in time," Harry Frobisher said. "She has a two-hundred pound husband and he'd have flattened your head."

"What's happening?" Marcel asked.

"We're going down."

"Why wasn't I consulted?"

Harry Frobisher said blandly, "The pilot wishes to beg your pardon. He's consulting you now." They were grinning together. It annoyed me very much. "They're going to give us the crimson-carpet treatment. A reception committee, everything laid on. A nice hotel and *filet mignon* for supper."

"Good," said Marcel, and now he opened his eyes. "I haven't eaten for six hours. See that the champagne is properly cooled."

The co-pilot looked at me again, struggling with his resentment. His expression said frustratedly: they're ridiculous, what can you do with creatures like that?

I chuckled coolly and said to the prisoners, "Why don't you shut up? All you're going to get is dry bread and a hole in the ground."

Then Marcel yawned hugely, stretching himself like a beast; and the steel chain tightened with another tinkle, jerking the arm of that large black man, Charlie, sleeping soundly at his side.

"Look at him," Marcel said sadly. "Not a care in the world. I'm hungry and sex-deprived, and all he does is sleep."

Harry Frobisher looked past Marcel at the Negro, Charlie. He said affectionately, "He's a growing boy. He needs all the sleep he can get."

He was a big one, that Charlie: a black monster. When

he stood up he made a tall man feel very small. His shirt had been torn open during the trouble in the bar, nobody had sewn it up for him in prison, and the solidly thick pectoral muscles you saw through the rent stupefied you. He was a pleasantly inoffensive man—innately placid, no doubt because he didn't know any other way to behave— and he slept with a light delicate smile on his thick lips. I wondered peculiarly what had brought three such diverse tramps together: an Australian (as one presumed him to be), a fat talkative Frenchman with the cheap conniving chatter of Place Pigalle on his lips, and a dreamily complacent, heavyweight North American Negro. Marcel seemed to know exactly what I was thinking and he looked at his two chained intimates and grinned impudently, "Evil companions. They've been the ruin of me."

The co-pilot couldn't bear it; he frowned angrily. "That'll do. Why don't you be quiet, you animals," he said.

Then suddenly we were ripping through the low evening haze, not two hundred meters above the blunt crater, and we saw the whole island, the black-green sides of the darkening mountain, the thin frothy swathes of the beaches, gleaming flatly in the last rays of the sun. The lights of the tiny town were already twinkling. The island was all dead volcano; it rose from the sea like a hunchback, as obese as a worn-out satyr with all the sap gone out of him; a fat, tired extinct old mountain. A child might have lumped it out of olive-green wax, sticking a finger carelessly in the peak while it was still soft: and that was the crater. We flew straight across it. There was a little white pall over it—smoke, I thought at first, but obviously cloud; it looked as soft as a bride's veil. And from the crater of the mountain, radiating like the spokes of a wheel about the axle, the deep vegetation-tangled ravines ran down to the sea.

21

You could see the patches of gray ancient pumice. Most of the island, of course, was old lava. Only the pink of the coral beaches looked new.

Except for the town—and the radio-telephone mast sticking up like a fragile black matchstick on the slope just above it—there was nothing but jungle and gorges cutting deep into the swelling sides of the mountain. The natives' villages were a little way along the beach from the town. None of the Melanesians—nothing but ants and wild hogs —lived in the interior. I'd been up a little way, torn and rasped by saw-edged ferns and brambles. A hell of a place, a wilderness. I understood that there was an isolation hospital for leper children high up on one of the humps.

Then the island hurtled past us—it took only a minute and a half to cross it—and the steel-gray Pacific was rushing below, but I kept my eyes on the twinkling lights of the town and came round, looking for the opening in the reef to touch down in the lagoon.

There was enough light to see the dangerous low water fringing the coral arms of the reef; the deep channel wound through the opening in it, and I saw a couple of freighters and a schooner tied up at the jetty. We went a long way out and came right down, brushing the water with our floats, bounding up off the wave tops with rubbery jerks; then we were through the reef and I throttled back and let the old crate sink on her belly, flinging up a hissing bow-wave, tilting over clumsily as if she wanted to bury her nose in the sea. You had to pull the wheel hard back. She was a frightened old cow of a seaplane the minute she felt cold water under her.

Then the engines were grunting softly, all tired out from the long journey, and we were plowing forward to the jetty and I saw the little motorboat coming out to moor us. Our wave rocked a couple of night-fishing outrigger canoes inside the reef. The natives stood in them,

22

spears poised, balanced easily like acrobats, their matted hair fluffed out—they had astonishingly wiry mops—waiting for the water to subside so that they could go on with the fishing that was important to them. Ten years ago the seaplane had been a frightful novelty to them. Now they gave it less attention than the village *curé* gives to the urinal planted discomfitingly just outside the church.

Marcel nudged the Negro, Charlie. "What are you trying to do," he grinned, "sleep forever?" and the black man opened his eyes, instantly polite, and said, "Pardon me, Marcel. I guess I must have dropped off."

Marcel stared through the porthole at the lights of the town. "No reception committee," he said sadly. "Goodbye, *filet mignon*. I don't even see any champagne."

Suddenly the co-pilot swung round on him. "That's enough," he said insupportably. "Stop joking. It isn't seemly."

"What would you like me to do for you?" asked Marcel coolly. "Cry?"

"Yes," said the co-pilot. He was such a humorless man, to him it was indecent that men facing four years' *travaux forcés*—that is penal servitude, hard labor—should have anything to joke about. "If I were in your shoes," he shouted, "if I knew what was coming to me, yes, I would cry."

"*Merde*," said Marcel, and the co-pilot's face went brick-red; I thought he would hit the man. I said, "They'll cry. Don't worry. But let them cry in their own time. Grab the mooring rope."

"Jail-fodder," grumbled the co-pilot. He flung open the door, seizing the mooring rope and jumping out. For the first time I noticed the puckered, pitying face of the navigator. He was much too young. I had just cut the engines —it was suddenly wonderfully pleasant, with all the gritty vibration gone. Sometimes the hands jerk with little electric tremors for about an hour after a long flight. I kicked the Melanesian constable hard in the shin to get him awake. They are immune to pain; nothing moved in his face. I tossed him the key and he unclamped the chain from the bulkhead, still leaving the prisoners linked. The navigator and I jumped out on to the jetty. The three prisoners stood in the fuselage doorway, hesitating, adjusting their eyes to the twilight, with the Melanesian constable shoving them out.

"After you, *m'sieu*," said Marcel. His lumpy face obtuse, the Melanesian jabbed his backside with the rifle. "I appreciate your argument," said Marcel. He led the way, the shackles clanking like a bag of nails as all three jumped out.

The dusk was blue and scented. There was a little glitter along the main street of the town. A few shop windows, doing late business, the sudden glare and greasy rush of accordion music as a bistro door opened, the glow from the church doorway; listening carefully, you could hear the soft tuneless chanting of the native choirboys practicing. Hymn books at eleven, the pagans—and witch-doctors when they come to puberty. A useless business with them, religion, don't you think? You know how it is with the French? Wherever we go we take a little of our country with us. We are a very nostalgic race. You will find townlets in the Pacific that might have been lifted bodily out of Provence or Languedoc, the same cobbles, the same crumbling stucco, the same green shutters, the same wine-bottled windows; only the fantastically tall co-conut palms and the pink coral and the monstrous hermit crabs on the beaches are different. I like it that way.

The truck was not on the jetty to meet us; evidently it was more importantly occupied. So we decided to walk the short distance, the prisoners ahead, the black constable immediately behind. People were sitting at the tables outside the bistros, taking their evening drink. There was a group chattering politics excitably at the corner. Eight thousand miles from Paris—and still politics. . . . A few boys and their girls drifted along the sidewalk; their young laughter came sweetly to us.

Suddenly the navigator grabbed my arm. "The chain," he whispered nervously. "People will observe it. Do we have to have the chain?"

I stared at the three men trudging ahead. Curiously enough, they didn't seem to be troubled by—what would you call it?—their badge of shame. Maybe all human pride had been rubbed off them; there was no mud you could sling at them that could sully them now. I glanced inquiringly at the co-pilot.

"On your own responsibility," he said. He was still in a bad temper. "You know your orders. You're to hand them over to the prison guard securely and get a signature for them."

"What's the harm? What can they do?"

"They can run for it, can't they? Animals like that, what have they got to lose?"

"But there's nowhere to run." Except for the town and its attendant radio station there was nothing but suffocating jungle and insects: where could they go? I pointed to the constable trailing along with the rifle. "Anyway, he'd shoot."

"He'd shoot," said the co-pilot sourly. "Only he couldn't hit an elephant's rump at five meters in broad daylight. In this light they'd be in the bushes before he discovered what the trigger was for."

That settled it. Humanity is all right for gentlemen; we were dealing with unpredictable scamps. Anyway, it was only ten minutes' walk to the Governor's block where the prison stockade was. I said to the navigator briskly, "Don't let your conscience work overtime. It doesn't seem to worry them much."

"I am ashamed," he muttered—he had brought the bright shine of his idealism to the Pacific; he would lose it with the down on his face.

"Attend to your business," I said, nettled. "You are not on your college campus now."

We passed the group on the jetty. They looked at the constable with the rifle, then at the three men. There came a sudden frozen silence. A few of them followed us curiously. When we reached the street the boys and the girls on the sidewalk stared. People stared from the tables outside the bistros. We walked close to the curb, avoiding the lights, but still they stared . . . if you led circus animals along the Champs-Élysées, what d'you think people would do? Of course they would stare. A boy in tight jeans called out cheerfully, "Can they do any tricks?" and I saw Marcel turn his head uglily. If he'd been free at that moment he'd have shown the boy a couple of tricks, with the heel of his boot.

Harry Frobisher and the Negro showed no emotion. They didn't even turn their heads.

Then we came up to the church. The Melanesian kids were pouring out; choir practice was over. The priest stood on the sidewalk talking to the black hoodlums as they milled around. I'd only seen him once or twice before. I knew that his name was Father Doonan, that he was Irish, that he hadn't been on the island very long. I don't think he was altogether accepted; he hadn't the French cast of thought, the subtlety of the Gallic mind; he never seemed quite to grasp the diamond-clear distinction we make between religion on Sunday and hard business the other six days of the week. He was a burly man, and the cassock made him look burlier. He had a keen, but diffident, smile, with a round face and fixed, intensely penetrating brown eyes. I don't know why the superiors of his order had sent him out here; maybe they'd had a little trouble with him—some of the religious can become too religious—and the Pacific was a conveniently long way off.

He saw us approach. He looked at the constable with the rifle and frowned; then he saw the three convicts shuffling ahead and his face went ridiculously stiff.

He didn't move for a moment, then he left the horde of black choirboys and came over and stood in our path. He didn't know which one of us was in charge, and he searched our faces. I said, "Good evening, Padre," and tried to push gently past him, and he said apologetically, "Good evening. Forgive me. But these men are chained." He made it sound as if he'd seen something unbelievable —an optical illusion—and he didn't get out of the way.

"We're going to the prison, Padre," I said.

He began clumsily, in bad French, "But these men . . ."

"We just came in with the seaplane. I have to deliver them to the stockade," I said.

"Do they have to be chained?"

"I have orders," I said.

"This is a street. People are watching." He was getting agitated—he tugged me aside as if he didn't want the prisoners to hear him and perhaps be humiliated. I thought cynically, 'Grow up, Padre. You don't know these specimens.' But he whispered, "One must have humanity. It debases all of us when we see fellow-creatures chained like beasts." He didn't suggest, I noticed irritably, that there might be anything debased about the fellow-creatures.

I shrugged. "It's dark. It's only a few minutes' walk."

"Then let them walk with dignity. Like men."

The co-pilot wasn't a good Christian. He said sharply,

27

beginning to use his shoulders on the padre, "Get out of the way."

"I'll walk with them," said Father Doonan. He stood there, barring us: he had begun lightly to perspire. "I'll guarantee them. Just take off the chain."

"You've no business to interfere."

"Please take it off," Father Doonan said.

Marcel clinked the thing slyly; perhaps he thought it was fun. I think he did it to needle us. He was still smarting from the jokes of the boys. I kicked the black constable irritably and he rammed his rifle idly into Marcel and started moving them on. The priest went quickly in front of them and stopped them. He still wouldn't get out of the way.

I said—I began to sweat also—"This isn't your affair."

"Men are always my affair."

"Talk to the Governor."

"You're also a man. You have good feelings. I am talking to you."

And, would you believe it, he stood there trembling, ridiculously worked up—his arms wide in the gesture of the crucifixion, which didn't make things less discomfiting —and people were gathering and it was getting to be embarrassing. For the first time I thought: 'Now I know why they got rid of you out here.' The navigator muttered distressfully, "Please. This is terrible. Do as he says." I got very hot. Why should I be made a spectacle of? What was I doing but my job? There was a crowd now, all watching the three convicts, and not too sympathetically, either; sullen and unshaven, trying to put a derisive face on it, they looked what they were, bad lots.

"All right," I said, to get the priest to shut up. I beckoned to the Melanesian constable and he unlocked the chain.

"I shall report this——" the co-pilot began loudly.

And I said angrily, "Report my backside to your aunt."

"Thank you," Father Doonan said.

Marcel did a theatrical business of stretching his arms; he yawned straight in the faces of the crowd. Harry Frobisher looked down. It was always hard to know what he was thinking. Then he stole a sardonic look at Father Doonan as if he distrusted the cloth, but this might be rather a special sort of priest. As, I assure you, he was: up to that moment I had never felt like hitting a priest. Harry Frobisher said huskily to Father Doonan, "For Christ's sake, I'm dying for a cigarette."

"Here," stammered the priest suddenly. He started searching in his pockets and he pushed a packet at them. "For the sake of Christ. Here, take the cigarettes."

Now I was truly in a sweat. It was crazy. Here in the street: the man was actually fumbling for a match. I shouted, "Get on."

Marcel grinned, "What's the hurry? I want to go in the church to say my prayers."

The co-pilot said in a stifled voice, "Say them in your cell."

"I shall complain to the bishop."

And finally we got them trundling on. Father Doonan followed us a little way and when I looked back he was standing in the middle of the street like a gendarme, keeping the crowd from trailing after us. When we got on some distance the co-pilot knocked the unlighted cigarette from Harry Frobisher's lips. The big Negro, Charlie, spat his out before the co-pilot could reach him. I saw him look at the co-pilot impassively as if wondering whether it was worth adding five years to his sentence by breaking his arm.

We got the trio to the guardhouse of the prison. When they were led off to the stockade and I had got a signature for them I was glad to see the back of them. I was clammy under my jacket. The priest had said to me: "You have good feelings." It was a ridiculous thing to say. I had a colored girl named Daisy in a shack outside the town, she was waiting for me with a bottle of brandy, and I got a little drunk and took her to bed. Those were the good feelings I had.

In the morning I had a slight hang-over; a headache and the taste of unslaked lime in the mouth. I was—for natural reasons—somewhat exhausted. I had nothing to do with myself, so I took the hair of the dog that bit one—a drink at the Pêche d'Or, the bistro—and then I went and sat on the step of the guardhouse, talking to the corporal of the guard. He was, like the Governor, a veteran of the Indo-Chinese war. He had a highly colored parrot —not a native of the island—that had a range of expletives that turned the air in its immediate vicinity blue.

The morning is the pleasantest time in the Pacific. The trade wind has swept away the sweet sickly smell of decay that you find in the tropics; the sky is radiant without heat, the sun has not yet climbed to its zenith; you can move freely without exuding pints of sweat. There was a coconut palm in the middle of the prison yard, and birds fluttered sweetly in its fronds. I talked about this and that to the corporal; he brought out a carafe of wine and we listened to the parrot monotonously cursing its life.

Then suddenly I saw Father Doonan enter the yard and go into the Governor's office. He saw me. He smiled friendlily. I acknowledged it aloofly with a shrug.

The corporal watched him reflectively, then he said softly, "He is for it, that one. The Governor is going to chew his sexual apparatus off for him"—those were not the precise words he used, and it was anyway not a nice thing to say about a priest. But I knew that the Governor had discovered what had happened yesterday evening.

You have seen the Governor? A martinet. He is not a bad man—on the contrary—it is just that like all military men he has a rigid sense of order and propriety, his backbone has forgotten to be flexible, he has had the sweet milk of reason dried out of him. Things must proceed as precisely as a barrack square—such men shouldn't control civil communities, they think they can run people like *Légionnaires*.

Watching Father Doonan go into the Governor's office, I said to the corporal, "That's a funny kind of priest."

"If you like priests to be funny. Personally I do not like them and he is not funny to me. He is queer, that one. He interferes in things. An Irishman. I am told that the Irish are mostly mad. Why could they not send us a Frenchman? If they had to send us one at all?"

"Is the Governor in a bad temper?"

"I would expect him to be. This Father Doonan teaches the *canaille*"—he referred to the Melanesians somewhat differently, in a way that is subtly French and practically unrepeatable—"unpredictable things. A choir. Stone Age barbarians," said the corporal, spitting, "and he gathers the black kids into a choir. When they grow up they will think they can sit on equal terms with us in church."

I said cautiously, "We are all equal in church."

"In church I do not cease to be a corporal and I do not cease to be white." Which was a potent argument; and then the parrot started shrilling obscenities and the corporal said fondly, "I have been offered fifty thousand francs for that talented beast. I would not part with him for his weight in gold."

I was curious to know what was going to happen—I also wanted to get away from the parrot—and I wandered over towards the Governor's office and hung about outside.

The windows were open. I could hear the Governor's dry incisive voice, the intractable military voice. I could only catch intelligible scraps, but I heard ". . . your province is not to interfere in administrative affairs. You prevailed upon the seaplane pilot to unloose three dangerous felons. The man will be reprimanded," and I thought wryly: 'Ah, me next.' "It was not your business, Padre. I do not interfere at your altar, and it is not for you to interfere with the conduct of civil affairs."

Then I caught the soft anxious voice, still speaking very bad French ". . . chained like beasts," and the Governor cut in, a little impatiently, as if he was teaching trigonometry to a backward child, "But that is incontestably what they are. I have seen their records. They are appalling. They are debased and unprincipled men. I have had to request you previously not to take too much upon yourself . . ." and I went away from the window, shrugging.

I said ruefully to the corporal, "He spits ice, that one." I meant the Governor.

"Only when it is called for. He is a man with a strong sense of duty. He has much responsibility to bear."

Then Father Doonan came out of the office, looking a trifle wan. He glanced at me and nodded, but the smile came with difficulty this time. I watched the burly figure disappear slowly, and I decided that now was the time to make myself scarce for a few hours to let the Governor's ice melt a little before he had me on the mat. But too late. The Governor looked out of his office and beckoned to me.

"Your turn now," the corporal said happily to me.

I stood stiffly in front of the Governor's desk, trying to look military and failing lamentably. He gazed at me flatly as if my leather jacket should have had brass buttons so that I could polish them. Then, quietly and without malice, that dry scraper of a voice of his began to tear me into strips. I had—I will give you his precise words—"turned loose upon the community desperadoes whom the authorities had found it necessary to keep under the closest possible restraint."

I said something about humanity; then, in excuse, that it was only a few minutes' walk to the prison block, anyway.

"How many minutes do you think these men required in order to escape?" he asked. Then he repeated softly, as if surprised at me, "Humanity. You abuse the word. If they had broken into the home of some innocent family in the night and perhaps killed them, would that have been humanity?"

There was a Melanesian constable with a rifle, I pointed out.

He replied with a grim smile that, from the reports he had received, the Melanesian constable was something of a sour joke. Tiredly, he waved me out. "I shall forward a report of the incident to higher authority. The department of the colonies will, no doubt, take appropriate action against you."

I got back at him a little spitefully. I told him that the co-pilot had discovered an oil leak in one of the engines and that we couldn't leave for Tahiti for four days. I'd hoped that it would annoy him: in fact, he was unmarried, the old trout, and he didn't really want to go on leave.

What could a desiccated specimen like that do in Tahiti but bore other pensionable colonels like himself?

I went back sullenly into the sunshine and sat, while the corporal grinned jovially at me. For once I was in sympathy with the profane gabble of that abominable parrot —I would have liked to turn the voluble beast upon the Governor. (Probably he would have reduced it to a frozen stupor with a crisp military bark, "Silence in the ranks!")

Then I saw a few native prisoners sweeping up in the yard and it occurred to me rather strangely that I hadn't seen anything of the three men I'd brought in last night. It was usual to give them their morning exercise inside the bamboo stockade. I said to the guard, "Where are they?"

He chuckled. "Where would you think?" He pointed down significantly. "In the hole."

At first I hardly believed him; I was shocked. There was a cellar with a slit of a window under the guardhouse; when it was necessary to lock up violent prisoners, or give them a touch of solitary confinement, they used the cellar for that. It was about five times the size of a coffin. In the heat of a tropical night, it could well turn out to be a veritable coffin for three men. "They've been there all night?" I asked painfully.

"All night," said the corporal carelessly. "And until the Governor gives me further instructions that is where they stay."

"They will die there."

"I've buried better," he said.

After that, another drink at the Pêche d'Or was indicated. Everything about the men had been exaggerated. Probably the corporal had exceeded his duties; maybe the Governor, knowing that the seaplane wouldn't leave today, would now have them brought out. I went back to the guardhouse half an hour later to see what was happening and as I entered the yard I saw Father Doonan talking to the corporal: he was carrying a tray with a coffee-pot and rolls. I stood back behind a palm tree and watched the corporal shrug his big shoulders stonily at him. Evidently Father Doonan—knowing what prison fare was like—had brought compassionately a little breakfast for the three men.

What they are going to need, I thought caustically, is not food but smelling salts.

Then I saw Father Doonan stand quite still, staring emptily at the corporal. He had been told. He put down the tray and made a distressed movement. I had never heard his voice raised, but now he cried out impulsively. He began to shove forward and the corporal put out his beefy hand and shoved him back.

"Where do you think you're going?" asked the corporal.

"They'll suffocate there," Father Doonan cried.

The corporal frowned humorlessly, as if the remark was ludicrous, "Don't worry so much about them. Reprobates like that always survive."

"They must be suffering."

"They're not here on holiday. What do you think they're going to Tahiti for? A summer cruise?"

"Fetch them out, I beg of you," Father Doonan said.

"All in good time. When the Governor says so, not before."

"Fetch them out. Quickly."

The corporal grunted—he was not being cruel, merely unimaginative: he was a typical *sous-officier,* and we turn out some very tough ones in France. He said loudly, getting a little red, "Don't tell me what to do, Padre. You're in the wrong department. I don't take my orders from God." He turned his back on Father Doonan and suddenly the glaring dusty yard was quiet, heavy with heat, heavy with drama; I saw two black policemen in their soiled sweaty khakis peeping nervously out of the guardhouse.

Why should I feel implicated? I was only ferrying the three felons to jail; if one of them failed to make it because the air in the cellar was stale, what had it to do with me? But I stood behind the palm tree as guilty as a spy. It was like a bad religious picture. The poses were all wrong. The corporal, wooden with annoyance, his back turned flatly, Father Doonan making useless fluttering gestures as if he would like to fly the three men out of the "hole," the silent native policemen peeping inquisitively out of the guardhouse, the Melanesian prisoners sweeping the yard frozen into black sweaty marble. You teach men like that to respect the Church, then suddenly they see a priest derided and in thirty seconds they are pagans again . . .

Father Doonan made a sound: it came out of his chest. He turned quickly and headed for the Governor's office. He didn't knock, he plunged straight in.

I moved over to the window to listen and the corporal glared impotently at me. I caught the priest's voice first, just a scrap of it, "You had no right to . . ." and then the Governor cutting in bleakly, "I have no facilities for keeping men like that in custody. It was the only place."

"Have you ever spent a night there?"

"You are being insolent."

"You have been inhuman."

"I warned you before, Padre. Attend to your own affairs."

"Three of them in a hole. It's wicked. Fetch them out."

"I will attend to the matter in due course——"

"No, now."

"Are you presuming to tell me my duty?"

"I swear," began Father Doonan passionately, "that if you don't do as I ask . . ." and then his voice was lost because the Governor broke in, and then there was just a gabble, the two men aiming words at each other, both of them right, both conscious violently of their jobs. Secretly I sympathized with the Governor. He had probably been a little needled by Father Doonan's interfering last night, so into the cellar with the men. It was his way of restoring his ruffled pride. Military types are peculiar. Priests are also a little peculiar; and this Irishman, believe me, more than most. Then the door was flung open and the burly figure came plunging out.

Father Doonan went straight across to the guardhouse and he said to the corporal, "Put me down in the cellar with them."

"You're mad."

"Do as I tell you. Put me down there, too."

The corporal gazed at him. He gazed over Father Doonan's head at the Governor who had come out of his office into the doorway. He made a crude sound of derision between his lips.

Father Doonan pushed past him into the guardhouse and started banging on the cellar door. The corporal looked stupefied. He went after Father Doonan and grabbed him by the shoulder. The Governor, in his doorway, was a small stone of a man; in a few insane seconds the discipline of his guardhouse was spectacularly in ruins. Father Doonan turned on the corporal who was yanking him savagely around and pushed him away. The corporal lunged at him again. Father Doonan picked him up— literally, I mean that, he was inflamed, he was a thick strong man, anyway—and trundled him to the doorway and pitched him out. The corporal sat crazily on his backside in the pink coral dust. And the priest went on hammering at the cellar door. The sound was terrible.

The Governor shouted to the corporal from his office— it must have been like swallowing bile—"Fetch them out."

The corporal got up. He glared at the Melanesian prisoners. Their black arms began stiffly, like marionettes that have gone rusty from disuse, to work at their brooms again. The corporal went into the guardhouse and I heard the clink of keys.

Father Doonan disappeared below. I made myself small behind the palm tree. Then the Negro, Charlie, emerged

37

slowly, supporting the fat one—I always think of him as the horse butcher—Marcel. The Negro got as far as the doorway, then folded up gently in the sun, the stalks of his enormous legs buckling, letting Marcel fall out of his arms. The Negro lay in the dust, gasping throatily. Can a Negro look pale? This one was pale. Marcel began horridly to vomit. The yard was utterly silent, as if even the birds had been chastened, and the man's retching sound was like a saw on wood. Father Doonan came out next, holding up Harry Frobisher, laying him down in the sun. He was sick, too. Father Doonan leaned over him, using his cassock to wipe the filth off his lips.

The Governor went back into his office. He came out with a bottle of brandy and crossed the yard. He gave the bottle to Father Doonan and said—I think even he was put out by the sight of the retching, half-suffocated men—"I'm sorry. This was not intended. It was only necessary to leave them there until the seaplane left."

"They'll be all right now," Father Doonan said.

He fed the three brandy. One by one, sunken-eyed, they sat up. Marcel began hideously to curse. Disgusted, the Governor turned his back; even that hardened object, the corporal, winced. "Hush your mouth," the Negro said to Marcel. "Behave yourself."

"They could have killed us. It would have been murder."

"Oh, shut up," said Harry Frobisher. "They'd have to think up something really special to murder you."

Then the three men saw the tray of food and fell on it wolfishly. Father Doonan helped them to coffee. I said before that there was something Biblical about the scene: the priest squatting in the dust, his face tense with misplaced pity, his cassock dirty, the three men champing like starved dogs. I noticed that Harry Frobisher kept stealing curious sidelong glances at Father Doonan. Suddenly he said to him, "That's twice you did it. What made you stick your neck out?"

"It's my trade," Father Doonan smiled faintly. "Sticking my neck out."

"One of these days you'll get your head chopped off."

"We're a big rich Church," shrugged Father Doonan. "We've got lots and lots of spare heads."

"You're crazy."

"I know," said Father Doonan softly. "I behaved very badly. I'm ashamed of myself."

After that, Harry Frobisher kept quiet; he just kept on looking at Father Doonan speculatively. The Governor hadn't moved, watching them impassively. He beckoned now to Father Doonan and the priest went across.

"They can't leave for four days," the Governor said. "I can't keep them here idle. It won't do to feed four useless mouths." Even in his moment of compassion his sense of order asserted itself—he had strong notions about prisoners. If they were warm and breathing they could work; if they had visible muscles they could break stones with a pick. "You're going up to the hospital this afternoon?" he asked.

"Yes," Father Doonan said.

"There is a labor gang going with the truck. If you desire it, you can take these three along. A little work in the fresh air will be better for them than sitting about in the bamboo stockade."

"I think they'd like that," Father Doonan said.

The Governor's face was a slight study; what prisoners liked or didn't like was immaterial. He said, "But I want no trouble. You'd have to vouch for them."

"I'll vouch for them," Father Doonan said.

"All right. You understand, then." The Governor looked at the corporal, who was listening, and nodded.

"Don't lose them," he said to Father Doonan, and went back to his office, a small stiff man.

In the end he had behaved magnanimously. I thought he had been, if anything, a little too soft.

The corporal nudged the Negro, Charlie, with his toe and the man got up. The others rose. The corporal gestured to the black policeman in the guardhouse and they came out. *"Petit déjeuner* is over," said the corporal coldly. "Into the stockade with them."

"Later, then," Father Doonan said to Harry Frobisher, looking up the side of the mountain. "It isn't a bad trip up there."

"Conducted tours," grinned the corporal stonily. "Only the best for our prisoners."

Harry Frobisher rubbed the coarse stubble on his cheek, grittily black in that cruel light, staring lingeringly at Father Doonan; then the three men trudged with the native policeman into the stockade.

The hospital—at was an isolation hospital for Melanesian children, most of them lepers—was about four thousand meters up the mountain. It was thought that it was the best place for it—it was cool up there, quiet and restful, it got the trade wind straight off the ocean. The doctor who ran it, the Viennese—you have met him?—used to say that the staggering view of the Pacific would have been worth ten million francs on the Riviera, but I think he was speaking ironically. What he meant was that the colonists didn't like an isolation hospital for Melanesian leper children to be too near to the town. The truck went up with supplies twice a month and Father Doonan always traveled with it. It must have been a stupefying journey. A rough gravel road, ripped out of the jungle, twisting round the mountain. That Aristide, who owned the truck, is a crazy driver; I would rather have a leg amputated than sit with him in his cab.

Father Doonan walked out of the yard and I came out from behind the palm tree. I went over to the corporal.

"Well, that sorted itself decently," I said, and the corporal laughed.

"Wait and see," he said.

"It was a nice gesture of the Governor's, don't you think?"

"I know what I think." The corporal stared with narrow begrudging admiration over towards the window and spat. "I was with him at Hanoi. He was the regimental staff officer. He has a smart head on his shoulders, that man." He went on—quite violently—"He knows what is going to happen. Then he'll have the priest where he wants him, like caviare on toast. He'll teach him a needed lesson." And suddenly I understood.

The three scamps would get a breath of freedom up there and it would be intolerable to them. They would decamp. What they didn't know was that there was nowhere to run: no villages in the interior, nothing to feed them or shelter them: when they were starved sufficiently they would come crawling back. The Governor would have the necessary vindication. Back into the hole with them . . . a fresh charge, and another two years added to their sentence. Men like the Governor, arid and unimaginative, feeding on their prestige, throw small shadows, and Father Doonan had shortened his pride. Someone would have to suffer for that.

The Governor hadn't been a staff officer for nothing; maybe it was a pity that Father Doonan's superiors hadn't sent him to college to learn a little strategy, too.

The corporal went back into the guardhouse and I went off to the Pêche d'Or for another drink.

I was sitting over a Pernod on the pavement in the middle of the afternoon when Aristide's truck came rumbling along the street. It clattered over the cobbles like the heap of junk it was. Aristide was driving, that greasy maniac, with the butt of a dead cigarette clipped to his lip. Father Doonan sat with him in the cab. He saw me outside the bistro and began a smile of recognition, but it had no time to develop for he was past me in a rush. Two mop-headed native policemen were crouched on the tailboard with carbines on their laps. Already they were well into their first doze; they would sleep steadily all the way up.

Six Melanesian prisoners sat on a pile of rattling picks and shovels, beaming toothily like children being taken for a ride. (And probably they were—as the Americans put it—being taken for a ride: the corporal wasn't above raking in a few minor offenders whenever his labor gang ran short.) The three men squatting in the back with them—well, you may guess who they were. Charlie was the first to catch sight of me over the side of the truck as it rolled by and he smiled blandly: nothing ever discomfited that big black man. Then Harry Frobisher saw me and the corners of his mouth went crooked; he grinned vacantly as if I had reminded him of something bad. Marcel merely beamed at me fatly. He licked his lips thirstily at the sight of my drink and made an obscene gesture with his thumb.

Then the truck was just a din on the cobbles, puttering ahead of its oily blue smoke. It turned off the bottom of the street and began the six-hour climb up.

I walked over to the other side of the street to watch it go. I heard the gears change roughly, then the bonnet appeared over the rooftops, whining dustily up the gravel mountain road. I wished—I don't know why—I'd had a chance to get hold of Father Doonan and warn him: be damned sure you come back with those three bums. But by now the truck was nosing into the scrub that grew on the lower slopes. It passed over that florid arrangement of toothpicks, the Old Wooden Bridge, that straddles the gorge. I glimpsed it for a fleeting moment, a grubby little toy, grinding through the trees. Then the thick green vegetation of the jungle closed about it; and that was the last I saw of it.

3

AT this point Aristide comes into the story. He gave me his part of it in the bistro. It was drenched with the endless burble of a jukebox, shrill accordion music nibbling at the nerves like a dentist's drill. Aristide was a little foul with drink to begin with—after the level, undiscursive narration of the pilot he was as garrulous as an old crone in a *charcuterie,* his language spiced so freely with expletives that one felt helplessly in need of an interpreter.

It was necessary to lean well back from him. He had just eaten something highly seasoned; garlic hovered like a blue flame about his lips.

He was short and plump and had heavily pomaded hair. He was straight out of a French farce, the glib eye-rolling corespondent; he never took his eyes off the *patronne's* busty daughter the whole of the time he talked to me.

But he tickled me right away by saying that he had owned the only truck on the island: and that made him important. It gave him the standing of a bureaucrat or a *rentier.* He not only freighted loads for the ships in the harbor, he was in demand for local affairs like weddings and fêtes. "I was"—he said proudly—"a figure on the island. Anything that needed four wheels, you either came to me or carried it yourself."

He used to haul supplies twice a month up the side of the mountain to the hospital. "It didn't pay me," Aristide said. "I only did it as an act of charity." (It came out that he had an added incentive: he had once grumbled to Father Doonan that the trips weren't economical and the priest had grabbed him brutally by the scruff of the neck and shaken him. I could picture that irate Irishman rattling Aristide's teeth, warning him sternly to remember the sick and the fatherless.)

"But I forgave him," Aristide said simply. "To be a priest a man has to be a little touched. And that Irish specimen was more than a little touched."

It wasn't a bad trip up to the hospital that afternoon (said Aristide). It was a veritable bitch of a road, all pumice and loose rock and gravel, and sometimes I went whining by gorges that would have curled another driver's hair. Certainly not mine. I would look down from the cab and a thousand meters below it was all quiet green plush, soft in the sunshine, billowing a little like waves on the sea. But that plush was the jungle: ferns and ropes of creepers and stunted palms. A rock would go slithering down from under our wheels and I could listen with my ears pricked forever and still hear no sound.

I am a religious man and I sometimes think that hell must be like that: no flame, nothing violent, just falling away silently into endless depths.

It troubled me not at all—the road I mean, not hell—I was used to it.

I could hear the three roughnecks cursing behind. You will have noticed that my language is apt to be a little colorful, but I was an amateur at profanity compared with Marcel. That fat one had a tongue that aroused my reluctant admiration; I could see Father Doonan's face puckering up. No doubt it was agonizing for them in the back. The Melanesians have bottoms like stone: they cannot feel anything. But for the others it must have been purgatory, bounced about like peas in an iron pod.

Father Doonan said to me, "Go a little slower. They are suffering."

"They'll suffer worse when they get to Tahiti," I said.

"Is it necessary to take pleasure in the thought? They are your brothers——"

"Then my mother strayed badly. If we go any slower it'll be dark before we get to the hospital."

We got there before sundown, in fact. The Viennese doctor was on the porch with the Matron to welcome us. The hospital stood on a ledge on the side of the mountain; it was petrifying to watch the red ball of the sun falling into the vastness of the ocean. Dr. Wexler grinned and shook Father Doonan's hand. The Matron—I will tell you something special about her later—flung her arms about him and kissed him. It must have been intolerably lonely for them up there. A colored nurse came out to giggle at us. I parked the truck over at the side of the compound and all the Melanesian prisoners tumbled out.

Our three special guests—Harry Frobisher and Marcel and the Negro—didn't move. Probably they couldn't. They must have been stiff.

I heard Harry Frobisher mutter, "I'm blistered all over."

"I'm a hospital case," Marcel said. "Call for the doctor. The hell with them. They're not going to get any work out of me."

"Be patient, you'll change your mind," I thought. One of the native policemen, the sergeant, jabbed the butt of his rifle at them and all three came crawling out.

Dr. Wexler and the Matron looked at them strangely. It was perhaps a little disturbing—disagreeable, even—to

45

see two white men in a native penal gang. "Who," the Matron whispered to Father Doonan, "in heaven's name are they?"

I heard Father Doonan explain . . .

"What did they do?" asked the Matron.

I caught Father Doonan's soft, troubled voice—the one word, "Manslaughter"—and the Matron's face froze.

"Now we're really scraping the bottom of the barrel," she said wryly. "Are we so short of labor? Better be sure they don't murder us in our beds."

But she laughed and slapped Father Doonan's back. She was an incurable back-slapper—if he hadn't been as solid as the Maritime Bank of the Pacific he would have reeled. A fine gusty woman; I'd often had my eye on her. Half an hour on the sofa with her and I'd have given her better things to think of than leprous Melanesian kids . . . She cried, "Supper is waiting," and they all went in.

A girl had just come unobtrusively onto the porch and she stood there, silent in the blue dusk, listening to us. It was the second nurse, Camille. She was a half-colored— a daughter of a Melanesian woman by some amorous French colonist; on the wrong side of the blanket, of course. Sometimes the results of such unions make one want to vomit: it had turned out differently with Camille. She had the soft European features, the somewhat darker than honey skin, and the walk of her native mother—they know how to walk, the Melanesian women, before they run to fat, so that the hips play tricks with one's eyes. Eighteen years old and a beauty; an authentic gazelle.

I saw Harry Frobisher and Marcel stare at her sidelong. The sergeant was nudging them irritably to get into the shed in which they were to sleep.

"That chick," I heard Marcel remark softly. "Just take a look at her. The woman situation isn't going to be so bad up here." (He was a hot one, that man. He had the husky ingratiating voice of a tout for some Pigalle night-spot.)

"For God's sake," Harry Frobisher grunted, though his eyes were still fixed on Camille, "don't you ever think of anything else?"

"Find me something better to think of," Marcel chuckled slyly, "and I'll think of it."

The Negro, Charlie, murmured, "Come on, let's get a little food," then he added with an embarrassed kind of laugh—both men were still staring at the girl, no doubt lecherously—"Stop flashing your eyes at her. You'll wear your batteries out." The police sergeant settled the problem. He dropped the butt of his rifle brutally on Marcel's toe so that he squealed. He led them into the shed after the six Melanesians and locked the door.

Camille remained to listen curiously to the rattle of the padlock . . . It was almost dark now and I could hardly see her face . . . then as silently as she had come she went back into the hospital.

Marcel was wrong about the woman situation not being so bad up here. It couldn't have been worse. I am a healthy virile man and I do not deny that in pursuit of my natural inclinations I have let my eyes rest on the colored nurses—after all, on the side of a lonely mountain one cannot have one's choice of the Folies Bergère. But the Matron watched them like a furious hawk. The pastime could get to be dangerous. There was nothing to do here but eat and sleep.

I went in for my supper. I went straight to my solitary bed.

In the morning I went out after breakfast to watch the prison gang at work. There is something delicious to the body in squatting idly on a stone in the sunshine and watching other men toil with shovels and picks. They

47

had already been at work an hour—they were digging a trench for a drain. The Melanesians worked as they usually worked: no harder than they pleased. Harry Frobisher was stripped to the waist, prodding the earth restlessly with his pick—he was thin and worn with dissipation; the ribs shone like sticks under his sweaty skin. Marcel, his plump womanish breasts quivering, made only a pretence of shoveling. Nobody would ever get an ounce of unnecessary sweat out of him. But that monstrous Negro worked as if he loved it; as if he enjoyed the dignity of labor.

The sergeant watched them dully with a carbine, an unlighted cigarette dangling from his mouth.

Round about midmorning the old emaciated native who did odd jobs up at the hospital appeared with Camille, carrying pans of food for the men. Camille walked gracefully, picking her way with bare feet over the rocks, her toes feeling sensitively for obstructions. She carried a steaming can of coffee. I saw Marcel stop work instantly. Harry Frobisher leaned on his pick, wiping his dripping face; he, too, watched her. Both watched her with a flat kind of hunger, the way men with empty bellies stare at food.

They had probably had no sexual gratification since being arrested. For men like that six or seven weeks of enforced celibacy is an intolerably long time.

"My pin-up," Marcel grinned agreeably. "I reserve her for me."

Harry Frobisher grunted, "Why don't you shut up? You and your hot pants. You never talk about anything else."

"Have you taken a fancy to her?"

"All I fancy is breakfast. I'm hollow inside."

Charlie said pacifyingly—he seemed to be very fond of

his partners in crime—"Hush. No hard words about her. It ain't worth a thing."

"I sacrifice her to my friend," Marcel said handsomely, and he nudged Harry Frobisher. "He can have her. Just put me next on the list."

Father Doonan had to come from behind the hospital with a bunch of the Melanesian kids. I think he had heard what Marcel said; he looked sharply at Camille and his face went anxious and grim. The kids were from the hospital, small noisy lepers, trotting and laughing and clutching Father Doonan's hand. The hospital held about twenty-eight of them. Few of them were bedridden. Most of them were in arrested stages: it is possible to do something when one catches them young. But some of them had the symptoms that affright one—you have seen the types? The wasted rickety bones, the caved-in ribs, the peculiarly thickened features that are typical of the disease; you know what they call it, the leper's "lion face"? One small black rapscallion had had his vocal chords affected so that he could only utter whispery sounds. One might pity them—I did, naturally, I am human—but I also have a horror of the disease.

Since Biblical times one has recoiled from it. Unclean, unclean!

I moved back from where I was sitting so that they should not come too near me as they trotted along. Father Doonan held their hands as he watched the men squat down to eat—he also saw Frobisher's eyes flit queerly to Camille as she stood back from the open trench, not seeming to look in the men's direction, yet intensely conscious of them. The priest went over and said something peremptory to her. She nodded and went picking her delicate way over the stones back to the hospital. ("That priest is a goddamned spoil-sport," I heard Marcel laugh.)

The gesture wasn't lost on Harry Frobisher. He looked

from under his lashes at Father Doonan surlily; he didn't like it very much. He sat in the dust, champing on his food, and when Father Doonan squatted beside him and passed round cigarettes he shook his head and turned away. Marcel and Charlie took them cheerfully and lighted up. The Melanesians stuck theirs behind the ears like hibiscus blossoms, where they looked ridiculous. (Not so ridiculous, actually; they would get a few francs for them from the sergeant of the guard.)

Suddenly Harry Frobisher said to Father Doonan brusquely, "This must cost you quite a bit."

Father Doonan looked surprised. "Cost me? What?"

"The good works. The cigarettes. What do you do, go round the town and whip up subscriptions afterwards?"

Father Doonan smiled faintly, "I don't think the town's charity would run to that. It's just my pleasure."

Harry Frobisher said coolly, "You know what you can do with it as far as I'm concerned."

"What's the matter?" asked Father Doonan. "You mustn't talk like that."

"The hell with you. I saw you send that girl away. You think she'd catch a disease just from looking at us. Keep away from the lousy jailbirds, you said, they carry germs."

"No, I didn't say that," Father Doonan began uncomfortably.

And then Charlie interrupted huskily, reproving his partner, "Harry, don't be so touchy. You didn't hear a thing."

"She went off like a scalded cat, for God's sake. I've got eyes in my head."

"I'm sorry," said Father Doonan. "She's lived most of her life up here on the mountain, she knows nothing, she's not very accustomed to men. Forgive me. I didn't mean it the way you suggest."

"That's your story," muttered Harry Frobisher. (I don't

know what right he had to be so angry; if I had a daughter I'd put my foot up her tender backside if she went near a dangerous malefactor like that.) "Suggest it better next time."

Then the sergeant of the guard got up and shouted. Breakfast was over. The emaciated old native went round collecting the pans. The Melanesians grinned lazily and the guard passed amongst them, kicking them back to work with his bare foot. The kids were frolicking nearby. One of them brushed Marcel—I saw him give a horrified mutter and start back as if he had been burned.

"Get away from me," he cried.

"It's all right," laughed Father Doonan. "They're not contagious. You don't have to worry about that."

"It worries me considerably. You keep those filthy little monkeys away from me."

Father Doonan winced. He rose. He took the hands of two of the kids, clutching them passionately, and said, "No, not filthy. Look, I'm touching them. I won't come to any harm."

"You've got God working for you. I don't have any influence in heaven, I've got troubles of my own."

"Yes," said Father Doonan, staring at the children, then looking compassionately at Marcel. "You've got troubles of your own. But you're wrong about not having God working for you." He shouted to gather the children together.

Harry Frobisher grunted angrily as one of the rickety "lion-faced" kids got too near him. He made a distasteful gesture. "Christ," he muttered. "Four years in jail isn't enough, we have to take leprosy with us, too."

Even Charlie, the Negro, looked uneasy—he didn't make the same fussy objections, but he stood well back, on the other side of the trench, keeping a good distance between him and the milling rabble of kids. I had taken up a safe strategic position behind a tree. If one of them had come within arm's reach of me I would have repelled him, with the toe of my boot.

The three roughnecks picked up their shovels and went back to work. I went back to sleep. That was the day's entertainment. What was there to do up there?

It was in the evening that incidents began suddenly to hot up. It sprang, of course, out of the queer hostility that the man, Harry Frobisher, had worked up towards the priest: shame, one presumes. Even the most debased human has a spark of self-contempt, a sense of his own inadequacy. It was dark. The new moon was up—the kind of moon you get in the Pacific, slender like a maiden, but not innocent like a European moon. It looked hot and wise and knowing: it had the old moon cradled obscenely like a fat satyr in its arms. I went out into the compound and wandered about in the bushes for a smoke. Frankly, I had given the colored nurse, Sonia, a significant eye, and I think it registered. I hoped after a discreet interval she might follow me out. We could have nested down in the undergrowth cosily and let nature take its course.

There was a long sheet of light across the Pacific, swept by the moon. I could see the blunt crater of the old volcano cutting sharply into the luminous sky, blotting out the stars. I sat down. I must have moved rather quietly; I didn't see for a moment that someone was standing a little way from me, staring across the ocean. It was Harry Frobisher. I suppose he had persuaded the guard to give him a few moments' freedom, maybe to relieve himself, maybe to stretch his legs and have a smoke. His face surprised me. The faces of men when they think they are not being observed are always revealing: this bum was relaxed, all the prickles and sullen resentment gone out of him; he was listening to the cackle of the birds as if it was music, staring out at the sea and the moon.

"Take a long look," I thought secretly. "You won't get privileges like this in Tahiti. Leg irons for you, my friend."

He heard a rustle. He turned quickly—it might have been a bird, but it wasn't—it was Camille. I watched without betraying myself; she stood silhouetted by the moon, staring not at Frobisher but over his shoulder, then moved forward slowly in his direction. She stopped a meter or so away from him.

"Who is there?" she asked.

"Who do you think?" he muttered ungraciously. (Courtesy is a lost, ridiculous virtue to men like that.) "They sent you to tell me my time's up?"

"No. Nobody sent me."

"Fair enough, then." He looked at her covertly now and grinned. "Grand evening, isn't it?"

"It smells very sweet."

"You could be ten million miles from everywhere up here. I'm putting it down on my list for my next vacation. You want to sit down?"

"Thank you." And she sat.

"I never heard so many damn birds," he said.

"They sing loudest for the moon," Camille smiled. "They say on the island—the colored people say it—that it is their lost lover and they are begging it to return."

"They'll have to sing a hell of a long time." He was still studying her face sidelong, plucking nervously at the grass. I should have gone, of course. But to begin with I am no gentleman, and secondly they would have heard me move. So I sat and listened; it was a little harmless fun. "You like it up here on this crazy mountain?" I heard him ask.

She said something rather surprising—surprising to him, at least—"I haven't been down to the town since I was a child and I don't know what there is better to like."

"There's a lot better to like," he said. "Streets, bars,

bistros, there's no movies, but——" he seemed to realize ruefully that it wasn't an impressive list of attractions and he chuckled. "Maybe you've got something. If I didn't have a pressing appointment elsewhere I wouldn't mind stretching my bones for a bit up here."

"What can you see?"

"Eh?" He sounded slightly confused. I knew why she had said that, but he didn't. He just sat looking at her vacantly, a little suspicious, then he said emptily, waving his hand at the horizon, "Well, the sea. Moon. Stars. Night. What would you expect me to see?"

"Tell me about it."

"You like my television voice?"

"I'd like to hear you tell me."

"See for yourself, can't you?"

"Please tell."

He guffawed softly, falling into the mood. I saw him shift a little closer to her, then try a furtive nibble at taking her hand. And since she didn't recoil he took it. He seemed faintly surprised at the lack of resistance. It had a peculiarly incitive sexual appeal on me; a lusty man imagines vividly what he would do in such promising circumstances. I would have taken more than her hand, believe me.

"All right," said Frobisher, with greater confidence—I guessed what he was getting confident about, and do not tell me I am a dirty old man—"over yonder there's Australia. You can't see it, being a few thousand miles off, but there's stars that can see it and they can see us, too. That big feller up there—I've seen him before. I don't know his name, but he's a kind of Peeping Tom, and some nights I've laid out on the beach working off a slight headache—from overwork," he bubbled softly, "not drink. And the same sly, slinky star's looked down at me, that fat shining one over there, and he's as good as suggested he's disgusted with my company——"

"Why?" she broke in.

"Aren't you disgusted with it?"

"No," she said.

"Not so far," he corrected her. And he went on with that ridiculous baby talk about stars when he could have been working into a clinch with her—did he think he had all night to manœuvre the ball into the goal? "Maybe I'm doing him an injustice," Frobisher said. "Maybe he's just personally interested in me. Now there's the sea. There's a lot of water there. I'll tell you how much water there is: if there was a thousand miles less of it, in any direction, I'd chance my luck nipping off into it and swimming myself free."

He stopped, pausing while I could have counted twenty. "You know why I'm here?" he asked suddenly.

"You are working with the other men," she said.

"You know any other reasons for me being here?" She turned her face to his—that cool, young, lily face, luscious and half-ripe in the moon (and he was wasting time, that long-tongued maniac)—and shook her head, and he said, him with his wry grin, "I'm here on the Governor's private invitation. He said to me, friend, you look all fagged out, I'm worried about you, take a little trip up the mountain at my personal expense. Give them my love at the hospital. What do they call you?"

"Camille."

"French?"

"French—of a kind. Half French. The other half, well, belonging here."

"You've got two nice halves. They go together a bit of all right."

"Maybe," I thought, "that sweet chatter is the right approach—this man has experience—the gazelle only turns and runs when it is scared." I noticed that his other hand had started wandering gently; he had taken first her fingers, then her wrist, then his arm slid about her waist as lightly as a bee sucks at a flower. Thirty seconds more and he would have her bosom—then we would see what we would see.

He said, "Relax. I'll tell you about the moon."

"What name do you have?"

"Harry."

"That isn't a French name?"

"I'm not surprised. I didn't get it in France. Lean over a little. That's fine. You all right, now?"

"Should you be holding me there?"

"Just a friendly feeling. It's a good place to hold. Take it easy, it doesn't cost anyone a cent." (I sweated here: the curtain was about to go up.) "I could talk about the moon," I heard him continue, "but if you want me to be honest I think it'd be an awful waste of valuable time. That's a commodity I'm a little short of. Time. They're going to give me a lot of it, but not in the way you think. It'd be a pleasure normally," he murmured, "to take, say, thirty, forty minutes over sweet talk, just kissing a little now and again"—he did it, the rogue, I couldn't see distinctly, but I could hear the faint, terribly erotic, sound of the kiss—"and in the end we'd just get to the same place. You're pretty sweet. Was that all right? You liked it?"

(Evidently so. She didn't answer. I certainly heard no protest.)

"Fine. Here, this bit of grass is pretty smooth. Put your hand here. Nice." And he kissed her again.

Then there was the sound as if someone was breathing after a long run. The bushes crackled and Father Doonan came sweeping through the trees. He grabbed hold of Harry Frobisher and said, "No, no," violently, picking him up bodily and hauling him away from the girl.

"You're always nosing into somebody else's business," Harry Frobisher started yelling—I think he had had a terrible shock: in such a thwarted sexual moment any man would be half off his head. Then the priest cried out emotionally and hit Frobisher hard—unbelievably hard, on the chin. The man fell back as if poleaxed. That Irishman, cloth or no cloth, had not the slightest inkling of his strength. He bent over Camille and I could see his mouth working to form the words, the delicate question . . . how much of her Harry Frobisher had fondled and how far he had got?

He was in a trembling, agitated state. I thought to myself, ten minutes later and you'd have had something to be agitated about. He just muttered, "Camille?" shaking impossibly, questioning her again and again, "Camille?" Then he turned as Harry Frobisher came lunging at him. The priest's first breathless anger was almost gone now and he simply put out his thick arm and pushed Frobisher away.

"What did you do to her?" he cried.

"Ask her," Frobisher shouted, whirling his fists; he hadn't the priest's strength and he couldn't get past that stiffly poked-out arm. "You want an illustrated leaflet? She had the soup and the joint and the sweet, the whole business, she'll tell you. . . ." I don't know why he lied; spleen and frustration, I suppose. He'd hardly got beyond the preliminary skirmishing, as I'd seen for myself. I would have got twice as far with the most obstinate girl in the Bois de Boulogne in half the time. The priest mouthed something despairingly, then as Harry Frobisher jumped at him ragingly he hit him again. This time Frobisher went back into the bushes and stayed there. I wondered numbly if his jaw was cracked.

"What sort of animal are you?" asked Father Doonan softly. "Don't you know she is blind?"

Frobisher lay in the undergrowth and glared at him. He didn't say anything for a while. Then he muttered, "I didn't know that."

"She hasn't seen anything from birth. I told you she knows nothing, she is utterly ignorant of such things."

Harry Frobisher said thickly, "I hardly laid a hand on her. Ask her if you want to. I swear it, she's all right."

Other people were hurrying across the compound, half the hospital must have heard Frobisher's crazed yell. Marcel and Charlie came dragging behind. The native sergeant came first and his face darkened—a foolish expression, for he was as black as jet—he took in the situation and he went over to Frobisher as he lay in the bushes and kicked him malevolently in the ribs. A Melanesian's bare foot can be as lethal as a club. The priest cried, "No, don't do that. It was my fault, leave him alone."

Will you believe what I am telling you? He was actually crying; I assure you, I saw his ridiculous face working and the tears welling in his eyes. He went over to Frobisher and half lifted him and cradled his head in his arms.

The Negro, Charlie, and Marcel were staring through the trees, and Marcel muttered with a kind of vicious admiration, "That priest is in the wrong business. He should be slugging out his living in the prizefighter's ring."

Charlie went over to Harry Frobisher. He pushed the priest's hands away from his partner grimly. He said with harsh reproach, "You shouldn't have hit him. Not like that, you shouldn't have hit him. He hasn't been eating for a long time."

"Forgive me," Father Doonan said. He looked distressfully at Frobisher's thin body—I don't suppose the prison diet is very nourishing—and he tried to help lift him, but the big Negro elbowed him chillingly aside. Harry Frobisher got up. The priest was still trying vainly to steady him, but Frobisher said, "Get your damned hands off me, you crazy Mick."

"I'm sorry——"

"Keep away from me, I told you. You've busted my jaw."

Frobisher went off, supported by his friends, the sergeant helping him on his way humiliatingly by planting the horny sole of his foot in his back. Father Doonan stood there, breathing the way an animal breathes when it is running from a dog. He looked helplessly at Camille and took her hand and said, "Go to bed, my child."

"I am on duty tonight."

He began, "I'll ask the Matron——" but he broke off, probably deciding it was safer to say nothing to her. She would have run amok through the prisoners' shed with a crowbar.

Camille was asking agitatedly, "What happened, Father?" and the priest couldn't answer, stroking her arm; he was still crying. Harry Frobisher had called him rightly —if picturesquely—a crazy Mick. (That means Irishman, yes?) The two went off together, and then I thought it discreet to come out. Nobody had seen me.

A great deal of fuss over a bit of uncompleted fondling. As the shepherds say, much bleat and very little wool. In Paris, if people kicked up such commotion for so little reason, believe me, *l'amour* would be a dying art. The colored nurse I had hoped for hadn't appeared. That made two frustrated men. So I went to bed.

During the next day the gang finished their work. Father Doonan decided that we would start driving down the mountain before dawn so that the men in the back of the truck (the unfortunates, he called them) shouldn't suffer the journey in the heat of the day.

Notice that expression: *he* decided. It never seemed to occur to him to consult me. . . .

I remember sitting in the dark cab in the hospital compound, so drowsy that my head kept falling over the wheel; a man of my natural vivacity requires his full nine hours' sleep. What was left of the night still glittered with stars; but the moon was sinking so fast that the crater of the mountain seemed to be sucking it down. The engine was warming up, jangling like a sack of iron: which accurately describes it. Dr. Wexler and the Matron were saying their farewells to Father Doonan on the porch. He looked as though he had bitten on a bad tooth—I think it actually hurt him to leave them to their loneliness up here.

"Don't forget the picture magazines," I caught the Matron's hoarse chuckle. "The spicy ones. The big bosoms. Don't get fussy about them, you don't have to look at them yourself." . . . and I thought, "What do you think he's made of? Flour and water? Of course he'll look at them himself."

"Behave yourself," grinned Dr. Wexler. "You're embarrassing the man."

"And some cigarettes," said the Matron. "None of our French duckweed. Get me some Camels off one of the ships." I thought cynically, he'll need to be very persuasive. American cigarettes fetched a high price in the town; Father Doonan could wheedle the sailors in the name of charity until grass grew on the ships.

"I'll try," Father Doonan said softly—but I didn't hear what else he said because our three guests, the gentlemen from the stockade, had begun to curse passionately in the back of the truck. They would be pulped sore before we arrived in the town; the Melanesians had coiled themselves into a heap of black flesh in the middle, leaving the sides of the truck to hammer the rest. "Animals," Marcel shouted, kicking the natives, but he was wasting his strength. "I'll be hamburger meat by the time this tumbril gets below."

'This is not a Cook's tour,' I thought coldly. 'You're getting no worse than you deserve.'

I wished Father Doonan would hurry up. The Matron was peering into his face, chiding him. "Don't look so sorry about going. We're not much company for you up here."

"It's good. It's quiet. It's restful."

"It's as restful as a cemetery on a rainy evening, don't kid yourself."

Dr. Wexler said, "Don't take any notice of her. We're much too busy to be lonely up here."

"Ah, *bonne blague*," she answered: roughly translatable as, the hell with that for a tale! She leaned over with a hearty guffaw and kissed Father Doonan. "Don't worry about us," she said fondly. "Go along, now. *Soignez-vous bien,* take care of yourself."

I said that I would tell you something special about the Matron. I was sworn to secrecy by a man who once knew her in Paris. When she was about sixteen—before the nuns got hold of her—she used to work in a house of assignation, what we call a "twenty minutes hotel." To put it bluntly, she was one of *les girls.* And here she was, nearly thirty years later, on an island in the Pacific, a sister of mercy, marooned up in a kids' leper hospital. One has to giggle; human nature is a peculiar thing.

Then Father Doonan climbed into the cab and he said with unnecessary brusqueness, to cover his emotion, "Try not to sleep on the way down. Be careful. You're carrying precious souls."

But I couldn't get started. The half-colored nurse, Camille, had appeared from the hospital. She was feeling the hands of the men, one by one, as she moved along the side of the truck. "Harry?" she was calling softly, "Harry?" and when she came to his hand finally he snatched it away as if it had been burned.

"This partner of mine," Marcel chuckled admiringly, "is a fast worker. Ten minutes with her in the bushes and she's yearning for him."

The Matron was glaring with consternation. Dr. Wexler called out strangely, "What is going on there?"

The Matron—whose eyes were better than his—shouted to Camille thunderously, "Come back at once."

"You'll be here next time, Harry?" Camille said gently —it was odd to watch her eyes turning, emptily yet sensitively, waiting for him to speak so that she could focus her attention in his direction.

"There isn't going to be a next time," Harry Frobisher muttered. He looked discomfitingly at his friends. Then the Matron ran over in a fury and started tugging the girl back.

Father Doonan licked his lips and said to me breathlessly, "Quick. Let's go."

I let in the clutch. We clattered out of the compound, out on to the first slope of the road. I could hear the picks and shovels and the human cargo bumping on the truck bottom as we began to hit the rocks. Then we gathered speed and went ripping down the incline in low gear, the tires spitting like a machine gun. We went shaking down the side of the mountain, first into the rain gullies, then faster along the coiling pumice bed of the road; stones scudded over the verge into the ravines, where they were swallowed as noiselessly as a python swallows a rabbit. It is not wise to stare down into those green gorges in daylight, something happens to the brain mechanism; it does peculiarly swimmy things to the stomach and the eyes.

I knew that Father Doonan was rigid at my side. He never—and why? it defeats me—completely trusted me.

As we skidded slightly over the broken earth, he said huskily, "This abominable truck has a demon. You've no right to give it its head."

"Leave it to me, Father," I said.

"I refuse to feel easy. Slow down. You'll kill all of us."

I said humorously, for it wasn't a bad joke, "Then we'll go to heaven in good company. We'll all sneak behind your cassock through the Golden Gates."

Father Doonan said in a strangled voice, "You're a maniac. Slow down." I shoved at the brakes experimentally, just to show him that it was dangerous to check the truck once it had started its run—even assuming that the brakes would slow it, which was faintly doubtful. After that, Father Doonan sat back quietly, refusing to look out, staring down at his kneecaps—not that there was much to see of the landscape, for it was still dark; the thing that took one's eye most urgently was the slim sultry young moon, sated with the old moon, falling out of the sky.

It was then that I noticed the strong smell of burning. I thought at first it was the engine—but it wasn't that kind of smell. I peered below into the ravines for the red glare of a forest fire, but it was dark and still; in any case, it wasn't the smell of vegetation and sizzling sap. It was more the reek of embers, the smell of the pit. I decided that it was the brake bands scorching. I stopped jamming at the brakes.

Presently the sun began to push his pink paw into the sky; there was a little light on the horizon, not much, not enough to frighten the stars; soon we would have the whole theatrical pageantry of the dawn. I was letting the truck steer itself—nothing extraordinary, it had done the journey often enough—when suddenly Father Doonan clapped his hand on my knee and said with a frown, "There is something wrong with the engine. It's running hot."

"Not hotter than usual," I shrugged.

"It smells badly."

I answered carelessly, "It has never smelled like a lily. Why insult the old iron monstrosity now?" Nevertheless, it worried me. The stench of combustion was savagely pungent, it assailed the nostrils. The truck was bounding up a dragging incline, losing impetus, and I let gravity slow it down and bring it to a halt. I pulled up at the verge and got out. On one side of the track was the dark tangle of the forest. On the other a sheer precipice: one could, if one was interested in records, lean over and spit half a mile. I lifted the truck's hood. The engine had not really had a chance to get hot. I walked round the truck, feeling the hubcaps. I detected no reason for anxiety. Then the breeze fanned my face and I saw Father Doonan stand twitching his nostrils into the starlight: it was the wind that was carrying the smell of burning.

"There must be a forest fire somewhere," Father Doonan said.

I couldn't see any reflected glare in the sky; that heavy cinderous reek would have needed quite some bonfire. "I don't think so," I said. It was altogether too acrid, it impregnated the air. If Mephistopheles had not had a bath for a century, that is how he would have smelled. I went into the bushes to relieve myself, then I took a bottle of wine out of the cab and said, "Rest yourself, Padre. We'll let our box of tricks cool down, just in case."

Father Doonan spoke to the guard at the back. The men in the truck climbed out stiffly and stretched themselves.

We squatted at the verge in the darkness. The three malefactors appeared to be in a sullen humor; they removed themselves some distance from us. Father Doonan sat by them and put cigarettes quietly on the ground in front of them, one for each man. Charlie looked at his woodenly and shook his head. It was the first time I ever saw that Negro betray antagonism. Marcel hesitated greedily, then shrugged. Harry Frobisher stared at his cigarette. He put his heel on it and ground the tobacco into the dust.

"All right," Father Doonan said, grinning palely. He made an effort to compose himself. "Maybe that's got it out of your system. Let's try again."

"What goes with the cigarettes?" asked Marcel ironically. "A hit on the head?"

I heard Father Doonan murmur, "If you won't forgive me, how can I ever forgive myself?" but Marcel interrupted him roughly:

"How the hell do you come to be a priest? One of these days you'll lose your license. You're too quick with the punch."

Father Doonan said nothing; he seemed terribly chastened. If anything moved in his face I couldn't see it in the gloom.

Marcel was staring defensively at Harry Frobisher. He went on doggedly, "Sooner or later the girl's going to get what he would have given her. It couldn't happen to her from a better man. Did you have to crack his jaw for that?"

Then the Negro, Charlie, repelled Father Doonan by saying to him dispassionately, "We'd like to be by ourselves. We have a right to our own company."

Father Doonan said faintly, "Yes," shrinking under the rebuff. "You have that right. Excuse me," and he got up and moved away.

The fastidious slobs: what right had they to human dignity? The situation wasn't without its comedy. I grinned to myself. There was a little wine left in my bottle and I upturned it to catch the last few drops——

——And that was when it happened. I can recall the

shock it gave me as vividly as one recaptures one's most violent emotions—one's first woman, the agitated boyish fumbling one never forgets, the first sexual spasm—you know how these things are etched into the brain. The ground gave a soft liquid tremor, a wave passed beneath me; and I sat foolishly, the bottle uplifted, the drip of wine trickling down my chin. There had come a sudden brief silence, the birds hushed noticeably as if anticipating the shock; there was a deep rumble like the sound of an express train passing by. But the rumble was not in the air about us, it seemed to come from the very belly of the earth.

I sat stupidly watching a gush of loosened gravel sliding into the ditch. That was all; the night was calm again; the stars hadn't shifted in the sky. But the earth is our one sure refuge—when that betrays us, nothing is ever the same again.

Father Doonan was standing near me and I heard him say out loud, huskily, "I have just felt the Devil pass under my feet."

The Melanesians had risen. They turned their flat faces up to the crest of the mountain. Perhaps some tribal memory told them what it was. We were all very quiet, waiting for it to happen again. But the earth was solid; it had had its little joke, and enough was enough.

I said to Father Doonan, "Let's get on, I don't want to get caught in a landslide up here." But he didn't answer, frozen in some kind of nervous anxiety—his head cocked to one side, as if still listening out for the Devil. That was a terrible thing he'd said. I got into the cab in a sweat and beckoned to the natives to climb aboard. And I think—I am not sure—that out of the corner of my eye I saw the three men go. One moment there were three dark shapes in the starlight, made almost imperceptible by the over-hanging trees. Then I couldn't distinguish the black shadows—I heard a rustle in the forest—and they were gone. I was in such a natural panic that I couldn't have cared less. The native policemen first discovered that they had absconded.

They gave a shout and started brandishing their carbines into the darkness. They ran over to Father Doonan, pointing into the forest, and he hurried to the trees, shouting to Frobisher and Marcel and Charlie to come back. . . .

I thought dully. "These men are crazy. They have no food, no shelter: if they get themselves lost in the jungle they will leave their bones to be cleaned by the ants." Father Doonan ran into the forest, yelling, his voice echoing, and I was afraid that if he strayed too far he'd leave himself permanently in the jungle, too.

After a while, he reappeared with the native policemen, saying helplessly, "They've gone."

I do not deny saying spitefully, "Good riddance." I just wanted to get down to the town.

"Something terrible will happen to them," he said, making an agonized gesture.

I retorted properly that nothing worse than a Tahiti jail could happen to them. "If they've made a break for it," I said, "that's their lookout." I wasn't going to cry for them.

He started, "We must try again——"

But I interrupted furiously, "We can't search all the forest. You'd need an army for that." I wouldn't let him speak; my insides hadn't readjusted themselves; I was still in a cold sweat. I waved to him insistently to get into the truck. And then it happened again.

The soft belly-rumble, the tremor in the earth that loosens one's bowels, that indescribably unnerving sensation: the wave passed under us and I gripped the wheel ridiculously for support. With it, this time, I caught the bitter smell of burning; I think the wind had changed and brought it around. I had a peculiar feeling that the air was thickening; something was happening that was outside ordinary human experience. There was a faint haze like thin snow in the starlight.

I got out of the cab and turned my face up and smelled it—felt it—brush my face. I peered at the hood and drew my finger along it. It was covered with a fine white ash.

I blinked dismally at Father Doonan. He was staring up the mountain. I had the totally crazy notion that he was worrying about the hospital; and we were already three-quarters of the way down. I had had enough. I started up the engine and flung the cab door open to suggest that he could get in or not. He got in. He looked very pale.

We drove on. The sun—as happens in the Pacific—literally rushed up. The edge of the sea was on fire for a moment, the stars were puffed out like candles, and the sky was alight. The deep ravines were still black where the sun couldn't reach them. But the ridges and the gullies glittered, and a haze of white ash covered them: the way icing covers a birthday cake. It swirled in the air snow-like—but warm as it drifted through the windows into the cab.

I spat it out. It irritated the nostrils. It tasted like Old Nick's snuff. I had never been so frightened in my life.

Then we rounded a bend in the road, catching sight of the town below us; and looking up, I saw the old crater of the mountain. I had always seen it blunt, tree ridged, worn out and silent—and suddenly, like a dirty old man who has discovered some pills that give him vitality, it was agog. A thick flurry of smoke rolled out of its upturned mouth. It was steamily white, flaked with ash—the steam dissipated itself as it rose and caught the pink rays of the sun, but the burden of the ash trailed solidly down the ravines toward the town.

Father Doonan stared at it. He didn't encourage me: he crossed himself.

I did the journey down to the town faster than I had ever done it. We rattled over the Old Wooden Bridge at a formidable speed: it made the whole structure rumble. And when we rolled into the street, clattering over the cobbles, the entire town was up—barely twenty minutes after dawn—standing on the foreshore, trying to see the crater over the rooftops, and I looked back (my eyes refusing to register it) at the dark slurred trails our tires were leaving in the feathery whiteness of the road.

4

THE seaplane pilot comes back into the picture here. In fact, he was able to pick up the thread of the story at almost the precise moment Aristide relinquished it—he had been peering out of his hotel window just after dawn (stark naked; he slept as virginal as Adam in that climate, he said), shocked out of sleep by the first subterranean tremor. And, dumbfounded, he had seen Aristide's truck come driving along the street in what looked like a pale wintry fog; which was ridiculous because a tropical sun was beginning to flash up.

The haze drifted with a muffling sulfurous languor in the windless air. The pilot was astonished to see the truck leaving dark tracks on the white-coated cobbles; like a snowy Christmas card, he said.

But even in that moment of confusion he was sufficiently alert to notice that there were fewer men crouched in the back of the truck than had gone up. The birds of passage had flown. I don't know why (said the pilot), but it made me very angry with Father Doonan. They had made a fool of him. So much for human nature; next time the priest would learn to trust faithless scamps no farther than the bars of their prison cell.

Most of the population had come out into the street. Chiefly they were in pajamas, staring up at the top of the mountain, coughing and muttering; for some unnatural reason they seemed afraid to raise their voices. A veil of fine ash had drifted on to the window sill. I brushed it off with my finger bewilderedly. I had been fast asleep when the first tremor came; I opened my eyes to the taste of a bad dream—and the taste was terribly real, it was actually sneaking in through the open window—with a vague memory that the bed had throbbed beneath me. The second shock came quite a while later. I was wide awake now and I heard the soft grunt in the belly of the earth, a kind of regurgitation as if the island had swallowed something bad. In fact, that was the inconceivable notion I had when the tremor followed: that the earth was hiccuping.

The bed creaked sharply; a picture swung very slightly; and scraps of plaster fell off the wall.

It was getting light now. I had a natural fear that the hotel, which was only stucco and tiles, might collapse on me. I dragged on a coat and joined the people in the street. The air was foul with that acrid stench. It was rolling down from the crater like a gray curtain, guided by the ravines down to the town. It had chopped the radio-telephone mast in half; the upper part of the structure was cloaked as if by a fog. There was no fire, not even any rumbling, just a quiet steamy billow on the top of the mountain.

And soft creamy ash all over the street.

I heard the drugged, sleepy voice of a woman mutter,

"This is no joke"—it was the wife of Gaston, the *patron* of the Pêche d'Or. She was in her nightgown, torn warm from her bed, exposing more than her husband would normally desire others to see; he was probably too fuddled with shock to care.

"I never saw anything like it before. Somebody had better do something about it," he complained thickly—as if the Governor had fallen down on his duty.

When people are frightened they say some very foolish things. They huddle together like sheep.

I watched them covertly in the pink light of the dawn. They lined the foreshore, facing the mountain, all of them confused, silent when they were not coughing, the women in wrappers, the men scratching their chests, trying to wash the sediment of sleep out of their brains so that they could get a grip on the situation. Which, obviously, wasn't very pleasant: nobody likes to live a lifetime under a dead old mountain to find that it has never really been dead, only slumberous. A few of the native house servants and gardeners—the tribesfolk lived in their own villages along the beach—were staring up at the steamy crater woodenly. Maybe it was an old story to them; nothing like it had happened on the island for four or five hundred years, but eruptive volcanoes are no novelty in the Pacific. A tradition of it no doubt lingered in the blood.

Jean-Pierre, the attorney, chuckled with a feeble attempt at comedy, "Somebody has been snoring too loud. Who woke the old bastard up?" But the joke didn't go down; nervousness lay all over them like a fur.

And we stood there, in shared uneasiness, for about half an hour as the sun swarmed up into the sky. There was a colored halo about it; I suppose from the dust suspended in the air. The shadows of the houses began to shorten. Then the palm trees began to sway and rustle as the breeze came up.

It created a small miracle. The dawn always fetches the wind and it went murmuring over the beaches, up the hillside, and the gritty curtain of smoke from the mountain began to roll away from the town. You could see it bodily changing its direction. In about ten minutes the haze was blown right out of the street; it was drenching the distant beaches, but the town was clean and golden with sunlight. And all of a sudden the top of the radio-telephone mast was clear: the iron filigree of the structure crept starkly out of the mist. I think it was that that affected the people mostly. It was as heartening as a Biblical sign.

Take trouble, dump it next door in somebody else's lap, and instantly people cheer up. There was a rustle of relief along the street and someone said, "Now we can set up a factory to start smoking fish."

"Don't ask me to invest money in it," the attorney, Jean-Pierre, laughed importantly. "It wouldn't keep anybody in business very long."

And one by one they began to drift back into their houses. I went up to my hotel room to get dressed. Then I walked over to the jetty toward the seaplane; it was rocking softly in the sparkling lagoon, and the co-pilot was there with the navigator, both on the wings, brushing the light coating off the engine nacelles.

The co-pilot called out to me truculently, "That's a hell of a thing, eh? I don't like it a bit."

"We're not going to be here long enough to have to like it," I said. "How long are you going to take over that damned engine?"

"It'll be finished this afternoon. I just want to get to hell out of this place."

"I'll ask the Governor when he's going to be ready."

"Don't ask him," the co-pilot grunted. "Tell him. Inform him that I have a nervous disposition."

Our shy navigator said reassuringly, "It's all right, really, it's thinning out." He pointed up the hillside at the shredding smoky curtain. "Look, it's nearly over. You can see it dying away."

It was, actually: dying away. A two-hour scare. It was just the remnants of the ash rolling down the mountain; there was still a pink plume of steam over the crater, very jaunty, the way a woman wears a feathery hat; but the ravines immediately below it were almost clear.

I had breakfast. I went over to the guardhouse. The corporal was in the compound. He grinned at me.

"Ah, *le touriste*," he said. "Well, we're putting on a special treat for trippers today. I hope the excitement isn't going to be too much for you?"

"Not enough to write home about," I said. I sat down by him. "It doesn't seem to worry you."

He spat into the dust, that abrasive, leathery-faced man. "I can show you volcanoes in Honolulu that have been smoking for three hundred years. Nobody grumbles. Here, the old beast in the attic"—he peered ironically up the mountain—"turns over once in ten generations to have a puff at a cigarette, and the whole island has a nervous convulsion."

"There are women," I shrugged excusingly. "And children."

"And too much fat living. Too much wine. They're too soft, they've had it too easy," he said.

While he was speaking my eyes wandered about the glaring yard, past that leaning skyscraper of a palm tree, past a couple of native policemen cleaning the windows, to someone in dark clothes—a cassock—sitting patiently outside the Governor's office. I stared hard at the man, Father Doonan. He was very still, head bent, queerly unrelaxed.

I lowered my voice to the corporal, "What's he doing over there?"

The corporal grinned again. "He had to come and eat dirt to the Governor. Didn't I tell you what would happen with those three rogues? Well, it happened. Now that priest has to start growing up." The corporal grunted and licked the grime off his lips. "The Governor taught him the facts of life. He has a tongue like a saber. It made the Irishman crawl."

I said slyly, "But you still haven't got the three men?"

"No," said the corporal softly. "And I don't want them, either. Let the jungle have them. It will know what to do with them."

He had everybody bleakly sorted out in that military filing cabinet of a mind. The priest was a natural trouble-maker, the townsfolk were too self-indulgent; as for the three escaped good-for-nothings, he wouldn't even make mental room for them—all he had for them was a hole in the ground.

I got up, still looking at Father Doonan, and said, "Well, what's he waiting for?"

"He's worried about the hospital. The telephone line has gone. He's waiting for it to be reconnected. A man like that has to have something to worry about."

I walked over to Father Doonan. He looked up, recognized me, smiling shyly—but wanly—and I said, "Is everything all right?"

He said, "Thank you for asking," and he meant it, he was truly grateful that I had asked. "I'm a bit anxious. We can't talk to the hospital. The Governor's sending out a crew to mend the line." He looked covertly up the hillside. "I just want to hear that they're all right."

"A little smoke," I shrugged. "A bit of a jolt. That couldn't have harmed them."

"I'd just like to hear from them," he said.

He sat there, making one feel uncomfortable, his cassock dusty, out of his *milieu*—a strange Irishman—and I said, regretting it instantly, "Well, I hear your birds flew off."

"It was my fault," he said.

"You couldn't have stopped them escaping if you'd had them nailed down. They're just a bunch of no-goods."

And he surprised me with his flash of anger. He cried, "Never say that about human beings—that they're no good. Everybody's good for something. I was to blame, it was cruel of me to let them smell freedom and expect them to come back. Even the Devil wouldn't have tempted them like that." I must have grinned, for he said, looking at me crookedly, "If you'd been in their shoes, would *you* have come back?"

Questions like that are unanswerable; I turned my back on him and walked off.

When I passed that way a couple of hours later he was still sitting there, grilling gently in the torrid sun, waiting patiently for the Governor to tell him something, staring with submissive anxiety into the dust. I had lunch— frankly, I refused to let the man detract from my appetite —then I went to the barber's shop for a shave.

I think that short session in the barber's shop was where the drama started getting frighteningly personal: it suddenly reached down over the footlights and dragged the audience on to the stage to take part in the play.

Louis, the hairdresser, had a small overscented establishment; it was apt to smell like a whore getting herself ready for business on a Saturday night. There were two chairs— he had a native assistant—and I sat in one and Aristide, the fat little truck driver, sat in the other, and he gabbled monotonously all the time. I didn't listen much—nobody listens to barber-shop chatterers—then I heard Father Doonan's name mentioned and I pricked up my ears. This Aristide was in something of an outraged state. Apparently Father Doonan had begged him to take him up the mountain in the truck to see if they were all right at the hospital.

Louis was shaving me and I turned my head slightly and mumbled through the soap, "So what did you say?"

"Say? I said in plain French: 'I have no holes in my head. We have only just come down from the mountain, what's the sense in going up again?' "

I reminded myself guiltily of the silent priest waiting in the yard, and I said, "He's worried about them up there. Maybe that old volcano means business——"

But Aristide cut in disdainfully, *"Folie*. It's like a woman with a bad temper, you just turn your back on her and let her blow off steam."

I have known bad-tempered women crack a man's head wide open for turning his back on them. "I hope so," I said.

"That Father Doonan," Aristide grumbled defensively, "is a little crazed. It must be the sun. Maybe he's not accustomed to the sun? 'Aristide,' he says, as if it is a mere bagatelle, 'take me up the mountain in the truck this afternoon. It will be an act of grace. Heaven will reward you.' "

Louis grinned. "I've never seen a check from heaven that my bank would take."

"He had no right to appeal to my finer feelings."

"When priests appeal to my finer feelings," said Louis, "I go conveniently deaf."

"Religion and business don't mix."

"Without prejudice to religion, I wouldn't cut a bishop's hair for free," Louis said.

But the words "for free" creaked; I was lying back in the chair and suddenly it seemed to float strangely; the motion was quite perceptible and Louis hovered stiffly above me, his razor frozen on my face as if we were posing for a photograph. I felt his breath on my cheek. I saw his eyes go blank. I didn't know which to fear more, that unsettling liquid motion, or the razor paralyzed on my face. Louis lifted himself off me. He gave a husky inquiring murmur. I lay entranced, staring at the mirror on the wall; and again it happened, I saw my reflection in it grow blurred as if the mirror had been jarred. There was a slight tinkle as the bottles of colored hair oils rattled on the glass shelves. Now—as if momentarily delayed—I heard a sound, a faint whiplike crack in the air.

It seemed to come from a great distance in the sky.

Then once again, the vibration, the chair floating distressfully, just for an instant. I saw the faces of Louis and Aristide gaping at me in the mirror; and then the mirror split gently across, dividing our features drunkenly, and a piece of glass went jangling to the floor. Louis shivered and said faintly, "Jesus. My mirror. What is going on?"

The crack in the sky—louder than any whip—came again, banging out a hollow echo this time. Louis put down the razor feebly, gazing at the quietly split mirror, and I got up, half soaped like a clown, and hurried to the door.

The street was filling up; they were pouring out of the houses, staring up. There was no doubt where it came from. I heard Aristide beg pathetically, "Is it *that?* It's done it again?"

I walked over to the crowd gathering on the foreshore, so shaken that it didn't even occur to me to wipe the lather from my face. The steam hanging over the crater had gone gray, curling over as its flat crown was caught by the breeze. It was an atomic explosion in miniature: you have seen pictures of those frightful toadstools; this one was only a baby, doubtless, but I cannot tell you how awesomely it affected me. I thought—staring hard, but not too sure because the sun dazzled my eyes—that a rain of débris, at least something more solid than smoke, was pouring out of the crater into the sky. Someone was shouting, with nervous passion, just down the street.

It was Gaston, from the bistro. His handsomely bottled window was cracked.

I felt Aristide at my side, tugging my arm. He was soundless with fright. I was frightened, also; perhaps that was why I said to him spitefully, "It's just like a bad-tempered woman, all you have to do is turn your back on her." My God, I reproached myself bitterly, but for that damned seaplane engine we'd have been able to fly out of here as fast as a bat out of hell.

Then there was a soft, almost disarming, belch; a little discreet rumble in the guts of the earth. I saw the filth from the mountain's intestines go gushing skywards—no doubt about it this time, stones, red-hot embers, spraying from the crater as if from a blowpipe. The ashes from the first bang were settling softly and wintrily—as if from some split feather bolster—in the street; everybody started waving at them ludicrously. They stank.

The roar of the convulsion came now. The ripple of the ground, doing things to the stomach, and then the sound of plaster and brickwork falling into the street. I saw—plainly, with my own eyes—three houses and a shop split like rotten apples from top to bottom, and bits of masonry toppling, glass tinkling, and then tiles go sliding noisily off the roofs. A child began to yowl. I felt a nervous twinge of sympathy; an inclination likewise to cry.

I am no coward: I have fought not inconspicuously in the war; and babies do not fly airplanes.

But the worst was now happening. The great radio-telephone mast, all gaunt iron, towering over the lower slopes of the mountain, was leaning over. It didn't lean very far to begin with, just a few degrees, as if someone had given it a careless shove. But it was no longer quite vertical, and I could see the iron struts in its side buckling as the flutter in the earth gave the structure another jar. It had a slow, graceful movement; the antennæ on its top performing a gradual arc. It went on leaning and leaning, until the angle at which it drooped was insupportable to the eye: then it went quicker and quicker, the struts crumpling midway down the mast, and it tottered with a sound like splitting firewood to the ground.

I think, to everybody in the street, it was a spectacle of uttermost ill-omen: the radio-telephone mast was the island's sole cause for existence. And when it went it was as terrible an event as if God had leaned down from His firmament and slapped us chasteningly in the face.

I wiped the lather off my cheek. I ran back to the hotel. The co-pilot and the navigator were leaning out of the window. As I approached, the co-pilot shouted at me furiously—the fury was nine-tenths fear—"Did you talk to the Governor?"

I called up confusedly from the street, "Talk to him about what?"

"When are we going to get away? Go and see him, for God's sake. Are you going to leave us stranded in this?"

"How are we fixed?"

"We can fly. Now settle it with him. This isn't our business, I didn't come here to be incinerated." He was still yelling at me cheatedly as I hurried down the street, "No delays. Don't make damned heroes out of us, I have a wife and two kids . . ." and then his voice was lost in another chesty rumble from below, in the rattle of more falling glass, in the stabbing gabble from the agitated crowd.

I went to the Governor's office, hurrying through the yard past the guardhouse. A couple of Melanesian prisoners had started painting the roof; they crouched on it lazily; for a moment the discipline of labor was gone. The corporal was outside. I said to him breathlessly,

"Well. This is a nice kettle of fish," and he shrugged . . .

"Ah, control yourself," with an angry grunt. "What sort of a baby are you? It'll pass."

I pointed to the peak of the mountain and said, "Can't you see what's happening up there?"

"So what do you expect me to do? Go up and urinate on it to put it out?"

"See if you talk like that tomorrow."

He grinned callously. "You'll be here to enjoy it, believe me. Going to see the Governor? Don't kid yourself, *chéri*, you're not going to fly away from us today." I'd gone only a few paces when he called me back. His weather-beaten face was split by a wide smile.

"Want to see something funny?"

I wondered what he was talking about; he nudged me to the guardhouse door and pointed inside. Three men sat wretchedly in the corner. You can guess? Harry Frobisher and Marcel and Charlie. I never saw such exhausted, beaten creatures. Their pants were torn; the pink of Frobisher's legs showed through the rents; Marcel was rubbing his scratched hands blindly over his face. All three saw me, and Harry Frobisher looked through me wryly, Charlie's expression remained sad and flat, and Marcel—that fat undefeatable clown—tried to grin, but it was pathetically feeble. They looked as if they had been passed through a mincing machine.

"They're hungry," the corporal said. "They got lost. They were frightened." His voice disarmingly gentle, he went on, "The prodigal sons have returned. They've come crawling back. We're laying on a wonderful dinner for them, the bath water's hot, we're putting clean sheets on their beds." The exultant corporal looked at them out of unsmiling eyes, and Marcel winced: he knew what ignominy to expect.

"Could one have a drink?" he asked.

"Ring for the steward. He is here to accommodate your every need."

"Water will do."

"I would consider it an affront to gratify you with less than champagne."

Harry Frobisher said defiantly, "Go to hell, you hard-faced bastard."

"You'll get a special taste of it from me, *mon enfant*," the corporal said. But when he came out into the yard with me his expression changed. He said resentfully, "The Governor's forbidden me to put them back into the hole. Too many priests around here. I ask you? Christian charity for pigs like that."

I went to the Governor's door and knocked on it and looked in. Father Doonan was in the office with the Governor, his voice raised edgily, "But you promised that the telephone line would be repaired——"

"If you want miracles go to church and pray for them," the Governor said. "I can only do what is humanly possible." He saw me over Father Doonan's shoulder and he beckoned me in; he was glad of the interruption. The priest was evidently fraying his nerves.

"What do you want?" he asked me.

I didn't know how to suggest that we would like to be gone, which was what I had come for, so I said foolishly, "The aircraft is ready. It is at your service as soon as you wish."

"It will have to wait." He shut the window decisively, ash flakes and smoke were creeping in. "Do you think we are leaving with this unpleasantness on our hands?" he demanded. "You must be out of your mind."

I remembered the co-pilot's enraged nervous voice and it prompted me to mumble, "But there is nothing we can do here, Governor. Perhaps we can be of greater service? If we reported the matter to Tahiti . . ."

"You may be required for more important services than that." And the cold military eyes shut me up, snapping tight on me like oyster shells.

I went to the door, hearing Father Doonan begin again, pleading anxiously, "They may be in danger up there. They are alone. Helpless. You must tell me how to get up to the hospital. . . ."

I closed the door on the Governor's taut overstrained voice, "Walk!"

"Walk," I thought. This was one hell of a predicament. I went to the beach and looked through the gritty haze in the air across the blue ripple of the lagoon, peering between the slanting palms at the seaplane nuzzling the jetty. I could see the co-pilot and the navigator busy furiously inside. They were too damned hopeful. They were eager to get away. "All right, children," I thought, "walk!"

That night the cap blew off the mountain. It happened a little before dawn. I had made up my mind to stay awake—I had a kind of premonition. I was sitting in a chair, but I had closed the window to keep out the acid cinders; the air was foul and I must have fallen into a stupor. When the crash of the eruption came it lifted me a clear two inches off my chair.

While I timed five seconds—cringing in the chair—I heard that shattering boom flinging echoes off the hillsides, overlaid by a vast hiss as if a gigantic steampipe had blown. I suppose that was roughly what had happened: the volcano's blocked steampipe had blown. I ran out of the hotel into the street with the co-pilot dragging on his pajamas behind me, muttering vengefully at the back of my neck. He was in a vicious state—he seemed to blame me, either for the aircraft's engine going wrong, or for not persuading the Governor to let us go, or maybe for not interceding with God to stop the eruption. The navigator (I didn't blame a boy of his age for being pale) followed us hastily into the street.

The whole crater was fringed with yellow-red flame. It seemed to snake up to the sky as if fanned by pressure from below, the way the corona of the sun streaks out from the dark edge of an eclipse. And I was astounded to see that the blunt rim of the crater was now a different shape. It slanted down to the sea; evidently a part of it had exploded off. Grumbling sounds were still echoing down from the sky line. The navigator had brought his binoculars and I took them out of his hand and stared up.

The bonfire up near the dark heaven was clouding thickly with débris shooting out of the hole; I could see (I think I could) trees near the crater burning, but most unpleasantly of all I could see thin red fingers poking slyly down the side of the mountain. I didn't need two guesses: lava was beginning to flow.

"Well, this is wonderful," the co-pilot said furiously. "Now I suppose I should send my wife a radiogram telling her good-bye."

I was as shaken as he was and I said, "Better send her a letter. The radio-telephone mast has gone."

"We're going to be fried. Doesn't that worry you?"

"You'll fry in good company. Don't make such a national disaster out of it, there's nothing to worry about yet."

The navigator said softly—he was a good boy—"We're all in the same boat. Look, there are women." He stared at the silent gathering crowd. "We should set them a good example, not start them off into hysterics."

"When I need a sermon," shouted the co-pilot, "I'll go and get it in church."

The remark drew my eyes over to the church. Father

Doonan was standing in the porch, gazing up; I couldn't see his face in the dawn light, but his body seemed rigid with distress. My mind reverted to the hospital. I thought, "Well, they must have had it quickly, the doctor and the matron and the colored nurses and the twenty-eight leprous kids." In such circumstances instant obliteration must have been a mercy.

I went over to the priest.

He looked at me poignantly, not recognizing me to begin with, his face working. He said, "I should have gone up to them. They shouldn't be suffering alone up there."

"They're not suffering any more," I said. "Not after that," and I pointed up to the inferno. . . .

But he wasn't listening; he was just murmuring, as if to himself, "I should have walked, crawled, anything. I should have gone up."

"You'd still be crawling by Christmas," I shrugged: the man didn't seem to have a single practical thought. I said, "It's idiotic to torture yourself like that," and left him. I was terribly tired, irritated, all on edge.

It is probably an instinct in all of us to hide away from fearsome events. I had the kind of peculiar whim pregnant women are supposed to get—I just wanted desirously to wash the taste of smoke out of my mouth. I went down to the beach and dragged off my pajamas and dived into the sea. I plunged through the cool surf, swimming a little way out into the lagoon, watching the firework glitter on the dark water, the crackling light catching the tops of the palm trees: I was the ostrich burying his head in the nearest watery sand. I swam over to the jetty and clung to the float of the seaplane; it was coated with grit.

Then the sun started coming up. And one way or another the sun is always a friend. The sky flushed quickly, and presently there was enough light for me, treading salt-heavy water, to see the hot filth spurting overdramati-

cally from the top of the mountain, the faintly lumines-
cent lava poking down the shadowed ravines like neon
threads.

I thought fatalistically, "If it has to happen, it'll happen"; but I didn't really believe it possible that I would
die. I rubbed the thighs that not many hours ago had
caressed Daisy's—we're most of us conscious of the perma-
nence of life in the middle of the act of sex—flesh that felt
altogether too warm and vibrant and unready for death
. . . "No," I thought, "the grumpy old beast of the mountain is just putting on a show." Fear belongs to darkness.
So I climbed on to the jetty and sat there, dripping,
wrapped in *nostalgie,* wondering why I wasn't hungry,
why I couldn't get my breath properly, why—if I wasn't
frightened—I only wanted nervously to yawn.

I was still sitting there when the navigator came running up. He stared at my naked body stupidly.

"We couldn't find you. The Governor has sent for you."

"He doesn't want me. He wants the fire brigade."

He said uneasily, "You'd better come. Everybody has
been searching," and I grunted and put on my pajamas,
hurrying back to the hotel to get dressed. I started off for
the Governor's residence.

I heard steps behind. Father Doonan was following me.

The Governor was in his office. I don't think he'd slept
much; he didn't get out of his chair. Even in his robe, unshaven, he looked more military than I did. His face was
set like a mask: you know the soldier's expression. When
you are nervous, try to look as if your mouth is made of
stone.

"You took your time," he said.

"I went for a swim in the lagoon," I said.

He stared at me as if I had uttered an insult, murmur-

ing bleakly, "You went for . . . ?" But what could he do?
I was a civilian type. Then he said, "I want you to fly over
the crater and tell me what it's like. I want a clear picture
of the situation before I finally decide."

I felt like asking, decide what? But it was beginning to
be obvious; he looked at me sullenly, then bent down and
blew the ash off his desk. The gesture was significant.

"Get off as soon as you can," he said. "I want your report within the hour."

I said dubiously, "We're not going to be able to see
much."

"I do not require co-ordinated aerial photographs. Your
personal observations will do."

"It's all smoke up there."

"Then fly beneath it."

"We are likely to hit the side of the mountain."

"Then I'll see that you get posthumous citations for gallantry," he said harshly, which was his way of spitting contemptuously in my face. "You are under military orders.
Act accordingly. I intend to declare an emergency. Now
go."

I went back and told the co-pilot. He gave me a bad ten
minutes, as if I had personally made the suggestion to the
Governor. Eventually I got him down to the jetty, and
then I heard those trailing footsteps again and I saw Father
Doonan walking behind.

I stopped. I was in no mood for harassment. "Did you
want something?" I asked.

"I heard you speaking to the Governor. I'm coming
with you," he said.

"You are? What do you think this is?" I asked crossly.
"A hundred francs a trip round the lagoon? What's it got
to do with you?"

"I can help you. I know where the hospital's located. I
want to see if it's still there."

"That's ridiculous. How can it still be there?"

He said coolly, very stubbornly, "I want to see for myself."

"And supposing I forbid you?"

His snub-nosed Irish face crinkled and he chuckled dryly, "I would have to throw you into the sea." What's more, he was big enough to do it; and sufficiently frantic with anxiety to try.

The navigator muttered compassionately, "It's an act of mercy"—I suppose he was a churchgoer—"how can you forbid him? Let him come."

I felt like turning my back on the lot of them, the jittery complaining co-pilot, the religious navigator, and the overwrought priest. I got into the cockpit with a shrug, Father Doonan crawling in awkwardly, adjusting himself in the seat behind the navigator like an unblooded chaplain going into battle with his men.

I started up the engines and warmed them awhile; people were drifting with haggard curiosity to the foreshore to see why we were off. We taxied across the smooth water to the reef, turned for the take-off, then I boosted up the engines on full throttle and took the old crate across the lagoon. Her belly left the water; she was a little unwieldy, she jerked up as the drag of the water and the gritty bow wave ceased. We lifted slowly, wheeling over the harbor, going through hazy air, then up into a suddenly translucent sky as we got above it.

I went out to sea a little to gain height.

It was really not very spectacular from up there. A dark green pimple on a tranquil ocean, smoking, hot with pus where it was suppurating; in the dazzle of the sun not much fire could be seen. The wind had caught the billowing steam, trailing it like a dirty ribbon far out to sea. We got up to about six thousand meters, then circled back over the island, corkscrewing above it, coming down slowly to see what was to be seen. Which was almost nothing worth while: over the crater the smoke was dense, whipping past the plexiglass of the cockpit like a Channel fog. It penetrated the fuselage and made us cough. I was nervous of getting too low with visibility as bad as that, but if we were going to get a look at the thing it was no use peering at it delicately from upstairs. I took the aircraft down.

The co-pilot grumbled, "What are you trying to do? Fetch a few souvenirs of rock back with us?" but I had stopped listening to him; I said snappily, "Watch our altitude and leave the flying to me."

The navigator was staring below, Father Doonan leaning intently over his shoulder. The navigator said, "I think we can risk another thousand meters," pointing down.

"Let's walk the rest of the way," the co-pilot scowled.

We went lower. Now it *was* petrifying: we were getting to close quarters. It was a bird's eye view of hell. Sinners should be flown over volcanoes and they'd be reformed overnight. The hot uprush caught the wings and we shuddered in the thrust. The smoke was black, mixed with small stones sprayed from the crater; they rattled on the plexiglass like hail. We were almost over the very center of the crater, a reeking tongue-fired pit, with embers gushing up from it abominably, fascinating me with horror so that I almost lost sensitive control of the wheel. The gas from the earth's guts was blasting forcibly into the sky, smacking us bodily; what scared me most was that a boulder might be tossed up and go through the fuselage: then *kaput* for us. I kept going because there was nowhere else to go but straight across it. I looked back for no particular reason and saw Father Doonan's face contorted; it had given him his first realistic appreciation of purgatory.

Then I saw the lava pink and creamy, nosing in three main streams over the lips of the smashed crater; they had already slid down the ravines some distance. Trees and bushes were burning in their paths.

Father Doonan gripped my shoulder. We were over the hot spot, out into comparatively clear air, and he pointed down at the ledges of the mountain, calling out, "Round about there. The hospital. Try again."

Through the whipping smoke I saw the road fleetingly as he spoke. I also saw that it was crossed in two places by smoking lava, and that the whole ledge of the mountain on which it coiled had collapsed into a gorge. As a navigable road it was now only a bad joke. I circled back to where Father Doonan was gesturing excitedly—where he thought the hospital ought to be. Well, it wasn't; there was nothing but a sea of flaring smoke from vents opening up in the ground.

Then I felt his big hand literally crunch my shoulder as he cried out passionately, "There, I see it, it's there." The co-pilot looked at him insanely. I hadn't seen a thing; I hadn't expected to. I stared inquiringly at the navigator and he looked at me dubiously, shaking his head slowly. I think the priest had *wanted* to see it; his overworked imagination had done the rest.

I shouted back over the roar of the engines, "You're mistaken. There's nothing there."

"In God's name. I swear it. I saw it. It's still standing there."

"Every priest wants his personal miracle," I thought sourly; I made a hopeless thumbs-down gesture and his whole face went crazy with pity and yearning for the lost hospital. He leaned over me, crying into my ear, "I saw it. I saw it!"

"Don't kid yourself," I yelled.

But to mollify him, for there was a kind of inner violence in the man, an emotional reflection of the volcano, I banked and came back so that he could have another look.

"Lower, lower," he kept saying, squeezing my arm, "we won't see anything in this." I went lower to please him. The smoke started streaking past us, we went down into it —my heart in my mouth, the co-pilot protesting thickly, the priest peering out—then for an instant there was a little visibility, a vista of jungled slopes and gorges; then the wreathing pall of fumes closed in on us again. Father Doonan cried, "I saw it, I saw it," gripping me so that it hurt, and I blinked at his face—it was as exalted as if he'd had a vision of the Holy Grail and it was burned into his brain. "It's there. They're still alive, it's all right," he cried.

Did I see it? I don't think so; who could pick out a little white hospital in that harassing sea of smoke? The navigator muttered hesitantly, "I don't know—maybe I saw something . . ."

But the co-pilot shouted, "You're as crazy as the priest, nobody saw anything at all."

Then three voices were battling in the fuselage—the co-pilot's bellowing with fear, the priest's imploring, and mine yelling agitatedly to them to shut up—for the side of the mountain was rushing straight at us, and I yanked with all my strength at the stick. The sweat sprang out on me as if a wet sponge had been dashed into my face. The co-pilot pushed at the throttles to boost the engines. "This is death," I thought, "and not a quick one . . ." Those few seconds hung like all eternity. The old seaplane wallowed and lifted its nose. A crag whisked below us, the forest was almost scraping our belly—branches trying to grab us —then we were over the escarpment with only centimeters to spare, rising into the smoke.

Father Doonan was crying into my ear. It was so ridiculous that I didn't believe what I heard. He had his hand on one of the parachute packs and he was gesturing down passionately, "Drop me, drop me."

I said stupidly, "You're out of your mind," and the co-pilot made a mad movement as if it was getting beyond him.

"Drop me, I want to go to them," Father Doonan cried. He pulled at me and I wobbled at the controls. The co-pilot pushed the priest away brutally, struggling with him; then we were out at sea, bursting into glassily transparent air, corkscrewing slowly to touch down in the lagoon.

I was shivering with rage as we ripped over the reef and scraped water, taxiing with tired engines over to the jetty. I climbed out stiffly, probably looking like an old man. As Father Doonan emerged I said to him, "You could have endangered the aircraft. I ought to report this to the Governor."

And I don't think he was even listening—he was still filled with his religious vision of the hospital. "You should have dropped me," he said reproachfully, his face griped with distress. "Don't you see? They're all alone. Somebody has to help them. I have to go to them."

"We nearly went to hell with you," I said. I left him standing there and went to the Governor to report.

I didn't tell him what had happened; I just told him that I'd taken the priest along with us to search for the hospital.

"Did you see it?" asked the Governor, looking at me sharply as if I had exceeded my rights.

I hesitated. How could I be certain? "No," I shrugged.

"Did anyone else?"

"Only Father Doonan. He said he saw it."

He said flatly, "That man would see angels in a public urinal if it was necessary to him." I mentioned that the navigator hadn't been too sure—he thought he'd seen something—but the Governor cut in irritably, "That boy is too young to be trusted to wash the back of his neck." Then he asked me to describe what it was like up near the

91

crater. I told him without mincing words. I said there were three streams of lava coming down the mountain; they'd advanced maybe a thousand meters, but I couldn't say how fast they were moving. That new vents were opening up under the pressure and that the eruption didn't seem to be slackening off.

He was a small gray man with a great load of responsibility: he had the lives of a community on his hands. He said after a while, very softly as if I wasn't intended to hear, "We have to leave. It isn't safe to hang on."

Then he went to the window. He gave me another of his exhausted gray smiles and beckoned to me. I looked out. Everything I had seen up on the mountain somehow slipped into horrifying perspective—as if the jigsaw puzzle had been rapped so that all the pieces slid cruelly into place. The picture I saw shocked me. I will tell you what I saw.

The beach was black with the Melanesian villagers packing their outrigger canoes and rushing them through the surf into the lagoon. The old, the young, the bits of precious belongings, the sucking pigs and the vegetables, were aboard, and the little fleet paddled out and collected in a precise kind of battle order, then headed for the opening in the reef. I watched the heaving dots diminish as they made out to sea.

"You see? They know," the Governor said.

5

BY midmorning it must have been obvious to everybody that evacuation of the island was inevitable and that it would have to be swift. It was accepted with stunned incredulity—the way an apparently healthy man accepts the harsh ultimatum of the surgeon's knife. I think it was the departure of the aborigines, the superstitious implications, that caused the community's morale finally to crumble. The mental surrender turned into a landslide; we were sitting on a boiling kettle that was almost ready to blow its lid.

Even in the dazzle of the sun at its zenith one had only to look up at the "old beast in the attic" (the corporal's description) to see the red fringe of fire about his lips. The ash had become so thick on the sidewalks that it deadened footfalls. In the funereal hush one could hear small muffled thumps. They were the sounds of distant cliffs collapsing, of trees being bulldozed by the lava's shove.

Perhaps, after all, soldiers make the best colonial administrators. Having no imagination, they are incapable of spreading panic from the top. And when they act it is with military resolution. At about eleven o'clock the Governor proclaimed *un état de crise*—a state of emergency, you would call it—and native policemen appeared quietly outside shops. Looting is a symptom of despair; in a wave of hysteria people are apt to grab anything that might of necessity have to be left behind. I noticed that the two freighters in the harbor were hastily emptying their holds—to make room for human cargoes—and that the schooner in the lagoon had pulled up its anchor and was being towed over to the jetty. I was squatting on the wing of the seaplane with the co-pilot, filling up with petrol to be ready for eventualities. There was only one eventuality that interested me; you can guess what it was.

As the schooner slid by, the master—he was a Norwegian named Captain Olsen—called over to me, "So it's *finis*, eh? As quick as that. What did it look like up there?"

"Somebody woke up the devil. He's in a bad temper. He's spitting brimstone," I said.

"If we don't hurry, my God, we're going to get our pants scalded off." The Norwegian grinned enviously at the seaplane. "You're lucky. In half an hour you can be seventy miles away."

I had to make a pretence of regarding it as a reflection on my character. I said coldly, "I've had no instructions to leave."

"Well, it won't be long now."

"Probably. But I stand by until I'm told to go."

The co-pilot burst out. "We're isolated." He had got himself into a bad spiral of nerves; one couldn't do anything with him. "There's no more radio communication. They could at least let us fly to Tahiti to report the situation. . . ."

The Norwegian said dryly, "And it would take them three days to send us a ship. If you want my personal opinion, by then the island will have ceased to exist." He looked confidently at the freighters and said, "I think we can manage best by ourselves. If everything is handled expeditiously—providing nobody tries to take the last bottle of wine and every sideboard—inside twelve hours we can all be away."

The co-pilot said sullenly. "And we can also be blown sky high," which started my nerves rattling again. I had had enough of his company. I left him complaining to the

Norwegian captain, "I am a married man. My wife has no use in bed for a cinder. . . ." and I went over to the Governor's office to see how things stood.

I sensed the mute, sullen despair of disaster as I walked through the town. Furniture and feather mattresses—the pathetic array of uprooted households—were being stacked on the sidewalks. The children had stopped playing to watch with curious eyes; they still couldn't determine whether it was some kind of interesting game. It was the women who took it hardest. Men earn the bread, but it is women who create the homes. In an instant's cruel decision the placid security of half a century was gone. But even in moments of catastrophe the French do not lose their acquisitive sense—the Pêche d'Or had its entire stock of wine crated in readiness in the street, and I saw Louis and his native assistant struggling to get the ponderous barber's chairs out of the shop. The most emotional of all was that fat little Aristide; they had requisitioned his truck and he was half mad with anxiety to know who was going to compensate him for it.

I said to him, "We're all in the same boat," and shrugged with resignation. (I could afford to—all I'd brought with me was a spare shirt and a toothbrush and I managed to get both of them away.) "Every man has to make sacrifices to the common cause."

"What are you sacrificing?"

"I have nothing to offer but my life."

"Then do not talk of sacrifice. A life has no negotiable value. I cannot afford to lose my truck."

When I got to the Governor's residence I saw the three birds of ill-omen—Harry Frobisher and Marcel and the Negro, Charlie—sweating in the compound, loading up the truck. I thought sardonically, "So the corporal is finally getting some value out of them."

As I passed, Marcel winked and whispered, "How about a cigarette?"

The corporal heard him. "Shut your mouth," he shouted, "and get on with the job."

"If you haven't got a cigarette," Marcel murmured viciously, "give me a knife. Sooner or later I'm going to stick something sharp into that man."

The corporal told me brusquely—in between kicking Marcel—that the Governor had set up headquarters on the pier to superintend embarkation, and that there was to be a meeting of the townsfolk in one of the warehouse sheds in half an hour. I dropped three cigarettes surreptitiously on the ground. Harry Frobisher gave me the bitter ironic look of a man who will always spit in your face in return for charity. I was almost tempted to pick up the cigarettes. I went over to the pier.

We have a saying—I suppose all languages have something equally naïve—that trouble shared is trouble halved. I am as cynical as the normal Parisian, and it has been my experience that when people share trouble they usually try to unload a little of their portion on to somebody else's back. The crowd that had gathered in the warehouse shed was engaged busily in arranging that. Most of them, I think, had resigned themselves with fortitude to abandoning their worldly goods; but Jean-Pierre, the attorney, was telling the Governor passionately that room was needed for his daughter's piano—*petite bière*, he called it, small beer, narrowing it down with his hands to the size of a shrunken head. . . .

The Governor said coolly, "Not in any circumstances," and turned his back on him. "Good," I thought, "now there will be a little discipline. We have a soldier who will give orders and see that they are obeyed." They were apportioning out the space in the ships' holds—so much to a family—and since the only space I needed for my possessions was in my pockets I sat near the door of the shed to get a little air; the sun was beating down brutally on the iron roof.

I noticed that the truck had arrived and that Harry Frobisher and Marcel and Charlie were dragging valuable telephone equipment along the pier and trundling it to the derricks of the ships. They were stripped and running with sweat. The Negro worked as if he loved to utilize his vast strength; I was fascinated to see those bulky shoulders swelling as he toiled. But Marcel hated work, his podgy body only went through the motions; and Harry Frobisher was patently exhausted. He needed a good meal; his ribs stood out disquietingly under his skin.

Then someone passed by me and entered the shed. Father Doonan stood at the back of the crowd, waiting patiently for the chaffering to be done. He was very pale; that peasant face of his had a set, almost frantically anxious look. "This man is going to cause a little trouble," I thought, wondering what it was, and I waited for him to begin.

He spoke quite suddenly. He said to the Governor, humbly to begin with, almost with a nervous begging smile, "Shall we leave a little room for the children from the hospital?"

And then the crowd turned and looked at him, queerly angry because everybody but the priest knew that there was no longer any hospital. But nobody said anything. They left it to the Governor to deal with him.

The Governor was seated at a makeshift desk at the end of the shed and he had to look over the massed heads to see who had spoken. When he saw Father Doonan a tiny crease—of worry, compassion maybe—appeared between his eyes. He knew that the smooth process of embarkation was going to be temporarily dislocated and he sighed, glancing at his watch.

97

"If it was necessary to make room for them," he said softly, "I should be the first to be relieved. Unfortunately, one has to face stark facts. It is not pleasant for me to say it. But the hospital has been destroyed."

"I saw it," Father Doonan said woodenly, and he had started perspiring. "With my own eyes."

"The top of the mountain is an inferno," said the Governor. "The report of the air survey bears it out. It is not possible that any of them are alive. We should be thankful that the end was mercifully swift."

"It is there," Father Doonan said again, "it is intact, I believe that they are still alive——" and then there was a suppressed mutter from someone: nerves were being stretched. Nobody wanted to be harsh to the man. He simply wouldn't recognize painfully obvious facts.

"You imagined it," the Governor said.

"No. Believe me, I saw it. We must do something for them."

"There was much smoke, the pilot informs me; you persuaded yourself."

Father Doonan said stubbornly—I have never seen such an implacable man—"I tell you, I saw it——"

"You are mistaken," said the Governor. "It is just not possible."

"Everything is possible," Father Doonan insisted, "if one has charity in one's heart. They are alive. I swear it. We cannot abandon them callously up there. It would be an act of abomination. There is not a man here who would not carry the guilt of the sin within him for the rest of his life."

I saw the Governor's eyes sharpen—glint with resentment. He wasn't a ghoul, and the priest's fervent appeal had been unhappily phrased. What did he expect of us, anyway? That we should form a volunteer fire brigade and go up with buckets to put the eruption out? Then grub amidst the hospital's embers for the cremated remains? I had flown up there and I knew what it was like: inferno was a mild word for it. A priest has to be careful with the feelings of the living, too.

The Governor stared at his desk, as if hoping that by not looking at Father Doonan he would keep his temper in check. He said coldly, "You have no right to reproach us. It is equally painful to me. But I have the lives of a whole community in my hands and I cannot delay evacuation. I repeat, you must accept the cruel truth. Everybody else has faced it. The hospital is gone."

Father Doonan said faintly, "No, they're alive up there and waiting for us. I know it in my soul." And because his voice went for a moment he stretched out his hands, pleading like an afflicted shepherd for his lost flock. He was still sweating appallingly: I have never seen a man sweat like that.

Out of the corners of my eyes—in the utter stillness—I saw that the three vagrants had stopped working on the pier. They were wiping their faces in the doorway, listening inquisitively to the drama in the shed. For I suppose, in a way, it was drama—when an obdurate man pours out the bleeding guts of his despair in sheer futility, human tension rises. It was rising unpleasantly in the shed.

Jean-Pierre said furiously, "It's no use preaching sermons, that won't bring them back to life. We have to think of the safety of the living; let's get on with the job."

"The job," said Father Doonan, "is the salvation of our helpless brethren marooned up there."

Gaston, from the bistro, sighed uselessly. "What can you do with the man?" He looked straight at Father Doonan and said, struggling to be kind, if brutal, "For God's sake, Padre, use the sense in your head. They were finished all in a rush. If they weren't burned alive they were suffocated, and if they weren't suffocated they were buried under lava. There isn't even a wood louse alive up there."

"Their side of the mountain's away from the eruption. They're still preserved; let's go up, in Christ's name, and take them down."

Jean-Pierre gazed at the priest stupidly. "Go up? Are you crazy? How?"

"Walk."

"Now I know you're crazy. It would take a regiment a week to hack a way up there. In a week this island's going to be a stinking slag-heap in the sea."

"Then give me the truck," Father Doonan said, looking down at his boots—I think he was grabbing at every possibility that came into his tortured mind—"and we can be up there by the evening. I beg of you, give me the truck."

"The road is gone," the Governor said.

Father Doonan began, "Perhaps——" but the Governor broke in sharply, "The road's impassable," looking to me to support him: what could one do but state the unfortunate truth?

I said, "The lava's cut it in maybe two places. A lot of it's collapsed into the ravine."

Father Doonan was staring at me strangely; he had no right to reproach me with his eyes. He said to me softly, "You should have dropped me when I asked you." He turned back to the Governor and said, "He has parachutes. He should have let me drop."

The Governor's face wrinkled; it took him a little time to absorb it. "Drop? Into what? Fire?"

"Not all the mountain is on fire. Tell him to take me up and drop me where it is clear."

"The man's talking fantasy," Gaston said roughly; but the Governor held up his hand and stopped him.

"It's out of the question," he said.

"You know that one way or another I shall go to them. Even if I have to crawl on my hands and knees."

100

"You would be throwing away your life."

"Sooner or later my life will be required of me. Yours, too," said Father Doonan, staring into the Governor's eyes. "Heaven may ask you some very hard questions if you forbid me."

"I have a moral responsibility for you."

"I absolve you from it," Father Doonan cried. "I am a priest, I have that right: you are free of sin. I appeal to you. They are in mortal peril. Help me to go to them."

A pin would have created a clatter in that shed. I stole another look at the down-and-outs listening in the doorway. Marcel was grinning with fat malice; the Negro had his head cocked to one side impassively, studying the overwrought priest's face; Frobisher was staring sardonically at the crowd. Then I heard a voice break out from the back of the shed with raw emotion, "Oh, let him go, for the lord's sake," and the Governor gave a grumbling sort of sigh.

He said, "One man can't make it. It's all for nothing, but even so I cannot let him go by himself." I found that he was looking queerly at me. As if I had brought about the ugly situation. He asked, "How many parachutes have you?" and rather surprisedly I held up my fingers to show four. "Four," said the Governor softly. He gave a bleak grin—it had no real humor. He turned back to Father Doonan. "Find three others to go with you and I will not stand in your way."

Of course he was sliding neatly out of a difficult situation—the corporal had said he was a smart strategist. He'd been put in a terrible position; there had to be a way out that would leave him with an easy conscience, and at the same time make it impossible for the frantic priest to fling away his life. It was obvious that nobody sane would go with the man. Also, it tossed a little responsibility back on to the town.

And the ridiculous thing was that Father Doonan's face lighted up like a lamp. He went over to the Governor gratefully, trying to speak, pressing his arm. Then he started moving about the crowd, murmuring hopefully in all directions, "Who'll come with me?" (He just didn't belong to this practical world.) He got no immediate answers, so he tried the direct approach. He said to Gaston —who liked him—"You?" and Gaston stared at him hard, making a sour little prune of his mouth.

"It would be for nothing, Padre. You heard what the Governor said."

"Not for nothing, my friend, believe me. Will you come?"

"I have a wife and two daughters. You have no business to demand such a thing."

That was when Father Doonan knew that all men aren't cast out of the same dedicated mold. He frowned slightly, his face glazing wetly, still moving about the crowd, touching an arm here and there, muttering beggingly, "Will you come?"

Louis, the hairdresser, called out chucklingly: "Ask me." He was sixty-five and a bit of a hunchback. Nobody laughed.

I saw Father Doonan touch the shoulder of a big upstanding lad, and somebody shouted furiously, "Destroy your own life if you want to, but leave my son alone."

Father Doonan went on—looking from face to face—still mouthing that foolish question, using embarrassing expressions like "for the love of Christ," "I beg of you," or "children, so many innocent children up there." I thought that the flesh of his face had begun to fall in. Most of the men spared him an answer, some didn't even bother to look at him, one or two had the honesty to say stiffly, "No," and I saw a few make the kind of gesture that says: it's stupid, it's suicide, I have a wife, I have children, I have to think of them. But mostly they didn't trouble to reply.

The distressing spectacle had begun to affect the Governor; his face was baffled and wry. In the end—finishing his circuit around the shed—the priest arrived at me. What was I but a bird of passage: what had it got to do with me? When he touched my arm gently I let myself stare through the doorway at the surf creaming in the distance, at the palm fronds swaying in the smoke-laden breeze. The bums were watching me intently. Frobisher seemed to be angry with me.

Jean-Pierre put finish to the business: he was a man with a savagely outspoken tongue. He said to Father Doonan bluntly, "Forget it. Stop looking for sacrifices for your altar. You're not going to get any victims out of us."

I heard Father Doonan's voice faintly, "I need so much courage . . ."

"What you need, more obviously, is sense."

"I ask you to remember. Thirty-three of our brethren are abandoned up there——"

"They were," Jean-Pierre cut him off. "Not any more. Be reasonable. The doctor and the matron," he shrugged, "well, it was in the line of duty. I'm sorry for them. But as for the rest"—it came out of him like a rush—"whether you like it or not, I wouldn't throw away my life for a bunch of diseased black kids, lepers the lot of them. Stop making fools of us. There's work to be done."

The Governor wanted to say something—flushing, suddenly angry with the attorney—he watched Father Doonan standing in the middle of the shed; the priest was gazing at his feet confusedly, no longer speaking, just making those fluttering appeals with his hands. Then Father Doonan said, "Some of you will want to come, I'm sure. I believe in you. I'll wait in the church a little while. I appeal to you, come to me there."

He went out and there was a distinct sigh in the shed,

like air going out of a balloon; as if a painful job, aggravating to everybody, had been done, with as much kindness as jobs like that can be done. The business of tagging family groups for embarkation went on. I saw that Frobisher and Marcel and Charlie were back at work on the pier (for the corporal had arrived), gushing sweat in the almost vertical sun. There was nothing to keep me there. I went back to the town to help the women stack their household things in the street.

An hour and a half later there was a message for me from the Governor. I was to be prepared to fly off that evening with some of the old folk for whom the voyage on the freighters might be a strain.

I was in the Pêche d'Or, sampling the last bottle of rum that the bistro was ever likely to sell. I drank up and said to Gaston, "Well, here's to better things. See you in Tahiti," and flung the glass into the corner, the way the Russians do. He stared at the splinters on the floor with an inconsolable expression, as if he had just realized that nobody was ever going to clean up that mess.

I went along to the harbor to get our aged passengers briefed.

I passed the church and an odd impulse made me look in. It smelled of tropical wood and incense: a little white-painted structure that had nothing of the Gothic majesty Europeans associate with a church. It seemed to be deserted—then as my eyes became accustomed to the shadows I saw a figure sitting on the steps below the altar. It was Father Doonan. He was still waiting. There was a faint sound. He was crying, I think.

It gave me a pang—of annoyance, chiefly, of acute embarrassment. I thought that men shouldn't be priests if they hadn't the capacity to understand the basic impulses of ordinary men. I withdrew quietly and walked over to the pier.

✳

The town was now almost deserted; the last few families, clutching hand-baggage and children, were making their way to the pier. The warehouse shed was packed. Everything was being crisply arranged: family groups were tagged at the buttonholes to keep them together, the permissible share of household gear was going on to the ships. The schooner—which was too slow to carry passengers, it would take a week to sail to Tahiti—was loading up with precious equipment from the radio station. The shed was suffocating; I stood back in the doorway to get a breath of air. The three prisoners were squatting on the pier, greasy with sweat, still naked to the waist, munching bread and cheese. Somebody had rewarded them with a bottle of wine.

As Marcel caught my eye he pointed to one of the freighters, guffawing, "I want the bridal suite with two bathrooms. Don't forget to remind the Governor to fix me up with a bride."

I grinned (what could you do with that irresponsible horse-butcher?) and said, "Finished work for the day?"

"I've retired from business. Permanently," Marcel said.

"When you retire," Charlie said hazily—like many Negroes he had a voice that sounded as if something brazen was humming in his chest—"it'll be to a little stone room with bars on the windows to keep unwelcome visitors out."

"You know what you can do with the visitors. So long as they let me out to a woman now and again."

Harry Frobisher said sharply, "I don't see anything funny in that." I don't think he liked them to talk about the prison; the prospect, unpleasantly imminent, was beginning to afflict him. "Christ, just wait till you've had the first two years of it. . . ." He looked gaunt; the hard sweat on the pier had taken it out of him.

"Better than bellyaching about it, Harry," the Negro comforted him gently. "Crying isn't going to melt the bars away."

And I was no longer welcome: maybe they'd been reminded a little edgily of their lot. Suddenly they were surrounded by the invisible fence that sets the condemned apart. I'd flown them this far—I'd had a hand in their destiny—I was sorry for them and I was glad I wasn't going to have to fly them to what finally awaited them.

Then I saw Father Doonan move past me and look tragically into the shed. He was hollow under the eyes, but somehow—with those round cheeks and the snub nose —it was the wrong kind of face for tragedy. Most of the crowd saw him. They made no sign. The shed rang with the din of kids treating the embarkation as a holiday. I looked at the priest sideways. There was no reproach in his eyes: if anything, pity. He turned vacantly and saw the three prisoners munching bread on the cobbles behind.

I think if they'd been separated—if one of them had been over by the ships—it wouldn't have occurred to him. Perhaps the number three, the Governor's minimum sacrificial requirement, had taken on some kind of superstitious significance to him? (As an agnostic, I think all priests are actuated by superstition, anyway.) He gazed at them strangely. Then he went over and squatted in the dust in front of them, staring straight into their faces, saying, "You heard what the Governor said? You know about it, don't you?"

Charlie nodded.

"Then you know what I want," said Father Doonan. "Will you be the ones to come with me?"

Marcel blinked at him. "What the devil's he talking about?" he asked.

"Hush," said the Negro. "He just wants to talk."

Father Doonan said humbly, "You've been up to the hospital. There are twenty-eight innocent children. The nurses. How can we abandon them?" For some reason it wasn't the Negro, but Harry Frobisher, he had picked on as the focus for his eyes. "They're our brethren. Come up with me and fetch them down."

"What the hell's it got to do with us?" Harry Frobisher asked.

"We're all the same flesh," said the troubled voice, beginning to sag a little with defeatism. "Their sufferings are ours. Let's go up for them."

"You've got some nerve, asking us. You've come to the wrong place," Harry Frobisher said. He went on chewing the bread as if it tasted of dirt.

And then Marcel burst out as if the affrontery of the request had suddenly sunk in—"You heard that? He's mad. He wants us to jump out of that flying boat."

"He can go on wanting. What he'll get is another cup of tea." I saw Harry Frobisher grinning ironically over at the shed. "All those good Christians," he went on, thumbing slyly in the direction of the crowd, "the solid churchgoers, can't you get just three of them to go with you?"

Father Doonan said huskily, quite without hope now, "They have their own problems. They have responsibilities."

"So have we," Harry Frobisher said dryly. "We've got a pressing appointment that's going to keep us busy for four years."

The priest bent his head, starting to sweat all over again —he was a profuse and anxious sweater, that man—scrabbling his fingers aimlessly in the dust. He muttered, as if refusing to let Frobisher's words make any impression on him. "They are in great danger. In Christ's name, help me to fetch them down."

"Don't be silly. They're dead."

And then (surprising me) I saw Charlie put his hand on his partner's arm and say gently. "But we don't know that, Harry, do we? That's the worst part of it."

"They're fried, every one of them."

"You can't say that, Harry. You just don't know." Marcel, I noticed, had stopped trying to follow the bewildering conversation—he just stared confusedly from face to face.

Harry Frobisher began angrily at Charlie, "What the hell's got into you——?"

"Let's think about it a little," the chestily resonant voice of the Negro went drifting on. What made Harry Frobisher stare hard at him?

"It isn't our business. You know what we'd be jumping into? The frying pan."

"What are we jumping into now, Harry?" Charlie reminded him softly. "Something so sweet? A nice stretch in a Tahiti jail."

"Better than——" and then abruptly Harry Frobisher stopped. He wiped his face: he streaked it grittily with dust. I saw him looking covertly at the priest. What was passing through his mind was obvious; it didn't attract him much, but it bore thinking about. I suppose when men have reached the pit they can go no lower—all they have is the strength of desperation then. He stared with queer inquiry at Charlie. I heard the cautious mutter between them . . .

. . . Harry Frobisher beginning nervously, "I never did anything like that in my life."

"The jumping? Not a lot to it. I done a few jumps in my time, I was in a parachute battalion during the war."

"It isn't our war."

"We aim to get a little relief out of it? We have to make it our war."

. . . And Harry Frobisher's glance flitted shakenly back to the priest. He said very softly—the bargaining whisper was scarcely audible—"What's the chance of getting a little off our time?"

Father Doonan touched him. "I swear I would do everything possible to have your sentences reduced. They are civilized people. I'm sure they wouldn't be ungrateful," he said.

Marcel began in a frightful outraged mutter, "Don't depend on me——"

"But we've always depended on you, Marcel," Charlie said coolly. "You wouldn't be the one to let us down."

"A lot of lepers. Nigger children——"

Charlie chuckled unoffendedly, "And what am I? White as driven snow?" and Marcel frowned painfully, looking down.

I was limp with astonishment: it wasn't the kind of conversation I had expected to hear. The derricks had stopped working for a moment and in the brief suspended silence I heard Harry Frobisher's nervous fingers rasping the thick stubble on his cheek. Suddenly, wretchedly, he asked, almot as if not wanting the obvious answer, "What's the chances of getting back?"

"Ask God," Father Doonan said calmly. "We're in His hands." He was peering up under his lashes into their faces, pitying them. Harry Frobisher was looking unnervedly at his comrades; Marcel had come out into an unwholesome sweat. "Then it's all right?" Father Doonan asked.

I was surprised yet again to hear Harry Frobisher's anxious murmur, "We've got your promise?"

"You would always have that."

Harry Frobisher laughed drably. "What have we got to lose? All right."

The priest was still staring compassionately into the three men's faces. He reached over suddenly and pressed their hands. "Come," he said gently, and they all picked themselves up in various degrees of unwillingness and followed him towards the shed. Father Doonan passed me in the doorway—I don't know whether he recognized me, his eyes were pinpointed to a kind of exultant squint—and he murmured in my ear, "I have just found God in the gutter." (A trio of unshaven hoboes; I didn't expect God to look like that.)

Marcel squeezed past me into the shed, giving a sickly kind of giggle. He was terrified. "They're trying to get me the Croix de Guerre. Order me an asbestos coffin," he said.

I watched Father Doonan push through the crowd towards the Governor's desk. "My friends are coming with me," he said proudly—it was ridiculous, the way he beckoned them forward. "Here are your three men."

The Governor's face emptied of color: it started flowing back, first the pink of insult, then the red of anger. While they still have authority one should never deride the officer class. Whatever qualities Father Doonan had, tact wasn't one of them. The Governor said bleakly, "These men are convicts. They have sentences to serve."

"They're only going up the mountain with me," said Father Doonan. "They won't be running very far."

"They will do you some harm. They can't be trusted."

"I trust them," Father Doonan said.

The Governor stared opaquely at the priest (he didn't spare a glance for the three unprepossessing objects behind —I don't think he even recognized their existence). In the little space left clear for them by the crowd Frobisher and Marcel and Charlie were pulling on their shirts, pretending that the ignominious argument didn't concern them. Frobisher's face, maybe, had a savage quirk. The Governor said in his court-martial voice—the frozen one—"It's out of the question. When I said find three others to go with you, it wasn't intended to include creatures like these——" but he stopped: Gaston had come pushing forward, saying roughly:

"What are you making such a song and dance about it for?"

"These men are dangerous."

"They're not going to be dangerous to us up there. If they want to go, let them. It's their own affair."

(Some voice in the crowd—whose, Jean-Pierre's?—said unfeelingly, "It'll save the Government the expense of feeding them for four years.")

The Governor put his hands flat on the desk: a gesture of defeat. He sighed. He'd been made to look foolish; now he was going to have to eat his own words. But he still had a trump card. He muttered, "And if by one chance in a thousand you come back, who's going to be waiting to take you off?"

Captain Olsen, the Norwegian master of the schooner, was watching the bunch of volunteers narrowly. Perhaps the pathetic business touched him. He said on the spur of the moment, "I'll stand outside the reef till the dawn after tomorrow. That'll give them thirty six hours."

The Governor said, "You have your crew to think of."

"My Kanakas will do as they're told," Captain Olsen said.

The Governor made one last abortive try. He searched me out with his eyes. He said woodenly, with deliberate meaning, "Is it all right with you?"

He was putting the onus on me and it made me angry. "I'm only the driver," I said.

"I meant, is it possible?"

I said, "That's what parachutes are for. If they want to jump, they can jump."

"Very well," he said, slapping his hands down on the desk. It was finished; he only wanted to get them off his back. He looked about for the corporal and gestured him over. He spoke to him. The corporal gave his charges—now he really hated them—a stupefied look. He muttered some objection, but the Governor said loudly, "I've had enough of it. Be quiet and do as you're told." He looked emptily at Father Doonan, washing him finally out of his mind. He said coldly, "The corporal will do what is required," and he went on with his work, sorting out the survivors; as far as he was concerned the four volunteers were dead.

Father Doonan glanced at Captain Olsen: his face shone. He murmured, "Till dawn after tomorrow. Thank you," repeating gratefully, as if he mustn't forget it, "Thirty-six hours. We'll try to be there."

Then he touched his *protégés* and led them out of the shed. Why should it give me a pang? I thought they were abysmally stupid, but it would have been nice if somebody had said to them, *"Bon voyage."*

I knew what the co-pilot would say when he learned that we were going to make another flight across the crater—and he said it venomously. It took us ten minutes to get him back to a state of coherence. He had my secret sympathies, of course. I am forty-two years of age. I outlived my little era of heroism during the war.

We would have to take that ancient washing-machine of ours down to treetop level if we were not to drop our passengers straight into lava; you should try manœuvring an airborne walrus up burning gorges, knowing that the spur of a cliff or a tall branch can come looming out of the smoke to give you a hideous half-second in which to come to terms with death. I had been a little too glib with the Governor in the shed.

But the Negro, Charlie, seemed to know what he wanted. Maybe there was a history of criminality with the army: I fancied he'd had more experience as a para-trooper than he cared to say. We fixed them up crudely in the gasoline shed on the jetty. Each of the four *suicidés* —the only rational word to describe them—was to carry a heavy machete lashed to his back; they might have to hack their way through undergrowth that called for a bulldozer. Also some coils of rope. And Charlie and the padre would take the extra knapsacks that held a couple of days' rations (mostly chocolate) and a first-aid kit. The corporal pro-vided what was necessary, then turned silently and walked off. Guilt-complex, probably—he never wanted to set eyes on them again.

I fixed the parachute harness personally on the four, and then Charlie sat on the floor, talking to the others softly; I watched him draw diagrams in the dust, showing them how to rip open the chutes, how they could be guided during the fall by pulling at the side ropes to spill air from under the shroud. It was a lesson in technique; it sounded too easy. I listened to the twanging confident voice with a dreamy sensation, thinking for the last time that they were mad.

Father Doonan, of course, was dedicated; mad, but holily mad. And Charlie was languorously at ease. Strapped up with machete and rope and knapsack, he looked like a black Martian about to make an inter-planetary trip. But Harry Frobisher's face was haggardly frozen; the unsureness of his expression wasn't pleasant to see. Marcel, in a peculiar way, was better off: lard-white, greasy with perspiration, he had fallen into a merciful stupor of fear. I couldn't understand what made tramps like these—devoid of morals, of what we call human dignity—cling together in such desperate loyalty.

Then Charlie got up, glancing searchingly at his comrades, murmuring in my ear, "The sooner we get off the better. It won't do them good to think about it too long." The co-pilot was warming up the engines and we went out to the seaplane and got in. We taxied out as far as the reef, turning into the lagoon for the take-off, and I glanced back with a final hesitant twinge to see if any of the four had changed his mind.

Only Father Doonan would look at me. I shrugged and we went roaring over the hazy water, grunting arduously into the air.

We climbed above the roof of the smoke and circled over the suppurating chancre of the island. The sight—since last night's explosion—was more devastating than last time. The smoke gushed out, billowing leadenly, forked a little with flame; threads of more flame trickled down the ravines from the wound of the crater and I saw ponds of pink-gray lava forming in hollows, piling up molten shoulders, pushing on down the mountain side. The eastern side of the mountain seemed to be burning: the forest could be heard crackling above the drone of the engines. But the western side of the island was comparatively clear, not of smoke, of course—that flowed everywhere—but of flame. The worst thing of all was the solid thump that echoed at intervals like a bad theatrical effect: a hard hissing grunt, an elephant's bellow, then an uprush of blacker smoke from the broken crater and a thin spray of stones into the air.

We rounded the lip of crater, then went down to the first layer of smoke, searching for what was left of the hospital road. I would have to pinpoint some part of the terrain, as near as possible to where the hospital had stood (still stood, Father Doonan said) and go in on that bearing to the dropping run. I couldn't see anything at first but fumes; an occasional flitting glimpse of gorges, darkening in the suffused afternoon sun. Finally I got the gray thread of the road. The upper part of it, no more than a third of it remained; the collapsed hillsides had obliterated the rest. Two ribbons of plushy pink lava crossed it far down.

But of the hospital, nothing—until I caught sight of a tiny white box flickering inconceivably out of smoke. I saw what I hadn't seen on the last flight.

I looked back at Father Doonan and gesticulated encouragingly, thumbing down. He knew what I meant.

Now we really went down. Smoke ripped past the fuselage; we flew blind for a few intolerable moments, then we were under the filthy canopy and the roof of the forest wasn't far below. I had got a bearing on the remnant of the road and I searched for a clearing. I got one—sloping a little, but the best I'd ever obtain; it was dotted with no more than a few scrub palms and ferns—and then I signaled to the co-pilot to prepare. He was ready to get our passengers out; he couldn't have been more eager. The navigator leaned over me and I showed him the clearing; he fixed it, got his course, and we headed a little way out to make the final run for the drop.

I couldn't come in too low; they weren't rooftop droppers, they would need a reasonable fall for the chutes to open out. I was turning for the dropping run when I felt a blast of air and knew that the co-pilot had got the door open. I was pretty sure of my direction and I yelled to the navigator, "Help him to latch the door back."

I waited on edge—searching for the clearing, fumes shredding coarsely by the plexiglass—for the co-pilot to shout that he had got them ready and poised for the drop: that was the time when I had to hold the seaplane steady: they'd need six seconds for the jump, spacing two seconds between each man, to avoid one fouling the other. The air was roaring through the open door like a wind tunnel. And then the co-pilot gave the shout.

I saw the clearing ahead—fleetingly through the smoke, maybe from seven hundred meters—I steadied the old crate and signaled back, "Let them go." And involuntarily I turned my head: it was an indiscreet thing to do, but I had to see them go.

Charlie was the first to leave us. I was fascinated to see that large Negro walk out of the air-blasted doorway as unconcernedly as if he were stepping from a taxi to the ground. The co-pilot had shouted, "One," and before his lips had finished mouthing it the man was whisked out of sight. The co-pilot cried, "Two," counting the seconds. Father Doonan crossed himself swiftly, put his hands together and made the rudimentary motion of an amateur diving into water . . . the air seized him like a feather and he was gone. Harry Frobisher stood grinning ghastlily in the doorway; I don't know whether he was frightened, or whether his muscles had stiffened.

He made himself lean forward and the solid pluck of the air did the rest. He was gone, if anything a little too early: the co-pilot was still yelling, "Three."

Marcel was the last, and bereft of company he cringed. The co-pilot cried, "Four," then again, wildly, "Four," and Marcel stood back from the lip of the roaring door, flaccid and pitiful, sagging as if overmastered by sleep. I sweated for the hapless fat butcher—what was *he* doing in this foolishly heroic environment? The horse-slaughterer's yard was where he belonged. If he'd hung there a fractional second longer he'd have drifted too far from the dropping zone, lost from his comrades; and I got ready to give him up. The co-pilot gave him the shove of brutal kindness with his knee and Marcel lunged to the door, with the sickening gratitude with which the condemned thanks the hangman for being quick with the noose. He went out with a rolling lurch.

Then the co-pilot and the navigator were struggling with the door, latching it, and it was suddenly blissfully quiet. I banked steeply. I got a momentary bird's eye view of our departed guests. I saw three of the chutes, already fully opened, with the suspended dots swinging as if in a gale. I couldn't see anything of the fourth—presumably the last, Marcel's—but something materialized out of the wreathing pall, a flutter of petals, and the segments of the chute opened out. What hung from it oscillated frightfully. Underneath my leather jacket I gushed sympathetic rivulets of sweat.

Then the four spaced blobs sank towards the opalescent smoke and one by one entered it, growing gray, as intangible as ghosts, and like ghosts finally melted. I never saw them again.

Part
Three

6

THE seaplane pilot saw the four men go down, treading for a fantastic moment a white billowing floor; he saw them disappear into the veil of smoke. A few of the Melanesian children from the hospital saw them emerge from beneath it and come drifting leaflike to the ground. They cried out. Dr. Wexler told me that he'd heard the seaplane circling, but this visitation, he said, nearly startled him out of his life. He ran into the compound with the Matron, watching incredulously as the parachutes floated out of sight over the tops of the trees. They had been preparing to leave—all the inmates of the hospital; the children had been gathered in the compound and numbered off in readiness—and the sight did something wonderful to the Matron's morale.

She believed violently in miracles. Dr. Wexler heard her mutter with ludicrous emotion—clasping her hands as if in church—"We're going to need four more cups, angels are coming to tea."

(Of course, he didn't know then who the four arrivals were. He said to me dryly, "Angels. Father Doonan, maybe. But the other three smelly ruffians? I'd have laughed up my sleeve.")

But before he picked up the thread of the story Dr. Wexler told me what had already happened to them. When the mountain first started having trouble with its digestion it worried them. Never in their experience had it shown the slightest sign of life. Now—so unexpectedly —those disquieting belches. The shocks got much worse during the afternoon. When dusk came they climbed up on to the roof of the hospital and saw a frightening red shine about the crater.

Smoke (said Dr. Wexler) is worse than mere indigestion; fire, if anything, is the worst of all. None of us, I assure you, slept very much.

Well, you know what happened in the night. Part of the crater blew off. . . .

It was a bad time—the middle of the night makes the mildest volcano hideously spectacular; in the darkness the weird flicker of flame, the cracking of great trees going down before the flowing lava, terrified us. Fortunately— or miraculously, as the Matron insisted—it was the other side of the island that was engulfed; all we got was the smoke. The Matron is a woman who can stand up to volcanoes. She got the children out of bed. She said it was no use letting them sit there, quaking with fright. And we all had tea.

Can you believe it? A tea party in the middle of an eruption. (I drank three cups.)

We knew by next midday that it wasn't going to be any good. If our part of the mountain didn't burst open, the fumes would suffocate us. We'd heard an aircraft come over the previous day, terribly low, but we didn't see it and presumably it didn't see us. It was no use waiting to be roasted—to be preserved for posterity, like Pompeii, in a casserole of hot lava. We had four mules and plenty of food; so we got busy and started packing up. The two nurses, Sonia and Camille (Sonia is the full Melanesian— Camille the half-colored), prepared the children for the exodus. We had lost the old native who did the odd jobs for us. He ran off foolishly in the night.

Of our twenty-eight children, four were crippled and quite unable to walk. We tried to make saddles out of carpets and bolsters to sit them on the backs of the mules.

122

When one has nothing but last-ditch courage it is surprising what one can do. The Matron—as you can imagine —was a rock of cheerfulness. She made it look to the children as if we were setting out on a late afternoon picnic; in fact, they were the least worried of all. I didn't know how far we'd be able to get. Fumes were issuing from far down the mountain; it suggested ominously that part of the road was gone. We thought that—with a little luck—we might at least get out of the area of smoke; that if people still remained on the island they might be searching for us. I told the Matron privately that I didn't think they'd be there very long.

She said briskly, "Then we'll just get down to the harbor and start swimming for it." (And she'd have done it, believe me.)

And that was when we heard the seaplane come over for the second time, circling about invisibly, then going out to sea and droning back. Finally it was gone. But it had left something behind; the children saw the things first, descending from out of the smoke. I watched the little black umbrellas floating down, catching the breeze and scattering behind the trees. I thought that they were bundles of supplies dropped to us on chance—until I saw one of the bundles kicking wildly and knew that they were men.

My first thought—a doctor thinks first of the preciousness of life—was that they were insane. The seaplane had contributed four more victims to the sacrificial cause.

We started scrambling through the forest, shouting at the tops of our voices. The first man we found—to my utter astonishment—was one of the convicts who'd worked at the hospital with the labor gang. Harry Frobisher. It wasn't easy to locate him—the smoke had cut down visibility, one couldn't see beyond a dozen trees—but there he was, lying flat on his back in a pile of ferns, trembling with shock.

He was muttering, "Christ, I made it, I made it," grinning up at us ghastlily, and I wondered just what he thought he had made: a hero of himself?

We helped him up. "Are you all right?" I asked. I saw him grimace.

"I've done something to my ankle. Let's find the others." He cupped his mouth and yelled.

We heard a voice respond not far off. We hurried through the forest towards it. Then Father Doonan appeared out of a thicket and as he caught sight of us he stood stock-still. He could never have been sure of finding us. A wild exaltation—the sort of expression you'd see in a priest at the most sacred moment of Mass—flooded his face. The children rushed over to him as if Santa Claus had arrived. I could see him counting them instinctively as I approached. "Don't worry," I chuckled. "We're all right. What made you come?"

"Somebody had to." He unlocked the muscles of his stiff face with a smile. "You can't make the journey down by yourselves."

"We were going to try."

"Now we'll try together."

He was blinking at the Matron—that Irish peasant—and she clutched him. All she could say at that ridiculously emotional moment was, "Did you fetch those picture magazines with the big busts I asked for?"

"Forgive me," grinned Father Doonan. "It slipped my mind."

The next one we found was the Negro, Charlie. Actually, he found us. There was a crackling in the undergrowth and he came striding over, a bulky monster, like something scarifying out of science fiction, still wearing his parachute harness, with a veritable mule-load of coils of rope and a machete and a knapsack on his back. He nodded briefly—as if he'd bumped into us on an afternoon jaunt. It was his partner he really cared about; the heavy black face became suddenly anxious, narrowing compassionately as he saw Harry Frobisher hobbling along. "You hurt yourself, Harry?" he asked softly, holding him up.

"I've twisted my ankle," Harry Frobisher muttered. "Everything happens to me."

"There's a doctor. You want to rest a while?"

"No, let's find Marcel. I'm worried about him. I haven't heard him utter a peep."

And that fat Frenchman was the hardest to find. We shouted for some minutes, the whole congregation of us, and there was no reply. I began to suspect that he'd fallen too distantly and been lost. He could have gone straight into lava—or been overcome by fumes from the ground. The thing that most surprised me was the almost violent concern exhibited by his friends. They yelled frantically, and yelled. Then suddenly one of the Melanesian children gave a piping giggle and pointed.

A man hung from a tree—as motionless as a body on a gibbet—suspended from the parachute cords that were caught in the branches. It could only be Marcel; such fantasies belonged only to him. Or perhaps he'd been lucky in his way? He had fainted almost as soon as he pulled the rip cord, he told us later; all he could remember was a sickening sensation of falling, the jarring tug as the parachute opened, then the sheer horror of discovering himself going down into a bottomless carpet of smoke. We cut him down from the branches and brought him round. I have never seen a man so greasily pale; after that I don't think death could hold any terrors for him. And can you conceive it?—the first thing he did as he regained consciousness was to clutch the hands of Frobisher and Charlie gratefully, the way a sick child yearns for its mother.

The unbelievable comradeship of the union of tramps. Harry Frobisher patted him comfortingly. "All right. You're not going to die. The devil's not ready for you yet."

"I thought he had me on his gridiron that time."

Charlie laughed huskily, "He's waiting to cook something special out of you."

And presumably out of us, also. Whatever the devil intended to do with his favored disciples, it was obvious that he had something equally special in mind for us. In moments of danger the mind casts about nervously to sort out the threatening noises—as we trudged back to the hospital I heard above the crackling of our feet in the undergrowth the background hiss of distant fire, creeping round the flank of the mountain, a sporadic patter that sounded like hail on a tin roof. The crater was throwing up unwanted muck.

The Matron was watching the three "angels"—the word was hers—with a dubious face as she plowed along. Harry Frobisher cursed softly as he stumbled. When I went toward him he waved me back with a furious scowl.

The Matron mumbled, "They may have brought us succor, but they've left their good manners behind."

We got back to the hospital and finished loading up. Give the devil his due—that man Frobisher was an inventive genius. The saddles we had made were no good. They slid off the mules as if greased. Frobisher lashed some linen baskets on each side of the mules to form panniers. The crippled children slid comfortably into the capacious hampers. I am not very good at such organization—it hadn't occurred to me that we should have to travel through thick undergrowth and along narrow defiles; that it would be necessary to move in single file; that the children who could walk would have to be kept strictly in line. Harry Frobisher ran a double rope from the front pair of mules to the second pair about twenty feet behind. The children who could use their legs formed a long crocodile between them, clinging to the sanctuary of the ropes. It reminded me of the homespun ingenuity of the Swiss Family Robinson. In the meantime the Negro and Marcel were loading up the supplies.

Do I give you the impression that it was all carried out with lazy affability? Well, it was not. We were very frightened—there was a leaden sheen in the afternoon sky, the smoke and the suspended grit that poured about us stank increasingly. Frobisher and Charlie and Marcel (the latter particularly) looked up uneasily and listened, muttering profanely as they worked. They were scared and in a terrible hurry to go.

Then Frobisher went into one of the wards to get the last blankets. I happened to be in the dispensary next door, collecting my surgical instruments, and I could see him through the hatch. Someone had come into the ward. It was Camille. She moved as the blind always move—as if they have sensitive antennæ. She stood in the doorway, trying to fix his position, for Harry Frobisher had seen her come in and he froze sullenly. He didn't want to draw attention to himself.

Camille murmured, "Harry?"

He was watching her covertly—people never like to stare the blind straight in the face. He muttered ungraciously, "What do you want?"

"I wanted to tell you. I'm glad you came."

He grunted. "I'm not. I don't know what I'm doing here. I must have a screw loose. I ought to get my psychiatrist to examine my head."

Camille laughed sweetly, moving in his direction. "No, don't say that. It's a very good head. I'm still terribly happy that you came."

Suddenly, quite roughly, he said, "Keep your distance."

127

"Have I done something wrong?" She paused.

"Just stay away from me. I have worries of my own. You want me to get another crack in the face?"

But she was moving once more toward him, troubled, murmuring, "Harry," in a confused voice. . . .

And he burst out furiously, "Didn't you hear me? I told you to stay away."

"Don't you care to have me near you?"

"I have enough trouble. Tag on to somebody else." Then he said something rather cruel—perhaps it was the deliberate cruelty of an emotionally exhausted person— "Don't use me as a stick. Blind or not, I don't like anybody leaning on me. If anybody has to do any leaning it'll be me on somebody else." By peeping through the hatch I saw him watching her with furtive resentment, in a sweat of inexplicable anger. He had a stack of blankets in his hands. He didn't know how to get past her. He started circling round her widely towards the door.

She said, listening strangely to his slurring movement, "Is there something wrong with your leg?"

"I'm still wearing leg irons. The well-dressed convict's never without them these days."

"Harry, I can hear you limping."

"When I need a crutch I'll fix one up for myself."

Eavesdroppers never hear people at their best—their defences are down. But so were Camille's: her defenceless-ness should have moved even a roughneck's hardened heart. She was very delicate—in German we we would call her *geliebt*. And I went quite hot with irritation; one hates to witness implacable churlishness toward the afflicted. I was about to bustle next door, like an old Viennese Sir Lancelot, to remind Frobisher that a civil tongue cost nothing—when I heard a bosomy sound of fury behind me and I saw the Matron glaring thunderously into the ward.

128

"What's the matter with that bandit?" she asked.

I shrugged. "He's giving her what the Americans call the brush-off."

She growled. "If he doesn't watch out I'll brush his face off with the back of my hand."

"Maybe he has an allergy to blind people——"

"I have an allergy to ugly-mouthed ruffians," she said. I had never seen her so angry; the mother hen had seen one of her chicks brutally rebuffed. Harry Frobisher came out of the ward with the blankets. He paused doubtfully, squinting at us.

The Matron said to him coolly, "Leave that girl alone. She doesn't have the habits of your barroom drabs."

He chuckled ironically. "I'm not exactly chasing her."

"You, you rapscallion. You'd better not try it, either. She's too good for you."

Then Camille came into the dispensary, searching anxiously for Frobisher with her ears. The Matron began angrily, "He's gone," beckoning Frobisher out savagely with her head. But he didn't move——

Neither did I, nor the Matron: for a subtle kind of vibration had started in the whole building. I found myself watching a glass jar of antiseptic with a passive fascination as it danced along a shelf like a goblin, smashing itself to bits on the floor. Next, a window split with a minute click, no louder than the rap of steel balls. Frozenly, the Matron gazed up. We could hear loosened shingles sliding down the roof to the ground. There is no sensation so disgusting as the senile fear one has when the earth goes liquid under one's feet.

Harry Frobisher said hoarsely, "Get out, we're going to have the whole outfit down on our heads."

The Matron steered Camille by the shoulders and we all ran out. A few of the children were shrieking; Father Doonan was flurrying them away from the porch into the compound. Marcel was crying out in a wild scared falsetto, "The mountain's sliding. What the hell are we waiting for?" He turned violently on Charlie.

The Negro's eyes rolled up to the dismembered roof and he said, "Get the kids mounted. We'd better run."

But he seemed unwilling to do anything about it—it was Father Doonan and I who were heaving the crippled children into the panniers, Sonia and the Matron gathering the others into a compact huddle—and when the Matron shouted fiercely to Marcel, "Help me," he merely muttered excusingly. He shrank back.

I cried accusingly, "See to the children."

"You see to them," Marcel said, licking his lips. "That wasn't in the bargain. I don't have to catch anything from them."

The Matron glared. Frobisher and Charlie hung back, frozen with revulsion. What can one do with the inbred aversion to the leper? To children, even? There was a bitter silence. I began spitefully, "If there's any danger of catching anything, it's that they might catch something from you——" but Father Doonan pressed my arm gently, looking with torn commiseration at the bums.

He murmured, "Don't expect too much of them, too quickly. Don't press them too hard." (Meaning, I suppose, if you want to make a silk purse out of a sow's ear it takes time.) I am over sixty and I don't have all that time.

Then Frobisher roused himself and grabbed hold of the mules. He was, at least, pale, sickeningly guilty. The Negro ran forward to him and they smacked the mules into a jog trot and we all went scampering off. We left the hospital compound at a crazy gallop, as if the hounds of hell were at our heels. We jangled down the road, the panniers on the mules rattling the poor infants' teeth; the rest of the children scuttled like a long black lizard,

130

clamped tenaciously to the rope that stretched between the two pairs of mules. The Matron's bosom bounced breathlessly: she was appallingly put out. We had got some way along the road when the ledge on which the hospital stood cracked. We felt the flutter one feels when a train whisks into a tunnel.

And—like Lot's wife—I had to look back.

The massive green ledge of the mountain crumbled. The earth split ten yards behind me, and as the whole outcrop turned into rubble, sliding down the flank of the mountain—steaming copiously with dust—the hospital went to pieces like a collapsing house of cards. Literally: it folded. One moment I was gazing at the neat little white painted building to which I had dedicated myself all these years. The next, there was a heap of crunching timber and half my life had gone in a rumble down the mountain side.

I said to Father Doonan thickly, "Does God take any pleasure in that?"

He said, "Something always rises out of the ashes of the old." (Small comfort.) He dragged my arm and we followed the pack train that had gone jangling far down the road.

We stopped about ten minutes later to catch our breath. We sat on the verge of the road, shaken indescribably, drenched with sweat. I noticed Marcel staring numbly up at the colossal gray pumice scar that had been ripped out of the side of the mountain; perhaps he was thanking the lucky stars that had got us away in time.

Or had God preserved us? And taken pleasure in that?

Frobisher went through the bushes for a natural reason, and as he disappeared into the undergrowth I saw Camille's head turn towards him and her ears remained listening out for him.

✳

We started off again: sedately—you cannot whip children along like ponies. Not many of them had shoes. Frobisher and Charlie led the front mules, Marcel smacking the rumps of the rear pair. Father Doonan walked in the middle, encouraging the children to cling to the ropes. The dusky crocodile pattered along, ruining the illusion of peril with their fluting giggles; young minds quickly rub away the memory of shock. I trudged behind Father Doonan with the Matron. Her temper was uncertain. She was like those pugnacious crones who sit behind the stalls in a Parisian market: turn over the produce with sour contempt and you have a virago on your hands. Affront the Matron personally, and she could respond with a flow of profanity that might curl your hair; abase her children, and she was capable of doing something disastrous to your face.

She was staring at Harry Frobisher and Charlie ahead. She moved on to catch up with Father Doonan and I heard her begin in a low voice, "Those animals——"

But he turned quickly and muttered affrontedly, "No, not animals—no, no."

"All right. The aristocracy of the gutter," she said sardonically. "I suppose we're dependent on them?"

"We need them," said Father Doonan. And he cut in sharply to stop her protests, "Don't worry about them. We're in good hands."

"With all respect, Father, I have to laugh in your face."

"Do that," he shrugged. "So long as you let me have the last laugh."

"You actually trust them?"

"Of course."

"What? Men who have no pity for afflicted children?"

"They have pity," Father Doonan murmured. "It's merely buried under the débris of their ruined lives." He squeezed the Matron's arm cautioningly—the men ahead were listening, I saw Harry Frobisher turn right round and give the Matron a savage look. "Be patient with them. Show charity, and we'll dig the pity out."

The Matron grimaced. "You'll have to dig deep."

"I have big shoulders," said Father Doonan. "I'm prepared to dig deep."

"You're being naïve." The Matron stared angrily into his face.

Father Doonan's temper began to shorten. He said, "I'm a naïve man. Now be quiet. These men are my brothers—I think we can trust them with our lives."

The Matron said loudly, "Well, just don't trust them with mine." It still simmered inside her—she was getting ready to erupt. She began again in a high carrying voice, "Look at them. Unfeeling barflies. . . ."

And this time I saw the Negro, Charlie, look round. Offended. He gave the Matron a dull hooded glance. If we were dependent on these people there was no need for the Matron to keep rasping them with her tongue—I wished angrily she'd shut up. But she went on and on until Father Doonan cut her off, squeezing her arm so hard this time that it hurt. "Listen," he said softly—I had to bend forward to hear—"there are people who will face shellfire and run away at the sight of a toad. To these men leprosy is worse than toads; blame them for ignorance, but not for running away. Think well of them. I swear they'll respond."

"With a kick in the teeth," said the Matron. "They'll murder us in our beds."

"Will you do me a favor?" Father Doonan said to her painfully. "Just hold your tongue."

"Were they the best you could fetch with you——?" and Father Doonan broke in passionately, angrier than I had ever seen him:

"Yes, the best! And the most willing!"

133

"You've scraped the bottom of the barrel." And the Matron said harshly, "My God, we're in the hands of the lowest form of life. The sweepings of the saloons."

That was enough; even she saw it. Her face sharpened nervously, for Harry Frobisher turned his head again and stared at her, his expression viciously demeaned. "Everybody's so sensitive," I thought hysterically . . . the smoke was rolling down the ravines, as solid as chalk, forming opaque pools in the hollows; the air had a bitter distant crackle where the forest was burning, where the lava was shoving it fast at our heels. I turned to look pacifyingly at Marcel. He was watching the Matron balefully; for one sad, unguarded moment I knew what she meant when she accused Father Doonan: *you've scraped the bottom of the barrel.* Marcel made the gesture of ultimate insult—only Parisians can do it to perfection—thrusting up two fingers in the direction of the Matron's backside.

I sympathized with the Matron, echoing her words: *the lowest form of life, the sweepings of the saloons.*

And I think that was the moment when I took the first realistic look at our ludicrous baggage train. A thin thread of chattering black children clinging to the life line of the ropes stretched between the mules, shuffling precariously along a crumbling road skirting a bottomless burning gorge. I rubbed my eyes at the Arabian Nights fantasy. I listened to the bells tinkling daintily out of the smoke on the harness of the mules—and for a moment of insanity I thought of the bells of Flecker's camel-borne pilgrims, beating through the desert silence along the Golden Road to Samarkand.

I was fascinated the first time I saw lava. Living effervescent lava. But fascination becomes charged with urgent personal emotion when the stuff is moving with gassy violence to cut one off—even a scientist's interest fades when he is in danger of being cooked.

We had just come round the flank of the mountain. It gave us a gull's-eye view of the side of the island that was being attacked.

We had been dramatically prepared for the sight. It was about ten o'clock in the evening—the sun was losing its glare, the light was, anyway, masked opaquely by the smoke. Beneath us there was that continuous phlegmy grumble; something old and beastly was turning restlessly in its bed. It was breaking up the road. Cracks appeared ahead of us, none wider than a couple of fingers, but when one bent to touch them they were disquietingly warm. And wisps of smoke crept out of them.

We led the children over the smelly fissures very carefully, like anxious parents negotiating steppingstones across a stream.

But what worried me most was the endless profane mutter that came from Marcel behind—he was never very fastidious with his tongue. He was hopping nervously over the cracks. Quite suddenly something cracked in him, too. He left his place with the rear mules and ran forward to his comrades. The trouble with scamps is that they are so gregarious—more than ordinary men they suffer the fear of loneliness, the communal despair that drives rats to leave the sinking ship. Harry Frobisher turned on him brusquely and told him to get back to his mules.

Marcel looked hagridden. He stood his ground. I heard him mutter, "We'll never do it. Jesus God, our feet are going to fry." (What an expression!—it made the soles of my feet go uncomfortably warm.) "Why don't we try some other way?" he cried.

That was my first chill breath of anxiety. I thought "How long are the rats going to stay with our sinking ship?"

"There isn't any other way," said Harry Frobisher. "Keep moving." But he wasn't very happy, either; I saw his unshaven face twitching. He said with drab humor, "Stay with us. Maybe we'll fry better in your fat."

"What's so funny about that?"

"It's the funniest you can expect in the situation. Buy me a drink at the next bar we come to; I may have something wittier for you then."

"We're dawdling," Marcel burst out. "Can't we move those kids a bit faster?" He started smacking the rumps of the front mules, yelling, "Get on, you damned pigeons"— too terrified to choose his words properly—"stir yourselves, you long-eared loafers, move, move."

The Matron said rebelliously, "The children aren't marathon runners. They're doing the best they can."

"Their best isn't good enough. They'll have to do better than that."

Father Doonan took Marcel's arm and said gently, "There's a long way to go. We mustn't wear them out."

And then Marcel came out with something spitefully ominous. He said—I didn't like the way he stressed the "we" and the "us"—"We could go quicker. And it wouldn't wear us out." He was staring significantly at Harry Frobisher and Charlie—the man's frantic voice made Father Doonan look at him guardedly. I thought, "So that's how the wind's blowing"; and went cold with apprehension again.

Father Doonan controlled his face and said humbly, "We mustn't talk like that. We're all together in this."

Marcel shouted, "Where does it say that in the contract? We're not going to be together long if you keep stopping to pick daisies on the way." The Matron was suffused with anger, but very nervous—I could see the effort she was making not to provoke Marcel. He started smacking the mules furiously again, and the animals broke into a clumsy trot, the children beginning to whimper, dragged on by the ropes, looking to us for comfort: and what comfort was there to give? The panniers on the mules bobbed wildly, the tiny cripples peeping perplexedly over the sides.

The Matron cried out pantingly, "If you can't behave like gentlemen, get along yourselves. You don't have to wait for us."

That was when Harry Frobisher surprised me. (I don't know why I particularly expected humanity from him—if anything, I should have looked for it from Charlie, though the Negro's loyalty to us seemed cynical and detached.) He wouldn't look at us directly, his eyes shining nervously in his strained face, and he muttered sullenly, "This isn't going to be any picnic. If we can't keep moving we're done." He was watching the sky. It was growing dark very quickly—the sun, lying on the horizon, had a sour orange glow, haloed uglily by the cinderous dust. The dusk was beginning to show up the red lick over the crater, and it wasn't the pink of the setting sun. Frobisher drove the mules on stubbornly, scurrying alone awkwardly on his damaged leg. So we went galloping pell-mell, panicky because the men we depended on were stricken with panic —our feet twisting and slithering on the broken ground, the Matron's bosom bouncing, the children gasping, the two nurses running silently, Camille clinging blindly to Sonia's arm.

Then my breath started whooping—the sweat ran down into my eyes—I would have given up (my heart, anyway, if not my legs) when Frobisher and Charlie, running ahead of Father Doonan, stopped dead in their tracks.

They had just rounded the flank of the mountain. I heard them sigh with harsh consternation, like impetuous lovers entering the bedroom to find the betrayed husband waiting unexpectedly in bed with a gun. The ravines—

darkening swiftly in the gloaming—were bathed in a vaporous gingery glow: they crept with lava. Red ants seemed to be scurrying like half-ignited fireworks along the edges of the glistening ooze; I think they were bushes flaming briefly in its path.

A volcano in action is like an inflammatory old man whose dirty habits—his coughs, his asthmatic splutters, his bedpan—have made him unfit for society. Magnified appallingly, an erupting volcano has the phlegmy gush of lava, the shocking violence of bursting lungs; the hemorrhage runs hot blood and it pours out in a ravenous flood. The exploded crater was like a ridge of glowing coal—the streams were marching down the mountain, shoved on by the endless roll of lava, molten and furnace-fluid at the peak, but solidifying a simmering crust as it went along. It had an animal kind of hunger: it was consuming every bush and blade of grass. The pine trees flared aromatically, hissing momentarily into torches, until the lava pushed them and buried them.

Down in that shadowed ravine—robbed impressively of the sunshine, like a stage producer's over-enthusiastic conception of hell—everything hot and insatiable seemed to be moving very fast.

I heard Marcel murmur with dreadful finality (and why that irreligious bum should cross himself I don't know, but he did), "We've had it"—meaning literally, I suppose, we've had our lives. No one answered him for a moment; it is possible to be awed hypnotically by the thing that is going to eat one up.

Father Doonan said to Marcel cheerfully, "No, we've had great mercy." I wondered what on earth he was talking about until he went on, "God is giving us the chance to show what we can do."

I didn't know whether it would console us much when the flood of rolling lava swallowed us up. Sixty-odd years

were catching up with me; I sat weakly on a rock to re-
cover my breath. I heard Harry Frobisher say to Charlie
faintly (maybe to spare our feelings), "It's going too quick.
Christ in heaven, we'll never get round it."

"Christ's in heaven," said Father Doonan. "And we'll
get round it. At least, we're going to try."

Harry Frobisher said angrily, "You'd better start praying for a miracle."

"That's my trade," said Father Doonan. "Just let's help
each other to deserve it. Let's push along."

Marcel said suddenly, on a rising note, "I'll tell you
something." He was staring at the priest peculiarly.
"You're mad."

"Mad with hope," said Father Doonan. He grinned
palely. "All we have to do is just keep pushing along."

"Push where?" Marcel demanded. "Into that? You
want us to be stewed?"

Father Doonan lined the children up along the ropes as
if not listening and said woodenly, "We're wasting time.
Come on."

"What's the matter with you?" Marcel shouted. "You're
making fools of us."

"We'll be fools if we wait here much longer," Father
Doonan said.

I looked at the Matron. She gave me a shrunken look.
She was all disarrayed by the hectic run; when women are
sweaty and untidy you can't expect them to be in a very
encouraging mood. Marcel was still breathing noisily, the
children were watching the lava with pleasurable murmurs
as it streamed down the ravine—only the mules were im-
passive: they were nibbling calmly at the grass between
the rocks. I saw Charlie give Father Doonan a tight frustrated look. "Listen," he began—it takes a big black man
to sweat spectacularly, I watched the fat globules start out

of his heavy face—"nobody's going to fly over that stuff. I don't see any sign of angel's wings."

Father Doonan just said. "Come on. And let's be friendly. As long as we trust each other everything's going to be all right."

Harry Frobisher said huskily, "You must have a special kind of insurance."

"And you," said Father Doonan. "You've got a special kind of insurance, too."

"We're being cut off. Use your eyes. We're only trying to be practical——"

Father Doonan interrupted, "Nobody knows what's practical till it's behind us," and he went on collecting the children in line stubbornly to carry on.

Then I heard the thing I had been most afraid of, and, naturally, it came from Marcel. He said, not to us, but to his partners whisperingly, "We could do it, maybe. But the kids are holding us up."

Father Doonan heard it. He turned on Marcel grimly. "You said that before. I don't want to hear you say it again."

"I said it," Marcel muttered pugnaciously, "and I'll repeat it. The kids are holding us up."

"That is unworthy."

"You could be right," Marcel said. "But unworthy men live longest of all."

"And then?" Father Doonan queried sharply. "When you meet God what will you say——"

"We'll take a chance on the conversation. We don't have membership cards for heaven," Marcel grinned. "We belong to the more popular club below." Then—quite horrifyingly—his nerve snapped; he started shaking his fist under Father Doonan's nose, exploding incoherencies in French out of his system, words like *assassin* and *criminel;* then, so that Father Doonan could understand him, "All we want to do is survive"—as if his survival lay just over the mountain and Father Doonan and the laggardly children were depriving him of it . . .

"Shut up," the Matron said suffocatedly to Marcel. She rose. She is a very passionate woman—she had transferred her passion to the hospital and its twenty-eight children, but if she had donated it to a man I think she would have given him a turbulent time. Like most passionate women, you could always depend on her to do something dramatically indiscreet. She shoved her hot furious face right into Marcel's and said in a voice filled with loathing, "All right, you tramp, you rascal. Be on your way. Go on, run, you're in such a hurry to get to hell."

"No," winced Father Doonan. "You mustn't even suggest it."

"They're going to drop us like hot potatoes. Look at their faces. The first chance they get they're going to run away."

"They would never do that," said Father Doonan—and the Matron shouted him down, for the first time impatient with him. "Of course they'll do it. Don't be stupid. They'll leave us flat."

"You said it," Marcel murmured.

"Then be off. Oblige us with the pleasure of your absence. Your company is no longer desired."

The Matron had shot her bolt breathlessly; she wiped her hot face, panting, nervous of what she had started and I whispered reproachfully, "You shouldn't even have put it into their heads."

"Oh, for God's sake. Somebody's always talking," Harry Frobisher sighed. He bent to fondle his wrenched ankle, grimacing as he pressed it. Charlie moved to him uneasily; Harry Frobisher shrugged him away. A jumpily unpredictable, touchy man . . .

And we resumed the pilgrimage, Frobisher hobbling

141

ahead, refusing the arm I saw the Negro offer, the mules treading fastidiously over the steamy cracks, blowing their nostrils, the crocodile of undismayed children strung out along the life line of the ropes, the Matron walking in solitary offended silence, leaving me to follow with Sonia and Camille.

Marcel came belligerently behind. He had to have somebody's company. He hurried his steps a little and sought mine.

"That priest," he grumbled. "He preaches too much. He won't be satisfied till everybody's dead."

"What made you come with him?"

"Every man has his crazy moment. I am already regretting mine."

I reminded him slyly of the carrot that had been dangled in front of the donkey. "You thought you'd get a little time off your sentence."

"Naturally." Disarmingly he shrugged. "But to appreciate it one has to live enough to serve one's stretch."

"It was still a very brave thing to do."

"Crap," he said, giving the word a Gallic inflection so that it didn't sound like an American expletive at all. "Heroics are for adolescents. They had to eject me from that seaplane. If they'd waited ten seconds longer they'd have needed a howitzer to shoot me out."

Comedians are rarely gentlemen. I chuckled—I was beginning to take a sneaking liking to that grubby buffoon. But his eyes had already wandered. He was staring coolly at the Matron's back.

"That woman," he said, "has a rabid tongue"—he used the word *enragé,* associating her with a dog. "She doesn't choose her expressions very carefully. I could consider myself insulted."

"She's a very excellent woman."

"You mean, morally? That wouldn't enhance her attractions with me." Some men have a way of looking at a woman—you see their eyes shredding away the clothes like orange peel, revealing the salient feminine features underneath. Marcel (I was positive) was contemplating the Matron's bare buttocks; he had even cocked his head sideways to get a better look at her breasts. He said, "She had no right to talk to me that way. If she were ten pounds lighter and a little less ferocious I would break her jaw for her."

"She would take you apart."

"It wouldn't be the first time a woman did that."

Then his attention—it was always as fitful as an insect's—strayed to Father Doonan once more. "And the priest is another queer. He isn't fit to wear the cloth."

I was astonished. "Why not?"

"There's an etiquette in the profession, isn't there? Priests are expected to be polite to their communicants. That ogre shouts at us, bullies us, as if we were Sunday-school delinquents. He'd better watch his step." And that ended his ill-humor; he gave a guffaw. He pressed my arm sympathetically. "We've got ourselves into some very strange company, *m'sieu*. If we survive this business I swear that from now on I'll associate only with the cream of the bums on the beach."

He went on to saunter by Sonia and Camille. He bent forward to look prospectively into Sonia's face. Perhaps she didn't please him sexually: she was quite black, with the compressed nostrils and full lips of the pure Melanesian. He peered past her at Camille. His eyes sharpened. But one saw the odd hesitation, the reluctance; blindness, even in an attractive creature, has a chastening influence on sex.

The Matron turned. Seeing Marcel by the two nurses, she frowned stormily. Marcel fell back instantly and trudged by my side.

143

"The hell with the vixen. This just isn't my day, I'd give my arm up to the elbow for a drink."

We were making awkward progress; the road had narrowed through dragging thorny undergrowth, winding along a thin shelf that sloped steeply down to the ravine. The mules trod it sure-footedly; I walked less confidently. The Matron and Father Doonan fell back carefully to keep the trailing lizard of the children compactly in line. I think I became conscious then of the electrically sultry glare—it was as if the retreating sun had left a backwash of heat in the sky. Everything had gone very quiet: the birds ceased to clack; the breeze that cooled the peaks no longer stirred the grass. One feels the same expectant tremor in the theater when the curtain is about to go up.

Our auditorium was a vast, twilight ravine—the pale stars were the dying houselights—it seemed just right for the theatrical action to begin.

We were squeezing along the broken road and I saw a heavy boulder lurch slightly. Nobody was near it; I had the confused impression that a colony of ants beneath was shoving it out of the way. I remember as a boy being taken to the railway station in Vienna; I would stand near one of the hissing engines, clapping my hands exquisitely to my ears as the monster let out a devastating roar. I went straight back to my childhood as the air was torn recollectively by that steamy bellow. The ravine split gently like a cracked apple—the bushes and brambles peeled back. Out of the fissure flooded a glistening lake of lava, rising swiftly, as if a rash prospector had tapped a reservoir of burning oil.

And the whole valley banged—all the navies of the world might have united devilishly to let off that broadside. My eardrums cringed. False sunlight poured into the gullies; like spent magnesium the fissionable flame went out. For a moment—as ragged as the last teeth in an old crone's

144

mouth—the crater was silhouetted. I saw one of the teeth leap out of the photographic dazzle and dissolve. Millions of tons of earth blossomed out of the crater to form the petals of a gigantic dirty flower. Gravity held them aloft as if the camera of the eye had stopped working—then the film ran on and the débris came raining down.

We stood in nervous rapture; actors never had so frozen an audience. I heard Marcel's foolish mumble, "We are all dead."

We shrank as the thin nuclear dust descended; the airborne boulders pattered distantly into the ravine. The rising lake of lava was alight with a green and purple flicker of burning methane; a bubble of pitch and molten rock, the personal brew of hell. But black-gray clouds of smoke were rolling down from the detonated crater to smother it.

The careful earth has its own fire brigade.

Harry Frobisher said simply: "Run."

We ran. We lurched down the road, overtaking the mules for a foolish moment, careering along with the confused beasts, shouting at them as one shouts at irritatingly stubborn urchins—we lost all sense of proportion, of dignity. I found myself shoving past Father Doonan, elbowing children out of the way. What brought me to horrified sanity was a black hand reaching nervously out of the heaving wicker panniers. I took the fingers of the sad little cripple shamedly and held on to them as I ran.

We were running into the overflow of the smoke; we entered it, held together by our harsh communal breathing, by the snorting mules, by the tugging ropes. The overtaxed children were sprawling dangerously out of their orderly line. Father Doonan caught me up and gazed at me: an angry Irish face muttering disgustedly, "Stop, stop, stop!"

I waved; it could have conveyed anything—guilt, blind

fright. He thought I was failing and his sympathetic arm grabbed me and helped me along. I caught his scrappy voice above the hammer of hooves and feet: ". . . We mustn't do this . . . we'll exhaust ourselves, we can't go so fast."

Burning mountains have no timetables; the gases from the lake of lava in the valley were rising; the children were beginning to cough. I gasped, "We have to keep going——"

"No, our heads, we have to keep our heads," Father Doonan cried.

I shook off his arm. He supported me again. He was yelling in my ear. "Panic . . ." but panic has its own momentum: reason is always slow to catch up with pumping lungs and hysterical legs. Then two of the children fell by the wayside and Father Doonan left me with a furious bellow and ran to lift them up. Without his arm I crumpled—I lay where I fell, watching the children pitch weakly all over the road.

The Matron and Sonia started picking them up—they looked just like toy soldiers, blasted by artillery in a kindergarten game.

The mules trotted on, taking the panniers with them. Harry Frobisher and Marcel and Charlie were still running; Frobisher loping awkwardly behind his friends on his bad leg. Father Doonan yelled to them, "Stop!" They slowed down reluctantly and looked back. Father Doonan ran on to rein in the mules, calming the twittering children in the baskets. He said grimly to Harry Frobisher, "Help us. Behave yourselves."

Marcel looked emptily down into the valley. He transferred his scared face to Father Doonan and shouted to his partners, "Come on."

"Wait," Father Doonan called out to them.

"Not this time," Marcel waved wildly. "He wants a mass funeral, come on."

The three men started moving—Father Doonan ran forward to restrain them. I caught his bitter amazed voice, "What are you doing? Where are you going?"

"Get out of the way," Marcel burst out; he came back in an incoherent flurry to shove Father Doonan off Harry Frobisher; the priest was clinging to him desperately. I heard Father Doonan cry out, "How can you be callous? How can you leave us?" but his voice broke; he was left standing desolately, Marcel had elbowed him off.

"There's no sense in all of us dying," Marcel grunted. He and Charlie took hold of Harry Frobisher's shoulders, helping him along; the three men turned their faces away from Father Doonan and went pattering down the road. Father Doonan ran after them. The frantic voices receded. There was a short cruel struggle—they flung him off.

Then there was just a fading gabble in the distance—we sat there feebly, spectators of disaster, a huddle of unnerved children, the Matron gasping thinly with disgust, Camille sensing abandonment, crying out uselessly, "Harry, Harry . . ." But I don't think he could have heard. And I don't think it would have made any difference, anyway.

I caught Father Doonan's last condemned cry after the running men, "The children, the children . . ." tugging finally at Charlie's arm. The Negro tore himself free. I heard his harsh answer, "Let go. I have to stay with my own." They were away now, going fast—Frobisher leaning heavily on Marcel's arm, hobbling comically like an injured duck. They rounded the bend in the road; for a moment their heads bobbed above the undergrowth. Then silence: the patter of their feet was gone.

The loneliness was suddenly oppressive. Father Doonan

147

was a small distant figure. His arms drooped slowly. He looked different: deflated. He came trudging back.

The Matron said heavily, passionately, "Good riddance," but she was scared. She looked at me—momentarily resenting my age and weakness. I was ashamed to meet her agonized eyes. The van of the army had flown, the rearguard left to its fate. She told the children to stop whining. Then she changed her face (that staunch undefeatable woman, I loved her) and said cheerfully to Father Doonan as he came up, "Don't let it worry you. We'll get along better without them."

"I don't know how they could have done it," he said.

"They're trash. What did you expect of them?"

"Kindness," he said.

"Kindness," she burst out, as if Father Doonan had brought a dirty word into a serious conversation. "They have the instincts of tigers. I knew they'd betray us." And she used the ugly word again, "Trash. Trash." But she was upset by the priest's flat, stricken smile. "Oh, you," she went on in a huff, "you'll never learn. You don't understand human nature," then exasperatingly she broke off. Father Doonan would never learn—nobody can teach an old dog new tricks.

He sat down with us at the roadside. He said faintly, "I trusted them. I think I loved them. I thought they were my friends." He wiped the sweat off his face with his fingers, and with the same sad gesture wiped the shame and distress off it, too.

He grinned at me excusingly. He was all right again. The Matron said, "We're going on, of course?"

"Of course," Father Doonan said.

"And cheerfully?"

"Cheerfully," he said. We sat watching the fire-shot clouds rolling down the ravine; I saw Father Doonan stroking the thin rickety legs of the child nearest to him as if regretting that he couldn't pump some of his excess strength into them. Then suddenly Camille got up. She started walking like an angry somnambulist down the road, stumbling over the stones. Father Doonan squinted after her oddly. The Matron's face went confused.

She got up hastily and ran after the girl, seizing her arm. Camille tugged herself free. We could hear scraps of that startling conversation—Camille muttering resentfully, "Trash," as if the Matron's words had needled her . . . then the word "Harry" repeated passionately as if it were a talisman. "Kindness," I heard her cry accusingly, "when did you show him kindness? What did you ever do to encourage him?" The Matron's mouth fell open; Father Doonan was listening, the way he might have listened to something nakedly upsetting in the confessional box.

"He's gone," the Matron shouted. "Now forget him. We're never going to see him again."

The Matron had chosen an unfortunate expression—one never talks of "seeing" to the blind. Camille said something painful, "I never saw him. But I believed in him."

Father Doonan lifted the weary children to their feet. The little lead soldiers were ready for another nursery battle. He went down the road to the Matron and Camille, who was crying; there is nothing so hurtful as tears in blind eyes. He said to her, "He jumped out of a seaplane to come to us"—as if that was a partial victory, putting his thick hand on the girl's shoulder. "Maybe they've just gone a little way ahead to see if the road is safe." (A polite fiction; the Matron's mouth tightened like a prune.) Father Doonan said to Camille sweetly, "Anyway we *both* liked him," and they went on, hand in hand.

The Matron said hopelessly, "You know what that man does to me——?" but I never found out; she choked it within herself, turning on me petulantly, "I've got stones in my shoes!" as if I were to blame.

The children strung themselves instinctively along the ropes, the mules trotted, and the bells started tinkling again.

✳

The light slid suddenly behind the mountain; darkness fell down on us. We trudged in prison file down the road, waiting for the moon to come up. The cauldron in the valley glowed pinkly; warm dirt sprayed us; we never once turned to look up at the hot furnace ridge. Father Doonan led us in a kind of precise routine: fifteen minutes' walking, three minutes' rest for the children. He said apologetically to the Matron. "They won't be able to sleep tonight, only cat naps. I'm sorry, there isn't much time."

Then the young moon rose. The road was silvery; now Father Doonan walked with the children, for everybody could see. He was humming, *"Sur le pont d'Avignon,"* encouraging them to join in. The small black faces, lit fragilely by the moon, were without fear: the brittle tuneless voices derided the percussions from the mountain. "Sing up," the Matron said to me rudely, and an old Austrian doctor whose shoes pinched (he would have preferred Schubert, anyway) sang *"Sur le pont d'Avignon"* ridiculously.

It was nearly midnight when suddenly Father Doonan jerked to a halt. He peered down the road. We stopped singing; we could see shadows at the verge just round the bend. One of the shadows moved. The Negro, Charlie, came into the moon.

Father Doonan looked warningly at the Matron. She said primly, "All right, I won't say a thing." We could see Harry Frobisher sitting on a boulder. His shoe was off. Marcel crouched near him, rubbing his bare foot. They gave us covert begrudging glances as we came up. The Negro said impassively, not raising his eyes from the ground, "His foot's pretty bad." They had just been a little unfortunate; they didn't seem to think they deserved any particular reproach from us.

I went with Father Doonan to look at Harry Frobisher's ankle. It was appallingly swollen: hot and pulpy to the touch. I laced it with lotion and bandaged it up.

Father Doonan said to Harry Frobisher softly, "You shouldn't have risked scouting out the road for us. It was good of you, but we have to share the risks."

He was trying to whitewash them. Scamps can be very touchy—try to absolve them too obviously and they become savagely conscious of their sins. Harry Frobisher lifted his head and glared furiously at the priest. He said, "What the hell are you talking about? We ran away from you."

"Not very far, though."

"We'd have gone farther. Stick your damned haloes. Get away from us, nobody asked you to rub your soft talk into us."

The Matron cringed with resentful horror. Harry Frobisher got up. He tested his foot, lifting his fist threateningly as Father Doonan tried to steady him. After that nobody said anything that might put tinder to the sparks. Charlie had cut a sapling into a staff. He gave it to Frobisher, who hobbled with us, leaning on Marcel as he adjusted himself to the crutch.

And we all walked in chastened silence. We had been almost happy ten minutes earlier, singing *"Sur le pont d'Avignon."*

7

I THINK Marcel had a feeling about me. He dropped back to keep me company, muttering a compliment that I was *sympathique*. Meaning, I suppose, that a doctor is expected to be ultimately impartial; a ruffian's body isn't much different from anybody else's—only dirtier. He plodded affably by my side. He started the conversation on a typical note: "Do you have a good medicine for thirst?"

"Alcoholic?"

"But naturally. There's only one other worthwhile thirst—for women." And he twinkled, "I don't see any of the ladies of the Folies Bergère about."

"Abstinence is good for you."

"Look, Doctor, I like you," he sighed. "Don't strain my affection by preaching like the priest." It gave him a thought. He stared through the darkness in the direction of Father Doonan, murmuring carefully, "Do you want him to keep his health? Tell him to watch out, he's beginning to get under our skin. He keeps pretending we're holy. He's making fools of us." And that, I thought, must be the final depravity: when a human being can no longer recognize undiluted goodness.

But whoever had been good to Marcel for twenty years?

I shrugged. "He's making a fool of himself. He actually thinks you are holy."

"Why?"

"Because all men are holy"—I should have added, "he thinks."

"Christ," Marcel muttered. "Another crackpot"—referring to me. He guffawed, "You should have been in some of the prisons I've been in. You'd have seen some real holiness." But the idea rankled. He stopped laughing and left me.

It was one o'clock in the morning; the volcano's artillery had opened up. Even soldiers, I suppose, get used to bombardment—the bowels loosen pathetically to begin with, then the monotony of fear dulls the nerves. We just ducked automatically as small stones pattered about us. We had been keeping to our steady routine: fifteen minutes' march, three minutes' rest. I noticed that it was becoming harder each time for Harry Frobisher to get up. I guessed that he'd ripped a tendon; probably it was giving him a premonitory touch of hell. Then Marcel came back.

He watched Frobisher swinging along clumsily on his rudimentary crutch. He was genuinely concerned for his friend; it strangely touched me. Why are we always humorously surprised to discover honor and kindliness amongst thieves?

He started off, "His foot's no joke, eh? How bad is it?"

"It hurts."

"You don't need a medical diploma to tell him that."

I said, "Well, he won't be doing any tangos for quite a while."

"No," Marcel said dourly. "And the opportunities are likely to be restricted. Permanently," he added, looking uneasily up at the sky. "Is he going to be able to get along with that foot?"

"A man can get along with almost anything when his life depends on it," I answered, rather a naïve sort of remark to make. . . .

But I was astonished to see Marcel nodding solemnly. He said, "How right you are. I once suffered the torments of the damned in a Marseilles cellar with a ruptured appendix—" (an exaggerated diagnosis, if I ever heard one) "—because they were afraid to call a doctor on account of the police . . ." but as he spoke his tongue froze cautiously between his teeth; even on a burning mountain, hopeless hostage to fortune, he was nervous of betraying himself. "Well, keep him going," he said, looking at me sidelong. "I'm worried about him."

Then he changed the conversation—switching his eyes to the Matron walking ahead. He began once more that thoughtful, sexually searching scrutiny of her buttocks and breasts, but friendlily this time.

He murmured, "Now that could be a very attractive woman if she'd only learn to control her tongue."

"She'll be interested to hear it," I said.

"A man likes a female of ripeness when he begins to approach maturity," and I kept my face straight—I thought Marcel had not so much approached maturity as overtaken it. But he was terribly serious. "I've taken a fancy to her," he said. *"Strictement entre nous,* I consider her to be my type." He was treating me as a friend and I should have been honored by his confidence; it tickled me, too.

I said demurely, "You're seeing her at a disadvantage. She's under great strain."

"That is why I forgive her for insulting me." He lowered his voice discreetly, "Listen, I've heard rumors about her. They say she used to work in a Paris cathouse" —a euphemism for a brothel—"when she was young. Do you believe it?"

I'd heard the rumor; and had half a suspicion that it was true: converted Magdalens make the best wives and nurses. It didn't reduce her stature in my eyes. I said, "Why not ask her yourself?"

"There are muscles in that arm. It would probably cost me a tooth." But he was intrigued; he narrowed his eyes.

He left me suddenly, hastening to catch the Matron up. I moved forward so that I could hear.

Marcel walked silently by the Matron's side for a moment, then I heard him make the first gallant approach. He said, "It's a nice evening, *chérie.*"

Her head turned slowly on its pivot: she stared at him bewilderedly. "Eh? What did you say?"

"I said, it's a nice evening," but this time, I noticed, he omitted the word *chérie.*

She blinked up at the sky, red with the furnace glare of the volcano. "Is there something wrong with your eyes?"

"Of course. They are dazzled by the company of an attractive woman." And the Matron stared hard at Marcel again: she wasn't sure if he was serious.

"What on earth are you talking about?"

"If you will permit the freedom in the circumstances, I am talking about you."

The Matron gave a hoarse (and, I think, gratified) chuckle. "It's a long time since anybody said anything like that to me."

"Then they have been delinquent. It defeats me. I find you a most captivating person."

"Look," she said gruffly—turning suspiciously to see if I had provoked it: I just shrugged innocently—"you're wasting your soft soap on me. You're not addressing any spring chicken."

"I am addressing a woman of grace and experience. The chicken may have left spring behind it, but it has reached the high summer of robust charm."

"You're crazy." But she didn't sound angry; women are never too old to be affected by the Casanova approach. (This Casanova, admittedly, was a shabby, not too subtle, droll-eyed Parisian; but who could be so particular under the eave of a volcano?) She murmured, "Try your blarney on somebody else. You're making a fool of me."

"If you have ten minutes to spare we'd see about that."

"Eh?" He had said something in a very low voice, affably; she was gazing at him incredulously. She said softly, "Say that again."

"Certainly." Presumably he said it—I tried to hear what it was, but it escaped me; it was uttered in the same low blandishing voice. She lifted her hand and dealt him a stunning blow on the ear. For a moment he looked at her ferociously—it must have hurt him—then he shrugged sourly and retreated a step. I don't imagine it was the first time a woman had boxed his ears.

She said coolly, "Keep that sort of talk for the drabs you pick up in the saloons. It won't get very far with me."

He fell back to join me. He didn't speak for a moment; he was grinning; he didn't seem to be terribly put out.

"What did you say to her?" I asked.

"What do you think? I made an improper suggestion. I invited her into the bushes for ten minutes next time we stopped. I said we weren't going to live very long, what could we lose?"

"You nearly lost an eardrum."

"*Une bagatelle*," he said carelessly. "There has to be a beginning with every woman. One can lose a battle without losing the war." But he was still rubbing his ear ruefully when he went forward to give Frobisher a helping hand. He threw back at me admiringly, "She has spirit, eh?" as if congratulating me for training her well. . . . Then the Matron let me catch up with her.

She asked grimly, "Did you encourage that roughneck to insult me?"

"Does he look like the kind of man who would require encouragement?"

"He wanted to play Romeo in the bushes with me. Do I look like a complaisant Juliet?"

"Juliet," I murmured excusingly, "might have come to

a better end if she'd let nature take its course. Women who have passed the age of romance don't get invitations like that every day."

She said snappishly, "In case it interests you, women have passed the age of romance only when they have lilies on their graves," adding contrarily, "You are growing into a dirty old man."

Then Father Doonan signaled for a rest. Our loose military formation broke up and we scattered gratefully to the roadside. The children fell asleep almost instantly; the moon shone on their curled black limbs—they lay, as children will in exhaustion, without grace, not seeking comfort. The Matron walked amongst them, scrutinizing them anxiously. In the ravine the shove of lava went on: the crater still oozed redly, suffocating the valley with its blood. I saw Harry Frobisher leaning on his staff; he was afraid to sit down because his leg would stiffen and it would be difficult to get up again. I went over to him and asked him how it was.

"It's holding up," he said, and he stared at me gauntly; defying me. I bent down to touch his ankle. He said, "Let it alone."

"It's all right, then?"

"You have any spare legs?" he asked ironically, and I shrugged and left him: who defies a doctor? Presently Camille started feeling her way in his direction and I caught the drifting murmurs . . . first from her, compassionately, "Harry, your leg" . . . and then from him, like a stung animal, "Stay away from me, I told you. Look after yourself." Camille didn't stir, *watching* him (one can talk that way of the blind) with her ears. Then she gave a troubled sigh and reached towards him—he shuffled perversely away from her on his staff.

Father Doonan got up stiffly. He took the girl's arm and

led her away. He was suddenly angry; he went back to Harry Frobisher.

He said softly—but there was no privacy, we all listened—"Why are you so churlish? She wants to help you."

"The hell with it. I didn't ask her for help."

"She has a feeling about you. Don't rebuff her so much."

I saw Harry Frobisher stare harshly at the priest and I thought, "He hates everybody, but Father Doonan for some strange reason most of all." The man muttered, "Why don't you mind your own business? That collar doesn't license you to stick your nose into other people's affairs."

Father Doonan began nervously, "But you came with me, you came as a brother," scarcely audible, "don't you see, that makes you my affair. . . ." Then Charlie got up ominously and stood between them: a huge black janizary guarding the privacy of his friend.

Father Doonan came walking back to me. He was hot with emotion—emotion always made him sweat.

"He's a prickly man. He has a chip on his shoulder. Let him alone," I said.

"I don't understand him," said Father Doonan, wiping his face.

"It isn't important." I was getting tired of all the emotion—to me the only reasonable emotion was the lust to survive. "You don't have to understand him. You're not his keeper." I went on irritably, "So what are you going to do about it? Fight him all the way?"

"All the way," said Father Doonan. And maybe because I was looking at him sourly he repeated in a passion: "Yes, fight him all the way."

I got up in a huff. What would be the trophy—a man's soul? He'd get a tarnished soul. I went to the other side of the road angrily and stared down into the ravine. The lake of lava simmered: red eyes winked, bubbled

and plopped. The spilling crater reared theatrically behind. The elf-light danced in the darkness, the greenish-
yellow burble of ignited gas. The stuff (my brain couldn't
find an adequate word for it) had a kind of rhythm, a
surge; doctors have a name, *paralysis agitans,* for tremors
like that. It nudged at the trees, cracked them, burned
them; and that was what made it obscenely human: the
appetite to consume. I came out of the horrid trance with
a jump—Father Doonan was behind me, touching my arm.

He said apologetically, "We mustn't fret each other's
nerves, there's too much at stake." Then he glanced back
at the three men grouped like hostile wolves a little way
down the slope. He lowered his voice wryly, "We're soon
going to need them, anyway."

"What do you mean?"

"I'm trying to remember what I saw from the air. I
think we're coming to the end of what's left of the road."

And I felt quite injured—nobody appreciates the still
small voice of disaster—when the road ended ruinously
only a few hundred yards round the bend. Charlie was
leading the mules. He shouted back into the darkness and
the train of dozing, trudging children pulled up. I went
with Father Doonan to see what it was.

A yawning split in the gravel surface warned us. Fifty
paces ahead the whole shelf of the mountain that carried
the road had collapsed. The wound was recent; the hillside still crumbled; dirt slipped in little hissing gushes into
the ravine. I stood blinking down into the barbecue of the
valley, wondering obtusely whether the rubble lay there,
or whether the crawling escalator of lava had carried it
away. Then Father Doonan made an anxious sound. We
were too near the edge. It yielded springily—we were
standing on nothing more than a precariously balanced

boulder—a lot more of the road was ready to collapse. We ran back.

We stared in balked silence. I thought wretchedly, "This is where God" (for God is always there to be blamed or appealed to) "has His last laugh." We couldn't go on, we couldn't go down into the grill of the valley, we couldn't go back . . . I remember weighing up the alternatives like a child with an unfamiliar alphabet, none of the words it formed made sense . . . but perhaps we could, at least, go up? When I saw Father Doonan lift his head to the tangle of vegetation that climbed steeply from the road I knew that he was going to make us go up.

The tilted cliff reared into the moonlight—I couldn't see the top to begin with: then I made out the black ridge that blotted out the stars. It was impossibly high.

Charlie had followed Father Doonan's eyes. He whispered sensitively, "Mules can climb 'most anything. But they won't be able to climb that."

"No," Father Doonan murmured. He sighed heavily (for us? for the mules?) and squatted on his haunches, playing with the dust.

"We turn them loose, then?"

I caught Father Doonan's desolate echo ". . . turn them loose." (He *was* sorry for the mules.)

"And the children?" the Matron asked harshly. "We turn them loose, also? They're not goats."

"They have to survive," said Father Doonan. "For a little while, if necessary, they'll have to be goats."

Marcel muttered, "And the cripples?" He was staring confoundedly at the panniers. "Who carries them?"

Father Doonan looked at him with surprise. "We carry them," he said.

Marcel's mouth opened. Harry Frobisher caught his eye with an ambiguous expression—I think for the first time Father Doonan had a reluctant ally in the man. It

160

warned Marcel, and he grinned fiercely and shut his mouth.

"We'll take a rope up," the Negro said briskly to Father Doonan. "We'll rig some kind of line for them." I presumed he meant the children, and he took a machete and a coil of rope from his pack. He and Father Doonan began to slither up the hillside. I heard their machetes chopping away obstructive vegetation—they disappeared into darkness—only the busy chop-chop and crack of branches told us that they were there.

"Never a dull moment," grumbled the Matron. She wasn't built for climbing; neither was I. She turned to the children, a schoolmistress setting them a difficult holiday task. She cried, "We can do it, children, can't we?" and then chuckled emptily: half of them were asleep.

She began to unload the packs off the mules. She sorted the necessities into piles—a few blankets, the medicines, the cans of food. They still made a voluminous load. She started reducing it, leaving spare clothes and shoes and a couple of bottles of brandy behind. She said to me falsely, "Mules can always live off the country," but everything that wasn't blazing around us was collapsing: she stopped making a pretence of it and condemned the beasts to death with her eyes.

Branches were still twittering down the hillside. Presently dark figures panted out of the scrub and a rope came snaking down. Charlie appeared breathlessly with Father Doonan. They shared out the supplies we were taking amongst us. Then the Negro looked at the leprous cripples in the panniers, gave a peculiar shrug, and plumped one of them straight on to Marcel's back. The man cringed for an instant, relaxing with a Gallic grimace as the thin black arms embraced him. Father Doonan chuckled. He took a second child, the Negro took a third. Charlie hesitated, measuring me against Harry Frobisher for the last child.

He began, "That foot, Harry . . ."

"I can take my share," Harry Frobisher said.

Father Doonan put the last one (the tiniest, a girl) on Harry Frobisher's back. Charlie tugged at the rope to test it.

He said with frightful simplicity, "Let's climb."

We did it this way: Father Doonan stirred the sleepy children, starting the first couples up the hillside, giving them an impulsive shove with his arms. They went wriggling up like monkeys, clutching the rope. Children don't know fear—until adults infect them. They giggled, clawing steeply through the undergrowth. Only I was frightened; and perhaps Marcel. Father Doonan and Charlie straddled ahead, guiding the children past obstructions, clapping hold of small bottoms when their feet slipped. We must have looked like inexpert commandos struggling up that rough hill. Harry Frobisher swore ferociously when his bad leg twisted. And every now and again Father Doonan gasped back to us to rest. Then we lay, sucking air, face to grass, on the hillside, not wanting to look down; not wanting to look up. Down was a pond of congealing fire; up was an impossibly distant ridge.

Marcel whispered dolefully in my ear (his breath always suggested liquor), "And I left a comfortable prison for this."

I said, "Shut up!"

"Somebody has to cheer us up."

"I don't want to be cheered up. I'm frightened."

So was he. Maybe it was fear that made him hysterical—perhaps he was just an irrepressible comic at heart? Immediately above him as we rested were the Matron's firm buttocks. Marcel's eyes fell on them glassily. He patted them. (At least, I thought he patted: but I heard the

Matron give an incredulous gasp.) "No Frenchman," Marcel gave a daring grin, "can resist a fine female bottom. This one was made to be pinched."

The Matron cried, "Keep your hands off me. You're mad."

"You should appreciate the compliment, *petite*. It's as good a specimen as I've ever pinched."

She struggled away from him; but tilted on a precarious hillside, where was there to go? She cried again, "You have no manners. . . ." but maybe she liked it? It was the first time I ever heard indecision in her voice. Marcel chuckled; the child riding him like a jockey giggled; I heard his intimate murmur, "I have a fiery nature," drawing me into the joke.

His coarse humor defeated me. I clutched grass resentfully, the way a falling trapezist clutches his net.

And probably that ridiculous interlude kept stark panic away. A rabid imagination is fear's chief agent—the great thing is to keep it occupied. When you go into danger, always take a fat comic along. Father Doonan's voice came down to us. We started the next lap of the ascent. I have never been very partial to heights. It was a terrible climb. Muscles that were good for the daily round of a hospital ward were betraying me. ("Senile, senile!" I thought.) I broke into a sweat—dizzy, despairing—afraid unreasonably of being left behind. I was counting mechanically the greasy tussocks I mounted: each one was a victory. None of us stopped when there came a gritty rumble—probably I was the only one who looked down ill-advisedly to see the slab of road we had just abandoned fall into the ravine.

The noise subsided: and left another, infinitely more poignant in its place. The scream of an animal in distress shocks the nerves like a screeching pencil on a slate. The mules were crying. We couldn't ignore that animal agony. We still went crawling on. I saw Marcel's face and it surprised me: I was shaken; but his frantic eyes were screwed up.

He said intolerably, "Stop. How can we leave the beasts to suffer like that?"

"There's nothing we can do for them. They've fallen into the lava."

"Then they're cooking . . ." and there was no humor in that incongruous comment; he was simply going crazy with the dreadful whinnying in his ears.

"Try to take no notice."

He stopped climbing and wiped his face. "Somebody has to do something," he muttered.

"Put your hands over your ears," I told him. "It won't last long."

"What sort of man are you?"

I could have told him that I was a doctor, that audible agony is occasionally part of a doctor's cross. . . . Then a figure slithered down from the darkness to see what was the matter: the whole human festoon clinging to the rope had stopped. Harry Frobisher began to tug at Marcel nervously, "Come on, come on."

"Listen to those beasts."

"What can we do about it?"

"They are suffering."

"Look," Harry Frobisher started despairingly . . . but he cringed, infected by his partner's distress. The wailing from below pricked like a dagger. I wished the mules would hurry up and die.

Suddenly Marcel said gruffly—his face was washed insanely with sweat—"Wait for me. I won't keep you long," and he planted his child-jockey on the grass, expecting it to take root there. I gripped hold of a thin withered arm to steady it.

Harry Frobisher cried, "You're crazy"—Marcel had reached up deftly to slip the knife out of his sheath. It reminded me for a disconcerting moment of a fat savior of a pork butcher hurrying to slit the throats of tormented beasts that would in any case soon find their way to his chopping block. (Does the sausagemaker regret the horrid moment in the shambles that has to precede the filling of the skins?) Marcel crawled away from us—I saw him as a wriggling silhouette against the glow of embers; then he was just a dark grumbling mutter going down the hillside. He was in a terrible state.

Harry Frobisher said to me shakenly, "I couldn't do anything with him," but I think he sympathized intensely with his partner's feelings. When the Negro came sliding down from above with an urgent inquiry on his face he said, "He's gone down there." He added, not meeting Charlie's wry face, "He took my knife."

"Did he have to do that?"

"Yes. He had to."

"It won't do no good, Harry, they're up to their fetlocks down there. . . ." and then the shrill needle-sharp screaming rose out of the darkness, and Charlie gave a sigh. He muttered helplessly, "That stupid man. He don't have to be casseroled with the mules."

"Somebody'd better help him. He's half out of his mind."

Father Doonan had just come crawling down to us. He made a preparatory wriggle. "Let me see to him. . . ."

"No, I'm used to him," said Charlie. "He's a little mad, maybe. I'll fetch him back."

The Negro went away from us in a swift plunge: he tobogganed down the hillside. We lay, pasted like flies to the tilted scrub, listening out guiltily for him—one had the startled impression that he had dived suicidally below. Harry Frobisher strained to catch the fading crackle of twigs. He cried out suddenly, "I should have gone with them."

"No," said Father Doonan. "You'd have been such a worry to them."

"That stupid dolt. He's so clumsy, he can't be trusted on his own. . . ." I presumed he meant Marcel. And Harry Frobisher cried out again, agitatedly, "What, for God's sake, got into him?"

"Goodness," Father Doonan said.

"Don't talk crap. It just got under his skin."

"That's where goodness lies, not far under the skin."

Harry Frobisher made an angry sound. Father Doonan tried to console him. "Don't worry about them——"

And Harry Frobisher burst out, "Who the hell else do I have to worry about? They're my friends."

Now he was rubbing his swollen leg. "Oh, God"—I heard the mournful murmur—"it had to happen to me, I'll never be whole again. . . ." I just looked at him strangely —how long was it since this haggard, debased man had been whole? Father Doonan was watching him fixedly. When he reached out to stroke the injured leg compassionately, Harry Frobisher twitched it away.

Then—I hadn't counted the minutes—we heard the first laboring pants of the returning men. We shouted out to guide them. They emerged, scratched and breathless, from the scrub.

Harry Frobisher muttered, "You took your time about it," but rolled close to Marcel to stare into his face.

"The elevator wasn't working," Marcel said.

"You're all right?"

"Me? Of course I'm all right. You didn't have to worry. The bad penny always turns up." (It does, too.)

Human beings are like chameleons. The Marcel who had suffered the pangs of hell listening to the anguished mules was gone; the sly, fatly unreliable back-street Pigalle tout was back. He said carelessly, "We finished one of them off. The rest of them were cooked."

The Matron gave an offended grunt. She couldn't understand it. She expected men to run to a predictable pattern: saints to be saints, rogues to be nothing but rogues. There isn't anything about human nature as simple as that. We waited for the pair to get their strength back, then Marcel said jocosely to his child-jockey, "If you're ready, *m'sieu,* climb up."

"Am I very heavy?" the child asked.

"I'll tell you when you get to be heavy," Marcel said with grave formality. "Then we'll change over, you can start carrying me."

The others shouldered their children. Father Doonan slithered up. We waited for his shout. We started climbing again.

We did it in three more debilitating stages—I carried only my skinny old bones and a few blankets, and I couldn't have managed one more. We reached the ridge of the hill in a last gasping dash. We tumbled exhaustedly to the grass and lay there. The children rolled over, whimpering faintly, and quickly fell asleep.

The other side of the ridge was dark—there was no sign of burning trees, no indication that lava had invaded it. It would come, probably: a dam would burst somewhere and the fire would start chasing us. I looked at my watch in the moonlight. It was almost three o'clock.

I sighed to Father Doonan, showing him the watch, "How long are we going to keep this up?"

"We have only tomorrow. We have to be down in the town the dawn after that. We'll keep it up, won't we, the schooner'll be waiting?" looking at me, not anxiously, but fiercely—he was showing signs of wear himself, that thick-bodied indomitable Irish priest. I stared into the pugnacious face rebelliously—he was expecting too much of us, and I thought, "We'll never see any schooner," but I didn't put it into words . . .

I came to consciousness with a jump. Somebody was shaking my arm.

The Matron said ironically, "Isn't twenty minutes enough for you? What do you want to do? Sleep a wonderful night away?" She dragged me to my feet.

The other men were ready, all humpbacked with the cripples in the darkness. The yawning crocodile of children was lined up. I missed the mules. The caravan bells had been solid; very comforting. Now there was only the crunch of insecure feet, the crackle of uneven bracken, no firm road, no signposts—I suppose I should have been grateful that there were stars to steer by.

I had missed the mules as a symbol when we started marching. We began to miss them physically before the night was halfway through. The blankets I carried wetted my shoulders with perspiration. I could remember myself as a *Wandervogel* of eighteen roaming the Vorarlberg forests with a guitar and a pack like Robinson Crusoe's . . . and here I was, stooping under a pygmy's burden like a withered tree in a gale. The memory of youth comes back to us sourly in old age.

But the men ahead—two of them, anyway—trudged straightly: the Negro and Father Doonan, of course, didn't seem to notice their loads. I think they were planting their feet very carefully, not to wake the children sleeping on their backs. Harry Frobisher went with a one-sided kind of lurch: half of him balanced the cripple on his shoulder, the other half went heavily on his staff. I didn't think he'd be able to carry his human share much longer—I felt with a doctor's acute sympathy the strangulating hindrance of his foot.

Marcel went like an ape: hunched, shapeless. He must

have been sure his jockey was asleep—he pumped out like a fire-hydrant a soft delivery of oaths.

Then the Matron (I wasn't troubled by any false gallantry to see that she carried a load greater than mine: she was at least twice as strong) waved to me impatiently to catch her up. She wanted to talk to me. Women will want to talk in the corridors of hell.

She began—as I expected her to begin, for I knew what was in her mind—with a baffled stare in Marcel's direction, "That creature defeats me."

I shrugged: never mind. Breathing was getting to be a burden to me.

"I don't understand him," she said. Not so very long ago Father Doonan had said of Harry Frobisher, "I don't understand him," as if human beings have the democratic right to understand each other—everybody clearly identifiable like bacteria on a slide. I didn't answer. Talking would drain my strength like a leaky faucet.

Then she startled me by saying, "Would you leave your purse open while he is about?"

"Only if I wanted to make a present of the contents to him."

"The man is a ruffian."

"Of course."

"He is a liar. He is a womanizer," and she chuckled hoarsely, "I discovered that for myself. But can you understand him? His insides turn to water when he hears an animal screaming in pain."

"Perhaps he feels more sympathy for animals than for men."

She said, "You're a cynical old German." I began to say that I was a Viennese, but she interrupted carelessly, "You're all the same under the skin. You know what I think? That cheap rapscallion is a very complicated man."

I thought she'd lived long enough to discover that everybody is complicated.

Then for the second time she startled me. "I like him."

"In that case," I said, "go into the bushes with him and gratify him."

"Is that a nice thing to say?"

"He seems to think it would be a nice thing to do."

"You disgust me. Sex isn't the beginning and end of everything." (Well, if it isn't I have been reading the wrong kind of books.) "In any case, I am a nurse," she said, as if nurses were a special brand of female—completely devitalized of the physical urge.

I said, "When a woman's undressed nobody would know that she is a nurse."

"I don't think he's had the benefit of contact with decently civilized women."

"He's been lucky. It's the last thing he'd want."

"It would do something for him."

"It would do even more for the women. They would cease to be decently civilized." Then I looked at her strangely, remembering the rumors of her girlhood in Parisian brothels. Were those wild forgotten instincts coming back? "Look," I said sharply, "leave him alone. He still doesn't know how he got here. He's as dangerous and unpredictable as a bear in a trap. He's frightened, he only came out of loyalty to his friends."

"Loyalty is also something . . ."

"We haven't tested his loyalty to us. Just let's keep moving and stay alive." I added tiredly, "As long as possible. I don't think it's going to be very long."

"And you feel no gratitude toward him?"

"I'm the wrong sex. I have nothing to show my gratitude with." And I dropped back. It was getting to be a fruitless conversation. But after a while—when my legs got back into their drugged solitary rhythm—I began to think a little differently of Marcel. I liked him. Not because he had the lost dim kernel of goodness—but because he was a companionable scamp. I like raffish creatures. I liked that ridiculous and rather pathetic trio, Harry Frobisher and Marcel and Charlie, because they tickled my fancy. The good and the virtuous don't make the best companions, you know. When you're too old to be defiled by bad company—when you have no money in your pockets to lose—the association of scoundrels can't do you any harm. It's usually good for a laugh.

Then I stumbled—almost fell flat—there were no laughs for me that night.

We were tramping along the treeless crest of the ridge. The moon wasn't very luminous; we didn't dare go down into the thickly wooded valley before daylight came. And the lumpy going was arduous. The children were straying like sleepwalkers. I know that the schoolbooks are full of such heroics, but I was almost ready to drop back silently and let them go on without me—thinking caustically, "They won't get very far, anyway."

Then the Matron shouted out in an exhausted voice, "You men, don't you think we've done enough? You want to march to Honolulu all in one night?"

Father Doonan turned around surprisedly. He stared at the travel-drunk children. He blinked pityingly and said, "Why didn't you tell me? We thought you were just getting into your stride."

He put the child off his back carefully into the bracken; it didn't open its eyes. He went and took the one off Harry Frobisher's back, looking at the man's drained, tortured face worriedly. Frobisher sank slowly to the ground. Marcel unloaded his burden; immediately he and Charlie went anxiously to their comrade. They settled him comfortably in the undergrowth.

And the Matron dropped beside me, her thickening

voice warning Father Doonan before her eyes closed, "No cat naps this time. Not unless you want to carry me and this useless doctor and all the children. We've got to sleep till dawn."

There's a point of exhaustion when sleep becomes madly desirable, only the twitter of overwrought nerves won't let it come. I lay in the thick grass—too tired to cross the wall of wakefulness—too restless to get much pleasure out of watching the sickle moon. The Matron slumbered solidly; the children were beehives of shiny unstirring flesh. Father Doonan was hidden from the moon in the shade of a bush; I didn't know if he slept. As always, our three fastidious escorts had removed themselves some distance, as if cynically respecting our privacy. More likely their own.

For a while I listened to their secret murmuring. It died away: a soft snore. Even the few birds slept.

Then my overalert mind started unrolling backwards like a camera film. It went back to the struggle up the hill . . . back still further to the Matron forlornly unloading the mules . . . and for some reason my mind clung like a burr to that picture: Why? It nagged vaguely: there was something wrong with it. The brain is terribly careful—it stores away inconsistencies. Suddenly I was wide awake; I visualized the whole thing again. Remembering the Matron grumbling tetchily as she discarded the spare clothes, the shoes, the couple of bottles of brandy . . . something pricked a warning to pinpoint that. As we'd started to climb I'd glanced back fleetingly at the pile of supplies abandoned at the roadside: my mind reprinted the picture, and in it no bottles of brandy glimmered in the moon.

I stared quickly—quite instinctively—at the three sleeping men. I woke the Matron. I said softly, "I think they've got the brandy. The bottles we left in the road."

She came out of her stupor stiffly. "How can you be sure?"

I told her. Anxiety crept into her face. I pretended to go to the bushes for a transparently obvious reason. As I passed Marcel I hovered over him for a moment, holding my breath nervously: the bouquet of spirits hung about his lips. Then I saw the significant bulge under his coat—glancing at the sleeping Frobisher I saw the bulge of the bottle's comrade under his. I crept back to the Matron, nodding. She roused Father Doonan, whispering to him.

We should have never exposed the bottles. Nobody tantalizes starving men by leaving good food (and liquor was food to our trio) behind.

Father Doonan's eyes shone worriedly. He started off, "I've been very careless . . ." already he was taking the blame; when everything went wrong it was always "It was my fault," "It was stupid of me"; I shook my head, but he hushed me down. He asked sadly, "Where are they?" He meant the bottles; I told him. He rose.

"Stay here," he sighed. He went very quietly towards the three sleeping men. We followed his stooping figure. He bent over Marcel. He extracted his bottle without rousing him. He moved to Frobisher, but a twig cracked—I saw Frobisher stir dazedly and begin to sit up—hastily Father Doonan slipped the second bottle from under the man's coat; there was a faint gleam as he brought his hands together; glass shattered. Sensitively I smelled the pungent odor of brandy fertilizing the ground.

The Matron's chest creaked horridly and we waited for the storm to break. Charlie was awake instantly—I have never seen rage and frustration well so passionately out of a man. Marcel's reaction was slower; he gazed at the

glisten of wet glass stupidly. Then—I do not exaggerate—
he gave a slightly animal scream.

Frobisher lurched up furiously, yelling with despair.
"What the hell did you do that for?"

"Don't wake the children," Father Doonan whispered.
"We're better off without the liquor, aren't we? It's so
dangerous . . ." but Marcel was overriding him with a
high whimper. He was fumbling with the odorous
splinters—was he trying to reassure himself poignantly that
it was only a bad dream?

"He's a fanatic," Marcel cried. The priest, of course,
was a fanatic—but fanaticism requires courage. I felt the
pang a trapped rat feels, seeing Father Doonan confronting
the three infuriated men. The Matron shrank. I heard
her say, "They will do something terrible to him." Harry
Frobisher went forward, balancing himself—even to an
agnostic there is something wryly sacrilegious about the
mere notion of striking a priest. Frobisher dashed his fist
violently into Father Doonan's face.

"Now you'll feel better," Father Doonan said. He wiped
something dark off the corner of his mouth; it smeared
blood. The Matron got up.

I warned her, "Be still. They don't know what they're
doing, they'll hit you, too."

She was muttering. "They will kill him . . ."

"Men like Father Doonan don't get killed off so easily."
(But, of course, history is full of do-gooders eager to get
themselves wiped out.) "You'll only make things worse,"
I said.

"The maniac. Look at him. He's out of his mind . . ."

"Then don't watch." I dragged her back. "There isn't
anything we can do."

I am a coward—but cowardice is the sensible brother to
prudence. I looked away, wincing, as I heard the succeed-

174

ing smack of Harry Frobisher's wild fist into Father Doonan's face.

Then I had to watch: it was too mesmeric. The man with the bad foot was utterly beyond himself. I wondered how much savage resentment had piled electrically inside him: hate, guilt, self-bitterness? I had the strange idea—I don't know what inspired it—that with every furious blow Harry Frobisher was punishing himself. Father Doonan was retreating clumsily, trying uselessly to avoid the blows; he could have protected himself by hitting back, but he was moving with his hands hung stubbornly at his sides. The expression on his smeared face bewildered me: where had I seen something like it? Those early Italian pictures of the martyred saints . . . Saint Sebastian pricked with arrows, Saint Lawrence burning on his grid. I had a feeling of revulsion; I stared mutinously at the ground. I was still holding on to the Matron—now she tore herself free and blundered over to Charlie.

I felt quite terrible, seeing the wakened children gazing distractedly at the priest's bleeding face.

The Matron began incoherently to Charlie, "Stop it——"

The Negro put her away obdurately. He said, "We been without a drink a long time, he didn't have to do what he did."

"That creature will maim him."

"He's a pretty big man," Charlie said coolly. "He can defend himself."

"He would not hurt a fly."

Charlie chuckled without humor, "For a man who wouldn't hurt a fly he certainly takes some chances. Maybe he'll think twice before he does it again."

I tugged the Matron back; her breath fluttered away. Father Doonan's eyes were puffed—he blinked woodenly, going back sufferingly before the frenzied rain of blows. Frobisher was yelling. "Why don't you put your hands up?" his knuckles banging again and again at the punished face.

"I hit you once before unjustly," said Father Doonan. "I'll never hit you again."

"Do something. What's the matter with you?"

"Get it out of your system. It'll be all right."

"You're crazy."

"Crazy," Father Doonan grinned one-sidedly; his lip was split. "Now be my friend——"

"—try that for size," Frobisher shouted. He dashed his fist into the bleared features. "How's that from a friend?"

Then he paused, his breath whistling. I heard his cruel mutter, "I've taken enough from you, you holy bastard." And teetering on his bad leg, he peered defeatedly into the priest's face. It incited him; he hit it again.

The Matron cried to Charlie, "That madman——"

"I don't know which of them is the madman," Charlie said. He was staring curiously at Father Doonan. He moved in front of Frobisher. "That enough?" he asked softly—it was half an admonition, half a suggestion.

"Enough," Harry Frobisher said tiredly. He looked vaguely at Father Doonan, sucking his knuckles. He hobbled off and dropped into the undergrowth.

The Matron took Father Doonan's arm and led him away. She began to wipe the maltreated features—one eye was a black swollen apple; the cracked lip oozed blood. She was shaking too much to do the job properly. I took over from her. She said rebelliously to Father Doonan, "Well, you did a bad day's work when you brought those barbarians along."

He shrugged. "I knew the time would come when somebody'd have to carry the children." And he added calmly, "Don't worry about them. You'll see, they'll turn out to be very good men."

"What did you say?"

"Hush. Quiet the children."

"The man is right. You *are* crazy——"

"Settle them. See that they get a little sleep."

She went off to them. And then something Frobisher had said came back to me . . . "I've taken enough from you, you holy bastard." I repeated it. "What did he mean?" I asked.

Father Doonan said, "I deserved everything he gave me. I've been shoving holiness into their faces until they got to be sick of it. I'm a very sanctimonious man."

He lay back in the bushes. I left him so that he could go to sleep. Harry Frobisher was a dim, half-erect shape in the darkness. "Be my brother," I thought cheerlessly— hostility crept out of the man like strangling ivy—and then I remembered Father Doonan's evangelistic cry, his passionate, "Fight him yes, fight him all the way!" God the Father—God the Sergeant Major—riding that cantankerous outcast to salvation . . .

"I'll choose better company in heaven if ever I get there," I thought. And I dropped into the bushes, too, closing my eyes restlessly, not expecting to sleep.

A hand pressed my arm. I woke: Father Doonan was leaning over me. The sky had changed; a pink heatless glow was trickling into its fringe. I looked at my watch. I had slept a full loglike forty minutes. Father Doonan whispered regretfully, "I'm sorry. But we have to go."

We all got up. The men shouldered the children. We formed line silently; we began to march once more along the ridge. Light was flooding softly into the valley. The smell of lava, the heat of battle, came with it. A bird, insensitive to disaster, began nonchalantly to sing.

8

I SUPPOSE it is impossible for a child—a crippled one—to ride a human being without establishing some kind of affinity with his mount. I'd got half used to Charlie droning intimately over his shoulder; the fleeting chuckles, the shared jokes, the child bouncing cosily on the saddle of the Negro's back. Then I saw Harry Frobisher making the same private little jerky head-movements. And that surprised me.

I wondered what he and the child who rode him could be talking about.

He was carrying a four-year-old girl named Fleur: a flower, but slightly withered, one leg wasted to a bony stick. Leprosy takes hasty toll when it seizes on the young. And I watched the child whispering, tittering faintly, twisting to peer interestedly at her host. Maybe what really surprised me was that this grouchily ignitable man had let himself be drawn out of his shell. I thought curiously, 'The disease doesn't seem to worry him any more; he's actually getting accustomed to it.'

The Matron was watching the couple secretly. We were trudging along the crest of the hill, waiting for daylight to enter the valley and make it safe for us to go down. She grumbled in my ear, "Somebody ought to stop it. He's probably telling the child a dirty joke."

"No joke is dirty to a child," I said.

It nettled her. "You were evidently brought up to be a snot-nosed little prig."

"I was brought up to respect tolerance——"

"—And to talk highfalutin' nonsense——"

"—And to remember that it takes all kinds to make a world."

"Not the kind of world I choose to live in." She threw an unforgiving glance in Harry Frobisher's direction. "You should communicate your noble principles to the savage who tried to destroy Father Doonan's face."

"If you'll forgive me," I said coolly, "for once I entirely sympathize with the man."

Her head swiveled belligerently toward me. "What the devil do you mean?"

"The good can get to be too damned good to live with. Sometimes ordinary imperfect people like you and me" (she started retorting, "Speak for yourself") "have to put them brutally in their places. They have to be hurt a little to teach them humility."

She growled, "Father Doonan *is* humble . . ." and I thought, 'Yes, humble like a crusader introducing the infidel to God.' Humble with a battle-ax. Father Doonan crying out exultantly, "Fight him, yes, fight him all the way!" Suppose the bum Harry Frobisher was satisfied with his seedy imperfections—suppose he just didn't want to be fought . . . ?

The Matron knew it wasn't much good getting into an argument with me. She gave a sullen rumble, "I don't want another word out of you."

"Why can't you live and let live?"

"Because the lives of men like that aren't worth living," she said with an intolerant scowl.

"How would you know?"

"You disgust me. Be quiet. You're an anarchist," she said.

Then the crest of the hill dipped. Smoke from the side we'd just left started pouring foully over the ridge. What was worse, the pink light of the dawn seemed to be mixed with a ruddier pink farther down the valley—I didn't want to worry anybody with premonitions, but I guessed that there was fire ahead of us as well as behind. The forest was dry. The rain of embers must have started it burning like tinder all round.

And then—we all got mixed up in the smoke—I found Marcel loping just ahead of me. He was burbling companionably to his young jockey.

". . . back me for the next race at Longchamp. For the Chantilly Gold Cup. We're an unbeatable combination," I heard Marcel say.

The child asked shrewdly, "You think we shall win?"

"We're a certainty. We're the punter's delight. We'll take the straight at a gallop, no need to use the whip on me, keep me eased to the rail, we'll come first in the field at a canter."

"And that will make us very rich?" the child pondered.

"Rich and famous," said Marcel. "I'm the best stallion that ever came out of a stable. Your fortune is made."

"Father Doonan teaches us never to covet money."

And I heard Marcel chuckle dryly, "Let Father Doonan try winning a packet at Longchamp, he'd be a different and better man . . ."

. . . But I didn't hear the rest because the Matron turned on me with an outraged breath. "He's debasing an innocent child."

"He's just telling it a fairy tale. They know they're not going to run any races at Longchamp."

She cried, "Are you content to hear that roughneck teach the young one to gamble?" and I clicked irritably with my tongue—we're all gamblers from the minute we come into a world that is nothing but a vast wheel of chance.

I said coldly, "You're a stuffed shirt, Matron. You must have led an insufferably pure life." And she flamed alarmingly. I seemed to have touched an uncomfortably sensitive nerve. She marched her red face away. Maybe all those rumors about her bawdy youth weren't so far out?

Harry Frobisher was still talking over his shoulder to Fleur, who seemed to have gone to sleep on his back. Something just at the threshold of my brain noticed that she was slumped like a small loose bag.

Then quite sharply—as if a tap had been opened—light gushed into the sky. The haze went green and saffron; spokes of the sun stabbed down into the dark valley. We all stopped to watch the topmost leaves of the stunted palm catch the light first—then the trunks crawling slowly out of the veil of smoke. Father Doonan shouted encouragingly. He started leading the way down into the valley, the children trotting after him in Indian file. I trailed after them down the slope.

I was still in the rear—coughing as I entered the reservoir of smoke—with Harry Frobisher lurching unsteadily in front of me, when my eyes fastened again on the child on his back. At first I wondered how Fleur could sleep so soundly under such a jolting, then a sharp professional curiosity wondered just what sort of sleep it was. Frobisher was supporting the girl tightly. But her legs dangled flaccidly, like a puppet that has lost its stuffing. I knew what was wrong before I reached out to touch her, turning the empty doll's face up to the light. I said to Frobisher hastily, "Wait, wait"—but we were all gathering breakneck momentum, trotting down the slope. I called to him again urgently—he pulled up uncomprehendingly, staring at me.

I shouted to the others ahead of us, "Come back."

Father Doonan returned slowly—like a puzzled general unwilling to give up hard-won ground. I said sharply to the Matron, "Keep the children away." She blinked nervously, holding them back. Then I whispered to Father

Doonan, "It's Fleur. She's dead."

His mouth sucked quickly with distress. He reached out instantly and took the dead child off Frobisher's back. Frobisher was gazing at me vacantly. He muttered, "Dead? What did I do?"

"You didn't do anything," I said. But I don't think he was listening—he was gazing stupidly at Father Doonan bending over the child in the grass. He kept on muttering, "What did I do?" until Charlie came up to tug at his arm.

"You heard the doctor, Harry," said Charlie. "You didn't do anything at all."

"But I was just talking to her——"

"You were talking to a dead child," I snapped. I was badly shaken—but I could have bitten my tongue. The man gave a drab chesty murmur and sank slowly to the ground.

Father Doonan looked at me. He was terribly pale. I said to him, loud enough for Frobisher to hear me as well. "She was very frail. It was just too much for her."

Father Doonan closed the peering inquisitive eyes—we don't like the dead, with their uncanny glazed perception, to stare at us. He got up and said huskily to the Matron, "Take the children down the slope."

"I would like to be here when . . ."

"But not with the children. Do as I say."

She gathered the silently intent children and hustled them down the slope. They sat on the grass distantly, still watching. They were all abysmally tired—they couldn't see anything wrong with a playmate taking time off for a doze. A few of them curled up instantly, imitating Fleur's rictus of death. Marcel had gone over quickly to Frobisher to sit in front of him shieldingly. Charlie and Father Doonan had started digging. The thick clump of the mattocks made an unpleasant sound in the still morning air.

182

Marcel began worriedly, "It was just a weak kid. You don't have to make such a tragic face."

"I carried her."

"I'm carrying one, too. It doesn't give me any paternal rights."

"I don't even know what happened," Frobisher said.

I said to him, "Listen." I didn't like his grim, drained face. "If it's any consolation, I never expected her to make old bones. Nine or ten—she wouldn't have lived much longer. She'd never have enjoyed her life."

He glared frantically. "How the hell do you know what anybody needs to enjoy life?"

"Not a sick wasted body, for certain."

"I've got a pretty good body," he said furiously—he was trying to look past Marcel to see what Father Doonan and Charlie were doing. "What makes you think I ever enjoyed my life?"

I thought coolly, 'In your shabby way you've enjoyed it; nobody stopped you changing it.' A few stones went rolling down the hill as I sat up. Men like Frobisher were that kind of rubble—they had only one direction, and that was down. After a while I heard the mattocks finish their clumping. I didn't go over to watch them put the child away.

Then Father Doonan started murmuring the burial service; the cold, comfortless platitudes came wafting across. "Man that is born of woman hath but a short time to live . . ." I watched Frobisher's face stiffen; and when the priest's murmur came to us, strong with assurance ". . . in sure and certain hope of the resurrection to eternal life," he tried harassedly to get up.

Marcel shoved him obstinately back. Frobisher bent his head to shield his eyes. I wondered if he was crying.

Finally it was all over. Father Doonan came over. He was breathless—as if he had been running. He stared hard at Harry Frobisher, as always in emotion, his face flushed and wet. He watched Frobisher trying weakly to get up. He seemed suddenly angry. He called Camille across.

He pushed her intimately over to Frobisher and said to the man loudly, "Take her shoulder. She'll help you along."

"What for? I don't have anything to carry now. I can get along all right."

Father Doonan broke in violently, "For once you're not going to argue. I've had enough of it. Do you hear?"

"I'm all right, I tell you," Frobisher insisted churlishly, backing off . . .

"You're going to hold us up. Take her shoulder. Do as you're told. You can help each other—she can be your crutch, you can be her eyes."

"What the hell are you yelling for?"

"Because you make me yell. You're such a stupid perverse man." Suddenly Father Doonan yanked Frobisher's arm compulsively round Camille's shoulder. She was murmuring reproachfully to the priest, "Please, I'll see to him, don't shout," but he went on shouting over her head at Frobisher; I couldn't imagine what had got into the man. "Now stay with her. Don't get me so mad."

"Any harm in letting her help you, Harry?" Charlie asked gently.

Frobisher gave him a trapped, slanted look. He began to adjust himself, leaning unwillingly on the girl. The Matron opened her mouth nervously—then she glanced at Father Doonan's stubbornly contorted features and didn't speak. I really couldn't understand Frobisher's savage reluctance to touch Camille.

I said to him impatiently, "You're making such a business of it. What's the matter with you? Why can't you co-operate?"

"Who asked you to interfere?"

184

"We've got a long way to travel."

"Then save your breath for it. Let's go."

And Father Doonan sighed. He picked up his child, grinning with fluttering panicky triumph—I wondered why—and we all got ready to march. Frobisher looked draggingly back over Camille's shoulder. He was staring at the rough earthy mound. It was set with a twig cross, the little Melanesian's Open Sesame if she got to the pearly gates (assuming, of course, that no color bar operates there).

"Rest on me," I heard Camille whispering to Frobisher. "I'm a very strong girl."

Charlie led off. We all went straggling down into the valley. Nobody seemed to have noticed that the sun had rushed up—for Fleur, finally. The birds sang discordantly in the smoke. Father Doonan walked behind with me. He watched Harry Frobisher letting his weight sag more intimately on Camille's back. They made an incongruous couple—he was like an offended lover who is too sullen to make it up. I tried to hear if at least they were speaking to each other, but his head was bent; the only sound he made was an occasional gruff mutter—the cautionary grunt a man makes, tugging at the reins of his pony—when she strayed blindly too near the trees.

"What's the matter with him?" I asked.

"Find out."

"It was a civil question."

"It's no business of yours," Father Doonan said. Then he burst out queerly, as if he couldn't contain it inside him, "You know why he doesn't want to touch her?"

"Because she's blind. . . ."

"Because she's blind," he overran me quickly. "Because he's never touched a woman except for one purpose"—he glanced at me, showing his teeth wryly, as if a priest wasn't supposed to know what that purpose was. "She's too helpless, he doesn't know what to do about it. You see, don't you, he's got the instincts of real goodness? He wants to keep her off so that he doesn't do her any harm."

"I know exactly what he'd like to do to her. He isn't the kind of man to think it'd do her any harm."

"You don't have a very nice mind."

"I don't know what a nice mind is. So what are you pushing them together for?"

"Sooner or later I have to trust him. It's his only salvation; I want him to know that I have confidence in him."

"If ever we come out of this, she'll be in the family way," I said unkindly. "If I were your bishop I'd have you unfrocked."

And for the first time he gave himself away, letting me know that he'd had trouble with his superiors in the past. He muttered uneasily, "They don't like us to take risks. But we have to sometimes, don't we? We have to help the worst of us along. We have to demonstrate our faith in them, we have to encourage them by putting them on trust." Then he started coming out with that hoary old aphorism, "There's more joy in Heaven over one reclaimed sinner than . . ." and I interrupted him gruffly.

"Oh, shut up."

A doctor has to have a strictly clinical attitude towards life. He takes men as he finds them, complete with their random gleams of mercy and their more conventional lusts. I watched Harry Frobisher and Camille hobbling along connectedly like a four-legged animal—the lame leading the blind, or, as Father Doonan believed naïvely, the blind leading the lame. He was too trustful for words. The opportunity would offer itself. The virgin would be raped.

I felt vaguely guilty about Camille. She had come in

such a vulnerable rush to the precipice of sex. I half thought of warning the Matron——

——Then the ground jumped underneath us as if a howitzer shell had landed amongst the trees. I looked back. Another piece of the crater was tossing itself into the sky. The morsel of crust soared over the uprush of gas as lightly as a plastic ball on the jet of a shooting gallery. And there was no room inside me for anything but panic—suffocating panic—the shameful senile desire of an old man to preserve himself.

We ran: it was like running futilely from the wrath of God.

The volcano had no doors for us marked "emergency exit"—none of those clinging bolts that let you out of a theater in case of fire at the merest push. There was a long rough canyon, a fold in the mountain, gathering smoke as efficiently as a gutter gathers rain. The canyon meandered stonily into the distance. The sun wasn't steep enough yet to reach the shadows where it twisted out of sight; but the gloaming was ominously ruddy. It wasn't imagination that prompted the idea that the forest was blazing down there.

Just to tease us there came a thin spatter of rain. But it was only a flurry of unconvincing clouds drifting in from the sea. The few drops rattled on the leaves halfheartedly, dying away.

And our breath died with it. Nature's belated fire-brigade wasn't giving us a lot of hope. We like God to lean down from heaven at such moments and say, "See? This is a sample of my miracles. I am going to make it easier for you." If anything, the miracle worked cruelly in reverse. (Of course, it was still terribly early in the morning. Maybe He slept.) The fold of the canyon became suddenly very narrow. The boulderous sides rolled up steeply. Our emergency exit turned into the merest crack in the mountain; a ravine hollow with witch-mutterings inviting us to enter the trap.

Walking far ahead, Charlie hung back. Sniffing, as if his eyes could see X-ray fashion round the gully, he said uneasily, "It's burning down there."

"It's burning nearly everywhere," Father Doonan said.

"We'd like to be able to run from it, though. There isn't an awful lot of room in this place to run."

"There'll be room," said Father Doonan. Adding with the kind of holy assurance that always maddened me, "If we have to run, they'll see to it that we have room."

"They" (I suppose) meaning the heavenly host. Charlie seemed to belong to a more sceptical Church. He shrugged dubiously, "I don't much fancy it. We're getting all closed in."

"Let's get on," said Father Doonan. "There isn't anywhere else to go."

Marcel bridled. "We could try going back."

"It's too late. I think we'll just get on," Father Doonan said.

Marcel's voice rose ironically. "You *think?* You're not making it an order?" He cried out rebelliously, "I'm a Frenchman. I believe in democracy. I like to vote on such things"—it didn't sound ridiculous coming from that chronic miscreant. I felt very much the same way myself.

"Don't be so angry with me," Father Doonan said.

"So how many votes do you carry?"

"All the votes of the angels," Father Doonan said cheerfully.

Marcel began to shout exhaustedly, "Can't you be serious? This is a matter of life and death."

"That's when one needs the votes of the angels, when it's a matter of life and death."

"This man is a fanatic. Somebody must talk to him," Marcel said.

Charlie shrugged with faintly sullen anxiety. "We could be putting our heads into a noose. It's burning down there."

"We've lived through so much," said Father Doonan. "Let's be patient, let's meet our difficulties as they come. There isn't time to go back, the schooner'll be waiting for us at dawn."

"We'd like to have a say in the matter."

"I thought you'd had it. Now let's get along."

But Marcel insisted, legalistically obstinate, "We vote." He looked at Charlie.

Charlie sighed. "I'm for going back."

"That makes two of us," Marcel said.

Then the Matron moved coldly towards Father Doonan: that made two on the other side. Next they stared at me. I said, choosing the coward's neutrality, "Leave me out of it. Forward or backward, the situation is equally hopeless." Now they looked at Harry Frobisher. (No one thought of looking at the two nurses: maybe Sonia's black skin disenfranchised her. Maybe Camille's sightlessness debarred her from a vote.) And Harry Frobisher surprised everybody, me not less than the rest.

He said, looking covertly at Father Doonan, "I'm with him," and I saw the priest glow as if a neon had lighted up inside him.

"With *him?*" Marcel blinked confusedly.

"You asked me."

"But one expects——"

"You said you believed in democracy. What the hell do you want, a loaded vote?"

Marcel shook his head as if to clear it. He gazed with bewilderment at Charlie; the Negro stole a look at his friend. He said stolidly, "Three to two. They have it."

And democracy started working; we all went plodding on.

I couldn't understand it. Had Harry Frobisher just gone unexpectedly mulish on his friends? Or had he sided with the priest because he'd begun unwillingly to believe in him? Of course, it was stupid—considerations of delicacy don't apply to people like that. . . .

But the Matron moved up to me wonderingly and whispered in my ear, "Well, wasn't that a funny thing? One never knows what they will do next!"

"Whatever is to their advantage," I said.

"Do you find it impossible to look for a little decency in your fellow creatures?"

I retorted, "You should have set me a better example. By going into the bushes and looking for it with Marcel."

That made her flounce—the sex *motif* wasn't very popular with her just then. "I'm beginning to trust them," she said.

"You know best."

"Father Doonan is right, we're all a mixture of good and bad."

"Chiefly bad when our lives are at stake."

"You're as sour as a green apple. Try to be a little more charitable."

And I said, scarcely recognizing my voice, wanting to shut her up, "We're all going to need whatever charity we can get." We had just turned the bend of the canyon—we faced a billow of advancing smoke, pricked sharply with red. The breeze was whipping it furiously along the trap of the gully towards us.

Marcel sighed painfully. Democracy had betrayed him —he would never trust it again. He said, and it sounded like a deathbed utterance, *"Nous n'avons plus de fortune"* —we're all out of luck. I suppose we could have run back along the canyon—one can always turn and run along the

190

tunnel from the fast express that is bearing down on one. Marcel showed his skull's grin to Father Doonan. "Now report it to your angels. This is a pretty mess."

The term he used was *pièce de merde*—gutter patois. I thought it exactly described the situation.

"But I anticipated it," Father Doonan said.

Marcel said flatly, "But you brought us along, nevertheless."

"Sooner or later we have to get round it."

"May one question your sanity?"

Father Doonan's voice rose impatiently. "The caves," he said. He gestured up the honeycombed sides of the canyon: they were riddled with holes, he exhibited them like a conjurer producing rabbits out of a hat. "It's shelter, isn't it? We won't be very comfortable, but we can sit it out."

"You'll say that once too often. Fire is approaching——"

And the priest cut him off brusquely—the conjurer's ability was being maligned. "I expect rain," he said.

Marcel shook his head to clear it; he was utterly at a loss for words. I wondered if Moses had said with such confidence, "I expect water," when he struck the rock. I think even Charlie was too bemused—too shocked—to summon up real anger. "You *expect* it?"

"Why not?"

"His angels," Marcel scoffed fiercely. "Didn't he tell you? He has a personal wire to heaven, everything's laid on. He has ordered a small private miracle. Nothing ostentatious, nothing Elijah would look at, but good enough for——"

And the Matron yelled at him insupportably, "Shut your trap." (How easy it is to forget to be a lady.) I felt terribly sorry for her; I'd always thought of her as a comparatively young woman. Lines I had never seen before had begun suddenly to age her face. . . .

". . . You talk like a lot of parrots in a cage." It was Harry Frobisher. "Finish the debate under cover. If we're going to hole up, let's get started."

"Children," cried the Matron, "there is a large tub of ice cream for the first half-dozen who scramble up with me into a cave." Ice cream doesn't grow in tubs in the jungle; maybe it was a glib promise she didn't expect to have to redeem. "Now up with you," and she slapped the nearest small black bottoms. They started scrambling up the loose rocky slope. The rubble slid from under them; a few of them sat ruefully on jagged stones. We went up the way people scale an escalator moving in the wrong direction. The platform slides betrayingly beneath us—we go through the motions of climbing without seeming to advance. Dislodged boulders rattled down.

Then I looked back—the incurable Lot's wife of the party, always looking back. . . .

A hot thread crept along the bed of the canyon—crackling carelessly like the outposts of an army too sure of victory to need surprise. The red regiments followed in a rush along the wind tunnel; the thorns spattered like firecrackers; the pines turned into Roman candles. The spectacle was wonderful. It is surprising how one loses one's taste for the spectacular when one looks like becoming part of it.

Then Marcel came groping alongside—stooped so that the child riding him like a tiny baboon should have a comfortable seat. That man never entered a conversation with a tentative paddle; always with a wordy splash.

"I prefer an honest crook any day," he said.

And it was up to me to say, "What do you mean?" or something similar—he had to be wound like a phonograph to keep his turntable moving. I said it almost automatically, "What do you mean?"

"All priests are humbugs. But ours"—for the first time

I noticed that possessive, begrudgingly affectionate "ours" —"takes your breath away. He is the archbishop of all charlatans." In case I didn't understand him—and I didn't —he grumbled, "He actually takes his mummery seriously."

"I don't know what you're talking about."

"You heard him, didn't you? 'I expect rain,' he says. The way a sailor off a ship with a thousand francs in his pocket says with just reason, 'I expect to have a woman tonight.' "

The comparison was odious. "Be quiet," I said.

"Now, look," Marcel said persuasively. "Don't get me wrong. Believe me, I admire the Church." He was scrambling alongside like an ape, the child bobbing dreamily on his back. "It invents miracles, but it doesn't expect anybody to believe in them because they don't happen nowadays. It gives you a nice comfortable ritual— the confessional box is generous—a few easy penances and everything is all right. But that priest," he said, feeling the injustice, "just doesn't play according to the rules. His bosses won't put up with him—" and for a dazed moment I had a vision of a jeweled and mitred football coach carpeting a humbly rebellious Father Doonan for not playing the game according to the rules.

"He's like an actor," Marcel complained, "who expects you to believe in every word of an impossible play."

"What's wrong with that?"

"It makes it uncomfortable for the other actors."

I said angrily, chiefly because my fingers were bleeding, "You're such a degenerate, you can't understand a very good man. He actually believes in it: goodness. If you had no shoes he would take his off and give them to you. Now do you know what I mean?"

"Yes. He would get his feet torn for nothing."

"Are you a Christian?"

"Of course."

"When did you last go to church?"

"When I was ten. But the label is convenient."

It was altogether too preposterous—a bony old Viennese Schubert-lover slithering pantingly up a stony slope with a self-paroled convict who had a black imp clinging like a burr to his back. Rubber seemed to be burning below. Sparks danced amongst us.

"You vagabond," I said irascibly. "Now I know why you've had such an abominable life——"

And he was so astonished that his little black rider almost fell off his back. "What are you talking about?" he cried. "I've had a wonderful life."

"You? You've been in prison . . ."

"Seven times."

"You've slept in gutters . . ."

"The best of their kind. I've never gone short of a drink or a woman. I've never worked an hour longer than I had to. What's wrong with that?" (And do you know, he was angry? Actually *angry*.) He said with passionate pride, "I have friends." He looked up towards Charlie, scrambling effortlessly over the rocks, then down at Harry Frobisher, trailing along painfully with Camille a long way behind. "The salt of the earth."

'Oh, shut up,' I thought petulantly, 'you make me sick.' I didn't want to talk to him. Marcel shouted jauntily back to Harry Frobisher, "Keep going, only another ten thousand meters." Then he said affably over his shoulder to his jockey, "Everything all right there, *mon ami?* You're beginning to weigh like a featherbed."

We had passed holes that might have sheltered a rabbit. I supposed Father Doonan was looking for something more commodious: a family-size cave. At length he shouted down to us. He had stopped at the lip of a dark cavity. The children scurried in after him—vanishing as if

194

a magical Pied Piper had led them straight into the hill. I had no kneecaps on my trousers—fingers raw—blinking sweat; since leaving the hospital I had oozed a whole pondful of sweat. The sparse scrub dotting the stones began to crackle, chasing us with fire, and Marcel gave a final yank and dragged me into the cave.

It was dark and cool and enormous. The children were ranged like an obedient class in rows at the back. The Matron and Sonia squatted with them. They looked as if they had just dazedly mounted the Matterhorn. Oily smoke was flowing up suffocatingly. I'd only that moment glanced below, catching a fleeting glimpse of the wounded laggard, Harry Frobisher, and Camille struggling over the stones—the pain in his leg must have been killing. Then I looked back once more and the couple was gone.

I said to Marcel, "Where are they?"

He said demurely, looking me in the eye, "They've just popped into another hole."

Father Doonan asked, "Which hole?"

Marcel said evasively, "I didn't see."

Father Doonan hung irresolutely at the lip of the cave, staring down. The hillside was as riddled as a warren; he shouted anxiously. There was no reply.

Charlie said softly, "They're under cover. Don't worry, they're all right."

"But Camille is with him," cried the Matron. "She will be——" and she broke off, the unspeakable words coming thickly to her tongue: she couldn't bring herself to say, "I don't trust her with that man." She sat back, bleared with fatigue. I thought she was going to cry.

And Father Doonan shouted down again. No sound came back. He made a move to scramble down to discover their hole; then the smoke poured up as solidly as milk, screening the entrance to the cave, and Charlie pulled him back with a cry, "It's too late."

He and Marcel—they were the only ones with any practical sense amongst us—were unpacking the blankets busily, draping them over the entrance, jamming the corners into crevices with stones.

Then we all crouched back in the echoing semidarkness, cosily entombed, as far away as we could get from the smoke that crept in under the blankets. For a while we sat in silence, listening to the undergrowth bringing the swarming crackle of fire up towards us; measuring the threat of its speed and intensity with our ears. Downhill the thorns spluttered raggedly. It sounded like a badly trained platoon at firing practice—they'd never be able to synchronize a volley, but it wouldn't make their bullets less fatal. Then nervous tension made me want to go to sleep. One can absorb just so much fear; cowards become reckless when they realize that there is no escape. But Father Doonan wouldn't let me go to sleep. He came crawling towards me.

"I suppose they're all right?" he said. He made an apologetic movement downwards—he was referring to the couple in the other hole.

I said, "They stand just as much chance as we do," but that wasn't what he meant.

"I wish we were all together," he murmured—it was as far as he could get towards voicing his fears. There are some priests—muscular Christians—who can talk about the sexual act in bald barroom language: but not Father Doonan. Perhaps he was waiting for me to refer to it medically . . . "I just want to be sure they won't come to any harm," he whispered.

Which was a way of saying: he wanted to be sure that no harm would come to Camille.

And his eyes didn't stir from my face. I saw the Matron staring at him hopelessly, accusatively, and I knew he didn't want to look at her.

"Don't worry so much," I said.

"He's a good man."

"What's the difference?"

"But he is, isn't he?"

"I've met worse."

I don't know why I went so angry. I just wanted to listen to the undergrowth crackling below—the air was becoming unbreathable, for the blankets wouldn't shut out the smoke. I tried to keep my voice down, but I was like milk frothing to the boil.

I said, "What's the matter with you? You told me you had to trust him. It was his only salvation—you wanted him to know you had confidence in him. Well, you put him on trust." I went on in a rush of recrimination, "Why don't you make your mind up? Either you believe in what you said or you're just a holy hypocrite."

And he grabbed hold of my arm. His face cleared instantly.

He said, "Forgive me. I had a moment's doubt." His face shone. "It was unworthy, I'll do penance for it. He's a *good* man," he repeated staunchly, stressing the word for the benefit of the Matron—this time his eyes moved over to her and he smiled assertively into her face.

She responded bleakly: she wasn't born the day before yesterday. She knew what was going on in the other cave.

Suddenly Marcel said loudly, "It's about time."

"For what?" asked Father Doonan.

"For something to happen. I'm still waiting to see how your angels vote."

"Please . . ." Father Doonan began nervously.

"You're the vote-getter. You're supposed to know how to pull the trick." Marcel's lips were pursed like a sullen child's.

Charlie said, "Hush a moment, I'm trying to hear."

But Marcel waved him down brutally. "He's the professional, isn't he? Why isn't he praying? He's falling down on his job."

"I have prayed," said Father Doonan.

"Maybe you haven't prayed hard enough. Try a stronger kind of prayer."

Father Doonan sat still, crumbling the earth of the cave awkwardly between his fingers.

Marcel lurched to his knees, crawling towards him to shove his hot rabid face close. He said angrily, "You're like all the priests, you know how to spin a tale." He raised his voice. "In ten minutes we're going to be smoked out of here. Why don't you pray louder? Let everybody hear." Then he started shouting—he was like a gourmet in a restaurant dissatisfied with the cut of the beef— "You're no good. You're an incompetent." And in his rage he said something so outrageous, "I'll make a complaint about you to God," that I had a stricken impulse to giggle. Even the Matron's mouth hung open: Marcel standing affrontedly at the bar of judgment, filing a charge against an incompetent priest . . .

I said to him sharply, "Be quiet. You're making a fool of yourself."

"Will you both be quiet," Charlie said.

He was bending forward to listen—the intent posture made me imitate it. There were two sounds now, the invading crackle of the undergrowth, a steady penetrating hiss. Charlie cocked his head chucklingly over to Marcel. "That complaint of yours traveled quickly."

"What do you mean, quickly?"

"It certainly triggered something off."

The Negro pointed to the entrance—the blankets hung patchily moistened, like a laborer's shirt soiled with sweat. I stared disbelievingly at the puddles forming at the lip of the cave.

Then it really began to rain. It was one of those black

squalls that come sporadically to the Pacific—for a time it is exactly as if all the buckets of heaven have been up-turned, but the skies soon clear, leaving the islands spar-kling in the sun like washed glass.

Marcel wouldn't raise his eyes above the level of Father Doonan's knees—he went to the blankets, looking out as if to convince himself. He caught my eye and nodded to-wards Father Doonan. I heard his defeated grumble, "He's too damned smart." I think, like me, he felt tricked; he'd been watching the conjurer's hands carefully and he still didn't know how the pigeons had appeared. He said, louder, "He must have a lot of influence up there."

"No. You have the influence," Father Doonan said.

For the first time Marcel let himself grin begrudgingly into Father Doonan's face. "Well, better not try that trick too often. They mightn't be listening upstairs."

We sat for about three-quarters of an hour with ears cocked to the drenching hammer of the rain. Father Doonan restlessly: he took his miracles for granted. He was worried that the storm might delay our rendezvous at the coast. There was the recurrent grunt of departing thunder; the downpour quieted; we looked out to see a dazzle of sun breaking through the electrically flickering inky clouds. The fringe of the undergrowth immediately below us was washed to a vivid green. But down in the bed of the canyon the fleshless stumps of the burned scrub steamed blackly: it was like a gutted house that the hose-pipes of the fire brigade have just left.

"We can go now," Father Doonan said. We all clam-bered down the hill, shouting out. Presently we saw Harry Frobisher issue from his hole with Camille. He leaned on her intimately for a moment; then he put his arm round her shoulder, propping himself on her possessively, waiting for us to catch up.

As the Matron came up she stared searchingly, first at

Camille, then at Harry Frobisher. She shrank a little. Her mouth drooped.

Marcel gave a comradely chuckle of triumph—how we all enjoy the vicarious sexual thrill—"Well, not everybody's been wasting his time."

There's a certain look about a man who has just satisfied the most urgent physical need. The face of the virgin who has eagerly succumbed to it shines transparently. It was there for all of us to see.

I said to Frobisher, "Were you all right?"

"We were more worried about you."

I thought angrily, "Only you didn't let it distract you from other things." Well, the raped virgin can't be unraped. In time—if we survived, of course—Camille would start to quicken with life. Would she then cry out vainly for the vanished father of her child? Father Doonan didn't seem to have noticed a thing.

We continued marching along the bed of the canyon. I tried not to look at the Matron's haggard face. For a woman who was reputed to have regarded her own chastity pretty lightly she seemed to be taking it very badly. Was it ravaged maternal instinct: or an echo of personal guilt?

9

I REMEMBER the slight shock—no, not shock, the skeptical thrill—I had when Father Doonan came over to me and said quietly, "I don't think there's much more than a quarter of the way to go."

The morning and most of the afternoon had passed in a drool of fatigue. The children were dragging: it wasn't possible to keep them in any kind of organized line. Every so often we had to pick two or three of them off the ground; the wilting babyish legs had to be kept working. It was an act of ruthless mechanical kindness; somebody had to wind the staggering clockwork toys up.

I looked at Father Doonan as if he'd said, "Only a little way farther and there'll be a fleet of coaches waiting to transport us to Shangri-la."

"Just one long lap down to the Old Wooden Bridge," he murmured encouragingly, "then it ought to be easy all the way."

"If it's still there," I said.

"Why shouldn't it be?"

"There's been a lot of fire. We don't know how far down it's spread."

He said sharply, "The bridge has to be there."

"Of course." You can't argue with a fanatic. He couldn't let heaven betray him at this late stage; he needed the bridge; so it had to be there.

He said to me chidingly, "You must try to have more faith."

I thought, 'If the bridge has gone, try walking over the emptiness of a sixty-foot gorge on faith.'

"Anyway," he went on in a nervous whisper, as if I was capable of destroying the morale of the entire company, "don't even suggest such a thing to the others. . . ."

"Why should I? If that's how it is, they'll see it for themselves."

"The Matron looks exhausted."

She was tramping ahead of us. She wasn't resilient any more; she had a different kind of shape.

"It isn't just exhaustion," I said.

"What, then?"

"Camille."

Father Doonan transferred his gaze to Harry Frobisher and Camille. They were intimately linked. They seemed to be possessing each other physically as they moved—I didn't know how it escaped Father Doonan's eye.

"She seems happy," he said.

"The Matron doesn't think she ought to be happy. After what happened——"

But he cut me off brusquely. "Nobody knows that anything happened." He went on angrily, as if I'd put it into the Matron's mind, "The idea is discreditable."

"Don't blame me."

"She's a good girl."

"She still is. And I don't know what it's got to do with her sexual state. But you said Harry Frobisher was good, too."

"He's done a lot for us. We'll never know what we owe them. All of them. Do me the kindness of thinking the best of him."

And it snuffed me out like a guttering candle. When a man appeals to your sense of gratitude to defy reason, there's only one thing to do: shut up.

The afternoon shadows were lengthening when we stopped for a meal. Nobody had much appetite. We just drank endlessly; we'd been able to refill our water bottles at mountain streams; as fast as we replenished the inner moisture we sweated it away. I saw Harry Frobisher studying me narrowly. He wanted to talk. Why to me? Because I was a neutral? He left Camille and crawled over—his leg had stiffened, and he winced as he groveled his way.

He started in a low voice, flicking a quick glance at Father Doonan. "I heard him say we don't have so far to go."

I wondered if he'd heard the rest of the conversation. I looked at his dourly amused features: he had.

"About a quarter of the way."

"Christ! I never thought we'd do it."

"We haven't done it yet."

"It looks all right, though. Don't you think so?"

"Three-quarters of a miracle isn't much better than no miracle at all. It has to be complete or nothing."

He chuckled, with affection almost, "You're a dry old stick." He probably thought he was doing me something of a favor when he stuck his leg out. "Would you like to have a look at my foot?"

It was incredibly puffed. It defeated me how he'd come so far on it. There was a lot of iron in the man. I had an uneasy feeling that if ever he reached safety (could there be such a state as safety to a man like that?) something very bad could happen to his foot. He'd never use it again properly; there were discolored gangrenous patches I didn't tell him about.

"Can you get along on it?"

"And if I can't?" he grinned coolly. "What are you going to do about it? Leave me behind?"

So I bathed and strapped it. There wasn't much more I could do.

Then he bent nearer and said confidentially, "You've got a dirty mind."

"Medically dirty. That's not as dirty as ordinary people's minds."

"I mean, about me and Camille."

"I know what you mean. You ought to know whether it's justifiable to be dirty-minded."

"Stick to your own business." But he grinned. Then suddenly he said, "Look, if we're going to come out alive" —like all rapscallions he was superstitious, he crossed his fingers quickly—"there's something I want to know. Where are Camille's people?"

"Dead."

"She doesn't have anyone?"

"Only her legal guardians. The Matron and myself."

"Would you object to her marrying me?" and the blunt question gave me a queer tremor. For a moment I thought he was mocking me; but if I'd made a cynical answer I think he'd have hit me. Some kind of sensitive nerve was dangerously exposed.

I asked, "Does she want to marry you?"

"Ask her yourself."

Camille's face was twisted in our direction; the antennæ of her ears were always reaching yearningly after the man. I didn't need to ask.

"You're a convict," I said.

He shrugged it off. It might have been a slightly unfortunate but transient condition, like measles. "Father Doonan seemed to think he could do something for us. Get us some remission, at least. We'd deserve something, wouldn't we?"

"You would." Privately I was less sure they'd get it. If ever we turned up at Tahiti, public opinion mightn't be altogether grateful; there's always something galling to a rescued community when the ones they have abandoned return discomfitingly from the grave. I said, "She couldn't sleep with you in the gutter. You could hardly expect her to live like a bum with you in the saloons."

"I know the manager of a plantation in Fiji. I think I could get him to give me a decent job."

"You wouldn't find honest labor an intolerable strain?"

He stiffened and said harshly, "Go to hell," trying to lift himself up. "I'm sorry I spoke to you."

I said in a contrite voice, "Wait. Don't be so hasty. I have to consult the other guardian, too." I called over the Matron. She approached. I said, "Sit down," but she shook her head stonily. A bad sign. She wouldn't even look at Frobisher.

"I prefer to stand."

"It's about Camille. This man wishes to marry her."

"We don't require any shotgun weddings. Tell him to take himself to the devil," she said.

"Perhaps you're being a little unjust." It was hard to be too persuasive, but I said as defensively as possible on Frobisher's behalf—he was watching my face intently, the Matron had frozen him with shock—"I really think he's sincere——"

"What would he know about sincerity?"

"You could at least listen to him."

"I will never permit it."

"And if there is a . . . ?" I left the word "child" unspoken.

"We have always looked after children. We will look after that one, too."

"I think the girl is in love with the man." I sympathized strangely with Frobisher—it must have been dreadfully disconcerting to listen to other people stripping him nakedly, talking about him as if he were a prisoner in the dock. (That wouldn't have been any novelty, of course.)

"Love?" she cried out obdurately. "Do you think it'll do her any good to talk like a sentimental novelette? She's too young to know anything about love."

I started off acidly, "You seem to talk with experience," but she broke in on me: I don't think she was listening, anyway. . . .

She was saying, "Love," in a dry condemnatory voice. Her tone brought up a picture of the cheap, plushily odorous brothels behind Rue Faubourg Montmartre—the fifth-rate hotels devoted to the passing trade; the girls in the bistro doorways; the arch mechanical looks; the pimps vulturously observant on the stairways; the *madame* with her bunch of keys in the hotel vestibule, as professionally classified as a wine waiter with his chain. The Matron repeated, "Love"—she substituted another word for it angrily, "Lechery. Yes, even Camille. Maybe we should have warned her. Well, if he's put her in the cart don't ask me to make it holy . . ." then she saw my face: she went gray with consternation and shut her mouth.

I believed everything I'd heard about her then—they say it's the reformed prostitute who wears the Salvation Army bonnet and tambourine with most passion. She was going to make somebody pay for those fetid brothels behind Rue Faubourg Montmartre.

"Let her choose for herself," I said.

"She can't. She's blind."

"He's not a bad chap——"

And again she cut me off, so inflamed she wouldn't let me speak. "What are you trying to do, whitewash the seducer?"

"Oh, really. That's a word for excitable old spinsters looking for burglars under the bed. Now who's talking like a sentimental novelette?"

The others had turned to stare at us. They were listening curiously.

Harry Frobisher gave an impatient stir. "Hell, what a song about nothing," he said under his breath. "Of course we did it."

The Matron glared at him wolfishly. "You *admit* it?"

"Why not? We both wanted it. When you don't think you're going to live very long you make the most of what's left. I'm going to marry her whether you like it or not."

"Over my dead body . . ."

Harry Frobisher smiled at her obliquely and said, "That might be the easiest way out."

I didn't warn the Matron that Father Doonan was coming up behind her. Our voices had carried; he must have heard every word. She gave a jump as he touched her arm.

He said to her softly, "What are you working yourself into such a huff about?"

"This creature has demanded to marry Camille." The

"this creature" annoyed me—as if he had no proper status as a human being.

"Camille told me. I'm glad," Father Doonan said.

"You are? You have no objection?"

"None at all. When the time comes I'll be only too happy to marry them myself."

"He has debauched her."

"I won't let you say that."

"He has admitted it——"

And white with rage Father Doonan shouted, "He admitted nothing that you didn't drag out of him in pique." Suddenly I knew exactly what was the trouble with him: he was two men under one biretta, a prize fighter and a priest; they battled it out endlessly inside him. I thought, "The prize fighter's the one who keeps putting his bishops on edge." Funnily enough, it was the prize fighter I preferred.

The Matron blanched and said nervously, "In that case I have nothing to say."

"But there is something to say. A few words of apology to your friend."

"My . . . ?"

"He could have been safe on a boat for Tahiti. And he's here, with a smashed leg, sitting beside us on the edge of an oven. That makes him your friend."

The Matron—religiously docile—never argued beyond a certain point with Father Doonan. She addressed a spot about two feet above Harry Frobisher's head, "I regret it," simpering a little as Father Doonan gave her an affectionate hug.

He turned her round, slapping her backside lightly. "Go and tell Camille you're happy about it."

"I've accepted the inevitable. Do I have to be happy about it, too?"

"If I say so," he said.

She swallowed her pride; I'd seen her more delirious with joy. As she went off, Harry Frobisher said loosely to Father Doonan, "You could talk the hind leg off a donkey."

"I'm sure you mean it kindly."

"You've got me so mixed up, I'm not sure what I mean. No hard feelings?"

"Hard . . . ?"

"I tried to alter the shape of your face for you."

Father Doonan touched it with an emotional chuckle and said, "It isn't the kind of face that could come to much harm."

"I wanted to hurt you."

"Of course. I needed to be hurt."

"Don't be so damned humble. I'm sorry. Would you give me a lift up? This blasted leg——" and Father Doonan went over to him hastily and helped him to his feet. They stood there together uncertainly, Frobisher still leaning on the other in the moment of strain. Father Doonan stared into his face and said in a breathless rush, "I have to be humble. You think every priest's faith is impregnable. Well, it's not. Nobody's so vulnerable—yesterday afternoon on the quay when you said you'd come with me I was so near to losing faith. You restored me."

"We came for what we could get out of it."

"You gave a lot more than you could ever get."

Harry Frobisher grinned. "Would it be worth a drink at the next bistro?"

And Father Doonan cried out gratefully, "Oh, so much more, so very much more than a drink."

It was the kind of incoherent conversation that makes ordinary balanced people squirm with embarrassment. I preferred Marcel's healthy approach when he sidled over to the Matron. (This was five minutes later; we had just started marching off.)

He said to her reproachfully, "You insulted my friend."

"He is scarcely insultable."

"He has a very sensitive nature."

"You exaggerate. I apologized to him, anyway."

"In that case I accept your apology on behalf of my friend." I moved forward to listen—my whole pilgrimage down that abominable mountain seemed to be one long process of eavesdropping. The Matron was walking stiffly by Marcel's elbow. I was rather surprised that she didn't seem to be making any effort to get away from him. And she said only halfheartedly, "May I be relieved of your company?"

"But I enjoy it."

"You are just applying soft soap."

"Naturally. All women love to be soft-soaped. That Matron's uniform doesn't necessarily make you less than a woman. I regard you as a wrongheaded but attractive creature."

She said, "Ha," loudly, but unconvincingly. I thought, 'Give that unabashed Casanova a session with her on a sofa—yes, even our Matron—and he'll extract her two gold fillings from her mouth.' "Flattery doesn't move me," she said. But she was walking straighter; she had a good buxom figure; she was protruding those parts that make men who like ripeness stare.

Marcel didn't neglect to stare. He said, "You have lived such a life of seclusion that you have forgotten what the body is for."

"It is all a lot of flimflam. Sex . . ."

"The figure that I am privileged to observe was created for such delicious flimflam. I see that I shall have to take your education in hand."

"In the bushes, no doubt?"

He said amiably, "If nothing better offers, no doubt."
Then he moved very close to her and all I could hear was

a persuasive mumble—he had lapsed into familiar barroom French; I caught the expression *"aime passionnément,"* which speaks for itself; then, *". . . l'heure de coucher,"* he was inviting an appointment in anything in the neighborhood that could approximate a bed. And she didn't recoil; if anything her bust grew more pneumatic. "My God," I thought helplessly, "the Rue Faubourg Montmartre is coming back in a rush."

She murmured indulgently. "You must not make indecent suggestions."

"You would not find them indecent if I could put them into effect."

"You are a monster."

"Much better. A healthily affectionate man."

Then she glanced at the child on his back and said modestly, "This conversation is scarcely fit for a young one to hear."

"He would applaud it if he were awake. What is your first name, *chérie?*"

"Margaret."

"Margaret," he said simply. "I like it." He slipped his hand carelessly through her elbow. I watched his round bottom bobbing along intimately by hers.

And less than an hour later he was dead. Dying with a grotesquerie that even now raises a shudder; that was theatrically overdone even for that raffish man. I thought God owed him a better death.

We reached the end of the canyon with the twilight. The steep boulderous sides vanished as if stagehands had whisked away the scenery flats on a light cue. The cue— the whole evening seemed shot with theatrical effects—was the quick arrival of the moon. It hung like an unrealistic paper lantern over the ridge.

But we could still smell burning—the stars were still obscured by a low drifting haze. The lava that we had almost been able to forget started reminding us of its existence; on our left flank a lurid glow was reflected from a simmering cauldron into the sky.

As we plodded along in the gloaming Father Doonan said to me humorously, "It's like a Chinese dragon, the flames look worse than the bite."

"I prefer not to test it."

"How do you feel?"

"Tired." Which put it mildly. I don't know how I kept my legs moving; I felt sorry for myself. And because I wanted him to pity me I showed Father Doonan the sole of my shoe that had flapped itself loose.

He started hesitantly, "Perhaps mine . . ."

"I'm not going to take the shoes off your feet."

"You'll sleep tomorrow night in a proper bed."

"Nobody's guaranteed it——"

He stopped me sharply. "I've guaranteed it," he said.

I glanced at his sunken face—"If he looks so exhausted," I thought, "how must *I* look?" Next to his thick body I was as frail as a straw. He was a little crazy with determination—quite suddenly it came to me how much we'd depended on him. He was the vital force behind our worn-out machinery; the steam (I suppose he'd have preferred to call it faith) that kept us moving. He believed so much in God that he was grimly resolved to hold Him to His bargain—the helpless and the abandoned, the Bible tells us, can always turn to Him.

I said, "And if the schooner isn't there, what then?"

"The Norwegian Captain's a good man. He promised, of course he'll be there."

Everybody was good; could basically be trusted in Father Doonan's chromium-plated little world. I thought 'If it doesn't turn out that way there'll be a terrible bill to

pay.' Then I saw Marcel shuffling along in the distance—
he was bent tiredly under his weightless cripple, he held
the hands of a couple of the children, he was chirruping
to them. I thought oddly, "How did that happen?" That
plump sleazy Silenus playing tenderly at nursemaid—what
had Father Doonan's peculiarly effective dynamite dug out
of him?

I nudged Father Doonan to look at him. "You've got a
candidate for your choir."

"Why not?"

"It's a little silly. The saint of the bistros. . . ."

"Where would you rather look for a saint?"

I muttered—well, I was too tired to be gracious—"Start
polishing his halo."

"Halo? Whatever would he want with a halo?"

I'd started a silly train of thought and I blurted out,
"He'd pawn it straight away for a drink. . . ." but I was
sorry the moment I said it. "Stop badgering me," I cried.

"You're doing all right. Keep it up," Father Doonan
grinned.

And suddenly the canyon finished—we were walking a
high ridge overlooking the stream of lava we'd run away
from when we abandoned the mules. We pretended not to
notice it, like an embarrassed party in the Royal Enclosure
at Ascot trying not to be aware of an old friend who has
come down in the world. We tramped along the ridge,
Charlie whooping the sleep-bleary children into single file.
We must have looked like something out of a moving-
picture fantasy: flushed redly by the lava on one side, cold
with delicate moonlight on the other: a string of half-
roasted chickens waiting to be turned on the spit. The
turf was spongy. It sprang like rubber under our feet.
We had forgotten how it could betray us—

—I don't think it was an earth tremor; probably it
was the overwhelming shove of the lava; the ridge opened

up. It split with the wet plop that tearing fruit makes. I thought with a shiver, "Marcel's fallen into it with the children." He was gone—I'd seen him teetering over the split, looking in the red flush of the lava like a lunatic acrobat illuminated by music-hall footlights. We crowded nervously to the edge.

And tragedy changed to a giggle. Marcel was nestled precariously in warm brown mud: he was hardly six feet below us. His rider clung sleepily to his back. The two children he had been escorting were perched glutinously in his lap. I thought with annoyance, "Always trust that man to do something clownish"—I was reminded of four chocolate figures being hotly coated in the vat. The cleft was appallingly deep; the ridge had split to its very root; I saw the first snakelike crawl of slag being shoved into the bottom of the pit.

The Matron came out of her shock. She cried down like a punitive schoolmistress, "Don't just sit there."

Marcel scowled up at us offendedly. "This is no joke."

He had made a quick floundering movement; he sank a little deeper, the warm chocolate oozed in a slimy ripple down the slope. It took him with it. Suddenly I stopped thinking of it as a joke.

"You are ridiculous," said the Matron. "Hand the children up."

But Harry Frobisher called down irritably, "Keep still." He was stretching down; Marcel was already beyond his reach. The three men fell instantly into the automatic pattern of rescue, Charlie and Father Doonan lying flat at the edge, letting Frobisher dangle into the cleft—he reached down his arm. He muttered, "Now send them up," and Marcel lifted the cripple off his back and handed him up. Frobisher took the slimed morsel; the other two children, tittering plaintively, followed. "Now you," said Frobisher, and I heard him breathe disconcertingly. The motions had sent Marcel oozing away from his grasp.

The Matron started to murmur (now she was vaguely frightened), "It is absurd. . . ." and Father Doonan glared at her (he was frightened, too). She grew silent.

I thought with a horrid premonition, 'Something terrible is going to happen.' I felt quite helpless.

Harry Frobisher called up to the others, "Let me down a bit more," and they eased him forward—for a moment the groping fingers touched. I held my breath, watching Marcel's muddy hand twining convulsively around Frobisher's; but the slime killed the grip, the urgent jerks dislodged the fat body—Marcel slid with a bitter, resentful cry farther down the slope.

In a hushed, calm voice Father Doonan said, "Keep utterly still."

"It is easy to give advice," Marcel answered, and I sympathized. He was bathed in sweat: the vat of chocolate steamed lightly. I looked down apprehensively into the pit. What I saw was a figure of fun, fun with a savage edge: the plump clown was brown with mud and deep in it to his buttocks.

I watched panic spreading over his features. He put out his hands softly, patting the stuff vacantly as a child paddles water. It was hardly more stable—there was the dismaying conviction that something relentlessly patient was sucking him down.

But he kept quite still, still but for the faintest tremble. He stared up at us appealingly.

"Don't take too long about it," he said.

"We'll give you a rope."

"I am in a stewpan."

The others were hauling Frobisher up—it was no use letting him dangle out of Marcel's reach—and Frobisher panted down reassuringly, "We'll have you out before you're cooked."

I thought forebodingly, "And are you so sure?" I wouldn't have breathed my doubts for a moment. But as Marcel's voice drifted up hollowly, "You will need a troupe of elephants to haul me out of this," I removed myself from the edge, I didn't want to look at his ludicrous predicament any more.

Once—oh, so very long ago, when I was a boy—I had paddled out to a man calling from the middle of one of the Salzburger lakes: cold gripped him before we could grab his scrabbling hands, he drowned before we could seize him. I remembered the suffused despairing face of death as it slid palely under the water. I thought, "If someone doesn't reach him soon, Marcel is going to drown down there."

"Surely we can do something for him?" the Matron whispered confusedly.

Father Doonan gave her a quick angry look. "Of course."

"He is sinking away from us——"

But Charlie broke in on her harshly, "A rope will hold him." Only not—or so I fancied—with much assurance. I saw Harry Frobisher's hands shaking. He sought the Negro's eyes secretly. The Grand Guignol had changed from burlesque to raw disaster—did the harlequin down in the muddy pit know it?

The buried voice came murmurously over the edge, "My time is yours . . ."

"Be patient," Father Doonan cried.

And the voice from the grave responded dolefully, "Only remember, I don't have all the time in the world."

They had uncoiled the rope, looping it to fit Marcel's shoulders. "We're ready for you," Harry Frobisher shouted, and they flung it down. I took my undesirable ringside seat once more. I gazed below. I was immeasurably shocked to see how far Marcel had drifted—he was very small down the fluid slope, and much less of him was visible. He had sunk to his waist in the simmering mud. My eyes were fascinated by the distant oven: the slag being shoved into the bottom of the pit by the invading lava. 'Marcel can easily be cooked in more ways than one,' I thought.

I willed him hard not to look down. . . .

"Gently," Harry Frobisher urged him. "Don't jerk, we'll drop it into your hands." He was whipping the rope like a fisherman, fluttering the hook of the loop towards Marcel's hands. The podgy fingers sought it gingerly. The man was too rigid with anxiety to stir. He found the loop and with a flush of triumph I thought, *Gott sei Dank, the fish is hooked!'* I watched the arms struggling out of the mud to insert themselves in frozen slow-motion into the loop. And the slime betrayed him—a tide of it started moving, and he floundered in a wild threshing of mud far, far down the slope. The rope tightened as his despairing fingers grabbed it, but the greasy hands couldn't hold it. It whipped away from him and he was gone.

I heard Harry Frobisher's throat creak and I wiped the sweat from my eyelashes to see Marcel, head and shoulders only, embedded distantly like a fly in amber. I thought dreadfully, 'This isn't mercy; they are prolonging his death.'

"I'll go down for him," Harry Frobisher said.

The Matron had retreated in a flurry—she knew the worst—she was in an abominable state. I saw her shut herself off amongst the clusters of sleeping children. 'A man dies and they sleep,' I thought reproachfully.

Then Harry Frobisher's words, "I'll go down for him," caught up with me—I was overtired, my reactions were slow—and when I heard Charlie say, "No, don't go, Harry," it was as if I had been daydreaming on a delayed conversation—the meaning had got all chopped up.

"Somebody has to help him."

Charlie said flatly, without cruelty, "Two instead of one, that isn't going to help."

"How can we watch him?"

Father Doonan said hurriedly, "It's so hard for you; no, it's for me to go." He started tugging at the rope.

Harry Frobisher shoved him away. "You're too big, you'll drown him," he said. He saw Father Doonan stare dubiously at his leg and went on, "This is a family matter," grinning without pleasure. "Anyway, I'm not going to need the leg." Docilely, Father Doonan nodded, yielding the privilege to the family—to me it seemed to be an argument without sense. Harry Frobisher called below, "I'm coming down for you, Marcel."

I will probably not live to be a hundred, but if I do I will remember that sad, doomed voice from below, "Stay where you are."

"Be with you in a minute . . ."

And again, the fretful cheep of a bird locked forever in a cage, Marcel's voice, "Stay where you are."

Harry Frobisher glowered. He was tying the rope around his waist. "Listen to him, he thinks he's encouraging us," he said.

"I wouldn't go, Harry," Charlie said.

"You would. If I'd let you."

The Negro looked obliquely at Father Doonan—for what? absolution?—and said, "No. Don't go. It's over. It's his ghost talking, stay where you are."

Harry Frobisher began angrily, "I never thought I'd hear you . . ." then his voice tailed off into a hurt grumble. He slithered over the edge, staring accusatively at Charlie, his face disappearing as the others paid out the rope. He went squirming down the slope.

He was part of the slime quickly. It was as if the stuff had a fluid hungry life; it was gratefully absorbing another victim. I could hardly make Frobisher out. A greasy ripple marked his progress. The head and shoulders of

Marcel waited. I saw Harry Frobisher reach him: almost. His voice growled up, "A bit more," but there was no more rope to let out.

Frobisher put down his arm. Marcel's hand went up to it, the fingers twined. Frobisher began to strain. I thought, 'This is an evil joke'—there was only a stump of the man left, it was like pulling a cork out of an age-encrusted bottle with the fingers: there was nothing left to hold. The comradely clutch kept slipping, the muddied hands jerking apart. I watched, knowing what would happen: and it happened. As the men's fingers parted Marcel slid away—a recoil, a little tidal movement, and he was three feet below.

Only a head protruded. I remembered something Marcel had once said—I couldn't recall the occasion— *"Nous n'avons plus de fortune,"* we are all out of luck . . .

The football of Marcel's head—it seemed to have been abandoned down in the muddy pit, as if the players hadn't thought it worth reclaiming—spoke. It said to Frobisher, "Now, enough. You did everything a friend could do."

"But still not enough."

"More than I'd have done for you, maybe," and Harry Frobisher made a rebellious sound. He dangled emptily at the end of the rope: he wasn't looking at the head. Neither was I. "Go along up," Marcel said.

Harry Frobisher didn't speak. Marcel said, "Don't make a long business of it. For my sake. This is a bad moment for false heroics. Go on up with you."

"There's no hurry."

"There is. A great hurry. I beg of you . . ."

I caught Harry Frobisher's angry voice, "What do you expect me to do? Leave you?"

I could hardly hear Marcel's reply. "Finish me," I thought he said.

"No."

Father Doonan and Charlie, straining on the rope, were staring at me intently—to report the conversation? I'd lost touch with the confused whispers from below; they echoed in secret conflict. Then I sorted out Marcel's bitter plea, "Friendship deserves a little something. I would have done it for you."

"There must be something . . ."

"Nothing. This is altogether insupportable."

"Wait."

"For what? *Je suis mort.*" (That terrible admission: I am dead.)

Again the urgent conflict of whispers. Marcel saying, "I suffer," and Harry Frobisher muttering, "No." And again, furiously, "No!"

Then Marcel's martyred voice rising, "Help me. In God's name!" At the end, even the unbelievers call on His name.

I saw Harry Frobisher stare down. The head was turned up to him; there wasn't enough of the man to picture his torment; you need a writhing body, something torturable, to express pain. Frobisher suddenly swiveled away. He began to climb up the rope—he made what I thought was a false drag: he slipped, his whole body started a convulsive floundering: it wasn't necessary to be so violent, he still had hold of the rope. But the mud gushed away from under him in his flurry, the tide flowed, and when I took my frozen attention away from him what had been left of Marcel was gone.

I turned to Father Doonan and Charlie. I let them read it in my face. I listened to Harry Frobisher's frantic panting—the harsh difficult sounds as he came crawling up. He swarmed over the edge, retching mud, and lay flat on the earth. The Matron looked at him drunkenly. I saw Father Doonan cross himself—I thought, listening to the familiar priestly patter, 'What good are his futile prayers now?'

I helped Charlie to lift Frobisher to his feet. He messed us unbelievably; he had brought half the pit up with him.

✳

There was a stream at the bottom of the canyon. Charlie went down with Harry Frobisher to get him cleaned up. In a moment of charity—I didn't quite like Frobisher's strained face—I offered to go with them, but Charlie said roughly, "No," and pushed me away. Maybe they wanted their grief to be private?

Nobody interfered with them. They disappeared solitarily.

In the meantime we got busy rousing the children. That was the bad part: they sagged somnolently. As soon as we got one parcel of them to their feet the rest slid uselessly to the ground. The small dark faces were senile; they didn't look like children any more. We propped them up—it was harassing, like trying to stiffen puppets whose joints had worked loose. But when Charlie and Frobisher came back we were all ready to go. Father Doonan had shouldered his crippled rider automatically. Now he cradled Marcel's jockey in his arms, getting ready to carry him, too. . . .

I was surprised to hear Harry Frobisher say, "Give him to me."

Father Doonan looked at him. "It isn't necessary. I'm not at all tired."

Harry Frobisher repeated bleakly, "Give him to me."

I wondered, 'Does he think he's doing penance? Easing his guilt by taking Marcel's burden?' Father Doonan continued to watch him strangely—I got the idea that suddenly he'd guessed; he froze a little but didn't argue; he drew his breath sharply and put the child instantly on Frobisher's back.

Then the battalion formed up. I noticed that nobody

turned to look back at the pit. Charlie took the lead; Camille moved instinctively to Harry Frobisher's side and he put his arm about her back. It was quite dark now. And we started what Father Doonan had called "just one long lap down to the Old Wooden Bridge," after which— I still quote him—it was to be "easy all the way."

10

THE ground began to descend steeply. Even in the star-light I thought I could recognize familiar lines in the mountain massif; we couldn't have been a long way from the town. We went with the ravine—it was the only way down to the Old Wooden Bridge. And the lava trailed along like a sultry creditor dunning us for a bad debt. I wondered if we'd ever get away from its ugly creaking presence, the sour breath of the burning gas . . . of course, it was alive and breathing, and nibbling bits of the moun-tain away. Hollow plops echoed from the cliffsides like the bursting balloons of a languishing midnight carnival.

I said to Father Doonan—I was in a macabre mood of near-collapse, which ought to excuse me: unshaven and half-blind with sweat—"The death rattle. Listen to it."

He said, "Death——?" with a repoachful laugh, wonder-ing what I was talking about.

"The island's dying. It's the last twitch of high fever. It's going to blow itself up."

"You've been saying that for a long time."

"A doctor knows the symptoms. It's near the end."

He said irritably, "Will you be quiet about it? There are children around . . ."

"They're too tired to care."

"*I* care."

"*You.*" I whipped up insanely—I just wanted to hurt him, he was the slave driver, the crazy Pharaoh with the whips. If he'd let me alone I'd have dropped gratefully into blessed oblivion a long way behind. I started yelling, wanting someone to suffer for my exhaustion, "What are you shoving us on for? You think it's some kind of holy mission? The Inquisition's out of date. Earn your damned saint's wings some other way, we're finished, we'll never make it, we're going to die . . ." and as his sunken face turned on me belligerently I cut in to get my bitter money's worth, "Leave us alone. You're punishing us for nothing. We're dead but walking . . ."

"When you stop walking," he warned me softly, "you *will* be dead."

"I have no objection. I just want to lie down."

"There's no time to lie down."

"There's always time to die . . ."

And he said obdurately, "I can't permit you to die. . . ." talking like an archangel on the Day of Judgment, selecting this one to live, this one to die. He put his arm round my shoulder with a pretence of compassion—but I felt his hard fist shoving me along. I dragged back. He shoved harder. Suddenly he said in a low jaded voice, "I'm very tired," and I peered at him surprisedly. So he had his breaking-point, too? He said faintly, "Don't weaken me, help me. I mustn't let myself break down."

I said savagely, "You? You'll never break down."

"Don't even let's talk about it."

"You've got to let up on us. There's a limit to what you can expect flesh and blood to do." We all talk in melodramatic clichés when we've given up hope. "The kids are

222

cracking up. Look at them." I made him turn his glazed eyes in their direction—it was like the aftermath of a juvenile brandy party, they were staggering unevenly. "It's cruel. It's for nothing."

"I told you before, not for nothing. I swear it, no, no."

"Everybody but you knows it . . ."

"Everybody but me and God. Let's trust Him most of all."

You can argue with almost anyone, but you can't argue with a man who has a special friend in God. I shut my mouth sullenly. I went plodding on.

The sole of my shoe had almost flapped itself off. I thought, 'That's going to be my last straw; when it goes, I go, too.'

Father Doonan went ahead to encourage the children— as if they were capable of taking notice—and his voice, "Not very far now, not so very far . . ." came ringing back. Charlie lagged behind to tramp by my side. Maybe he'd been listening; from the minute our pilgrimage had started—up on that fused grenade of a mountain—nobody'd had a moment of privacy.

He said affably, "You're doing fine. You know what the time is?"

"Gone midnight."

"And just another dawn to go." The banjo strings of his voice twanged reassuringly as he said, "That will be the best dawn I ever did see." But all the time he was stealing dubious glances at me. I knew exactly how he saw me: as the weak link in the bicycle chain. He came to what was in his mind really. "Lean on me a little," he said, nudging close.

"I didn't ask you for help."

"Don't be so proud."

"You're carrying enough. You're going to need your strength."

"I'm a pretty big man," he said humorously, "I have lots and lots of strength." But the veined eyeballs seemed unnaturally large—his sweat-oiled face had a bad leaden color—even giants could run out of strength.

My legs were wobbling. I didn't struggle as he propped my hand on his shoulder and straightened me up. "We'll get along crabwise," he murmured insidiously. "See, it's right simple? Not an awful long way to go." He had the arrogant tragic humility of the Negro—he looked at you over the fence of his color with mocking abasement. You never quite know how to take them, but he was still the politest black man I ever met.

I just wanted to get someone to agree with me. I said desperately, "You know it, don't you?—we're walking on a bursting kettle."

"I own no plantations on it," he said lazily. "When we're all off, it can burst whenever it wants."

"The whole island's a bomb, it's all ready to go off. . . ."

"You're telling yourself bad fairy tales," he glimmered at me amusedly. "You'll frighten yourself to death."

He knew I was infuriated with Father Doonan, and when I stared after him spitefully and said, "Do *you* think God's very interested in us?" he gave the faintest chuckle.

"Very likely not."

"You don't believe in God, do you?"

"I've lain in some pretty bad gutters, I've had plenty of trouble," he said with another of his glances of indulgent mockery, "but I never seen any sign of heavenly mercy yet." Who was it he reminded me of—someone Biblical— Job? "No," he drawled carelessly, "I wouldn't say I believe in God." Then his eyes narrowed: he was still staring after Father Doonan. And he said very softly, "But I believe in *him*."

"Why?"

224

"He takes responsibility. He behaves the way God ought to behave."

"He's half out of his mind. He's driving us more like the Devil——"

"Be quiet," Charlie said cruelly. He stopped being polite. "You're old, you're frightened you're going to die, you've gone sour on yourself. You can't recognize a very good man." I'd said something like that about Father Doonan—to Marcel, was it?—"You can't understand a very good man" . . . I was afraid Charlie might let go of me in his anger, so I made the pathetic face of age and exhaustion; I shrugged a kind of feeble excuse.

I muttered, "Saints are very hard to get along with."

"So are cynics," he cut me off contemptuously. And that settled me.

Then my legs started yielding like cracked stalks—they seemed to belong to a suffering animal. I thought wretchedly, 'Let the beast drop, take pity on it.' I said to Charlie, "I can't go much farther."

"You'll go as far as you have to," Charlie grinned.

"Life isn't worth it . . ."

"Life's worth everything. You talk easy," he said coolly. "You know we're not going to leave you behind."

"Why should you care?"

And the violence of the man's sudden thick-chested passion took me off guard. "We came a long way to fetch you back," he said savagely—I felt his shoulder muscles bulge under my hand. "A man died to help you along, a bum you had no use for, but he was my friend." I looked nervously up at the sweaty, entranced face—there was another Father Doonan, a black one, hagridden, obsessed. "We'll get you down," Charlie said implacably, "all of you, the kids chiefly. After that your life's your own; throw it away, it's no concern of mine. Till then, keep moving." And he dragged me along.

I knew what was wrong with him. He had to have some tangible return for Marcel's horrid death.

I watched Harry Frobisher stumbling along, Marcel's cripple perched lumpily on his back. I was tired enough to feel vindictive: I wondered how *he* felt about Marcel's death: he was the one who'd given his friend the *coup de grâce*. Doctors have to do it sometimes—we professionals get used to it—but when a man has to put the pistol to the head of a trapped human animal he cares for . . .

. . . The thought died like a match in a draught: Charlie's eyes were fixed on me like pebbles. He said with his mask-grin (he seemed to sense everything I thought), "He's a better man than you."

"I don't even know what you're talking about."

"He did what he had to. Don't say a word out of turn to him, he's suffering enough."

This time my legs folded. I don't remember keeling over—one moment I was erect, the next all dissipated, lying on my back staring dazedly up at the sky. The relief was ecstatic: like a drink of water to a parched man. I saw Charlie standing over me, I heard him say flatly, "Get up and start walking," but I closed my eyes, pretending a faint. 'Get away from me,' I thought ignobly, 'I'm not going to walk any more.'

Father Doonan came hurrying back. He leaned over me —through my drooping lashes I saw the stupefied face of the child tilted over his back. He said to Charlie, "What is it?"

"He's flat out."

"He has to keep walking."

"He won't."

"He has to . . ."

I lay quite still, shocked and resentful to hear Charlie murmur, "He's old. He won't do much more." Then he added under his breath like a careless conspirator—why should I have a dreadful remembrance of Harry Frobisher putting Marcel out of his misery?—"He's had his life. He's not so important. The kids are. I'd leave him behind."

Father Doonan said in a shocked whisper, "You don't seriously think I'd do that, do you?"

"No," Charlie said humorously. "But I would. I'm not you."

"He's a soul in distress . . ."

Charlie interrupted idly, "He's a bag of bones. An old, old man, he'll hold us up." I lay there with my eyes closed tightly—I felt like the useless bull, no longer worth pasturage, listening to the veterinary surgeons . . . I made a nervous little flutter; the flesh recoils instinctively from death.

Father Doonan said to me, "Open your eyes. Get up."

"I can't."

"You can. You have to. Start walking."

"Leave me behind."

"Nobody is going to be left behind," he cried. Then the thick angry arm reached down and yanked me violently to my feet. I saw Father Doonan's frantic face shoved into mine; he said huskily, "Walk—walk—walk." He repeated it like an insane litany. He took hold of my shoulder and pushed me along. My legs made the mechanical gesture of walking: they dissolved like water: I went staggering by his side. I was like the drunk being wheeled out of the party . . . I was sober enough to hate the persecutor, the priest who was using the whips of his faith on my poor back. "Nobody," he'd said madly, "is going to be left behind . . ."

Then I was leaning against him; we were a dark huddle of people cringing antlike on the moonlit hillside, the children beginning to totter, Harry Frobisher and the Matron holding them up; and the earth was suddenly as hideously intoxicated as I was. It leaned and floated. The sound of the island's retching was indescribable—what had happened in that instant was that the mountain had broken in half. It did it with the stench of brimstone, whooping fumes and tongues of gritty yellow flame into the sky.

The crater wasn't there as a recognizable crater, it was a bluntly leveled, exploded mass, most of it fraying raggedly into the sky; the thuds of the falling pieces made the half of the island on which we stood shudder. Nature puts on her best bits of pageantry in her worst temper.

What was the use of running now?

It seemed the most natural thing in the world to hear that insensate priest cry, "Run."

We padded afflictedly down the slope. We were descending steeply, too steeply, there was no doubt now that we were near the ultimate lap. We were the shipwrecked survivors on the raft, hearing the distant thunder of surf—but would the water last out? The spray of the finally disintegrated mountain straddled us . . . the artillery was uncertain . . . the burning meteors shot across the night sky, probably destroying the town. The lighter fragments bombarded the hillside below us: a scattering of fires sprang up. We watched them gather heat in the darkness as we stumbled uselessly on. We had been ambushed.

The Matron reeled near me, drooped, and lay inelegantly in the grass. I followed her example. I shoved my sobbing mouth into the earth. Charlie had said, "He's a bag of bones"—I had a quick numbing picture of God shopping for death in the heavenly poulterer's, prodding the ribs of the skinniest chickens . . . evidently I'd been selected. I didn't care very much.

The children were ninepins—exhaustion had tumbled them down. Father Doonan came looming out of the

228

shadows over the Matron. He said, "We haven't much time, we have to get along."

(The careful secretary, pointing to his watch punctiliously, warning madame that she was due at her hairdresser's, she hadn't much time. . . .)

She said in a thick voice, the *gamine* coming out in her, "Go to hell. I don't care."

"It'll be dawn in three hours. We mustn't waste time."

"I'm finished. We're all finished. The children can't go any more."

"They can go. They have to live," he insisted, and his voice trembled. "Help them to go."

"You ask too much of us."

"For them, everything." Next I felt his sweat-greased hands fumbling at my shoulder, dragging me. "Help them. Get up, get up."

"In a little while, maybe." I was still sucking in breath.

"Later may be too late. God's been merciful so far. Earn His mercy. Get up, get up."

I shouted, "I don't want to, let me alone. . . ." It took the last candleflicker of energy out of me. 'I'm old,' I thought mournfully, 'all worn out, I've chosen my grave, let me die. . . .'

Father Doonan dragged me to my feet. I fell against him like a dazed toper. Harry Frobisher hobbled over gauntly. Did I deserve his kindness? He let me lean against him.

His lips were cracked; he adjusted his crippled rider, whispering dryly in my ear (ridiculous comfort), "You'll live to buy me a drink yet."

And there, fire ringing the scrub around us, the roof of the mountain raging like an inferno, the island axed in half in its death throes, they hauled us bodily off the grass. One by one—me, the chief sacrificial victim, first—then the Matron . . .

She muttered drunkenly to Father Doonan, "There's a devil inside you."

His wild cry drowned her, "Let the devil have his use." . . . then the children, picking them up in heaps—damp yielding flesh, rickety legs, eyes pleading in stupor. They got them balanced somehow—Father Doonan and Charlie and Frobisher—they formed a line; even now a blind discipline held.

The the priest yelled, "Run," like the curate at the Sunday-school sports starting a race. Nobody ran: the thought was grotesque. But we moved. We reeled down the hill like a batch of reluctant conscripts, press-ganged into the slavery of fatigue. Charlie was making the pace— I could see him shambling erratically ahead—but the chief tyrant was behind us, Father Doonan, driving us obsessively, shouting . . . I remember thinking hysterically, 'Where does this holy maniac get the strength?' You have to picture sheep fleeing from the wolves of fire—the shepherd flurrying us on, keeping us together, gathering up the stragglers, shoving at us endlessly, endlessly. I hated him——

And every time that thick sweaty hand grabbed me, putting me back on my buckling legs, I wanted to spit in his face. I was dry of saliva. "Move, move," he kept breathing into my ear, that savage relentless hand yanking at me— then on to the Matron to give her the same cruel pressure— scooping up the fallen children, making the flagging, springless legs work.

This is what I heard the Matron say to Father Doonan— she'd just been dragged erect, clutching her bosom, staggering, "Let me die."

"Tomorrow you can die," he said. "Not tonight."

"I will never forgive you."

"I don't want your forgiveness. I just want your legs to keep moving. Go on, go on."

230

"You are a beast." (That wasn't her exact expression: it was French and obscenely untranslatable.) Nobody could blame her—you know what he had done? He had put his knee in her back. I thought, 'He's forgotten how a priest has to behave; this vulgar barbarian would give his venerable bishop a fit.'

The Matron shrilled resentfully, "Keep your feet off me," but she was moving. I suppose that was his victory.

Everybody has read about calamities. But not many have seen a volcano destroying an island—not many can know what it is like to run from the furnace when the chimney blows off and the slag comes racing out. You start with panic, you go into the terror of despair, then into a revulsion of sullen anger: you want to scream like a cock on a dunghill flapping his wings defiantly at the sky. You curse God a little, you contradict yourself by praying to Him—in the end you just yell at Him accusatively: what sense can there be in this ostentatious display?

We were always looking back at the shattered roof of the mountain. It was a mass of whooshing gaseous flame; the whole sky was its reflector. It drowned the moon that had just come flooding up—like an innocent debutante wandering into a marijuana party. How would a candle look against the harsh exultant dazzle of neon lights in Times Square?

And then suddenly we were groping through the fires that the explosion had started below. At first, tiny spluttering torches in the scrub. Charlie and Harry Frobisher trampled them out carelessly as they went ahead. Then the fires were more tenacious—the bombardment had really riddled the lower slopes with its phosphorous shells. We had to weave through a sizzling labyrinth of bushes; I could smell the children almost, like unplucked chickens being singed.

We ran that gauntlet. And Harry Frobisher, the demented scarecrow, was hopping ahead, yelling . . . he was pointing below, an improbable Moses showing us the Promised Land.

We saw the slender matchstick structure of the Old Wooden Bridge, burning fiercely at its near end. The crackling bonfire of the scrub was spreading like a quick rash about the struts. I heard Charlie swear—he left us to rush down, Harry Frobisher capering awkwardly after him. I saw them plow heedlessly through the ignited bushes, stamping them out, beating the flames away from the underpinning of the bridge. And we rushed behind them exultantly, kids, women, an old man who was getting to have a sneaking regard for miracles. . . . How had we come so far?

Miracles are chancy things—they come in gaudy packages like branded goods: the showier the packages, the more dubious the goods. Exultation blew out. We trailed dolefully down through the smoking bracken. The children made beds in it automatically and went to sleep; they looked like sacrificial left-overs after some cannibal feast. You have to imagine the bridge soaring theatrically across the gorge with its exaggerated arch, its photographable crisscross timbers—the early settlers are supposed to have copied it from one that spans a valley in Provence. The French are peculiarly fond of bridges; they are always singing about the bridge of the Seine, the shattered *pont d'Avignon*.

The whole near end of the bridge had taken fire. The men had banged out most of the flames, but the struts— the florid eighteenth-century underpinning—had charred to glowing embers. They seemed cunningly alive; little snakes of flame kept crawling out as the smoking wood re-ignited itself. About halfway along the bridge a few of the treads burned merrily.

Below it, the gorge was immensely deep; the moon-light couldn't probe its blackness.

Harry Frobisher put his foot cautiously on the bridge. He tested it tentatively. Charlie said, "Wait," but Frobisher inched on, shooting a nervous glance into the gorge. I would never have looked down. . . .

He said, "Let's get those treads out before they burn through." He was already six steps along the creaking structure; it was making pistol-noises like an old wooden house settling after a landslide. He edged farther, shuffling warily, tread by tread—stiffening with a frightened soldier's apprehension as the pistol-noises of the sagging timbers cracked out. I thought, 'Fate's an old bitch,' (I pictured the toothless crone cackling) 'all the time she's been making fun of us.' The bridge wouldn't last ten minutes. I expected it to go crashing like a pyre into the gorge.

And because I didn't want to see Frobisher go with it I kept my eyes on the charred struts that were beginning to tilt. There was no solid core left in them; the red embers flaked away to the charcoal. The far end of the bridge held, but ours, gushing smoke, smoldered treacherously——the whole thing lurched with a wooden hiccup; it reminded me of a polite drunk who has had one more than his head can stand. Harry Frobisher froze . . . no, a bad word, he was sweating like a waxwork figure in the heat. Father Doonan cried insupportably, "Come back." (It was like the refrain of a popular song—most of the time we'd spent rushing down the mountain, somebody'd been shouting perilously to somebody else, "Come back.") Harry Frobisher had the iron stillness that grips the angina victim: you felt that an indiscreet syllable might loosen the bridge.

He said, "Back where?" in a faint voice. "You going to set up a summer camp for the children here?"

"Somebody else might try . . ."

"I'm the lightest."

Not entirely—no lighter than my skin and bone. I suppose I should have offered to be a hero. It didn't enter my head.

Charlie was beginning again nervously, "Harry," but Frobisher cried out, "Shut up, you're frightening me." The bridge had settled at a slight angle; he started shuffling again towards the burning treads. I had the hysterical idea, unworthy in the circumstances, 'He's like a bumpkin learning a difficult dance. . . .' He came to the fire and knelt; he subsided as a camel goes down, joint by joint, cumbersomely. Then he started suffocating the flames with his coat. They hadn't taken very serious hold. He spat ridiculously on the reeking wood. He rose and put his foot on it—his whole weight. He said with shamed relief, as if he'd made a spectacle of himself for nothing, "It's all right. As safe as a bank."

I had had money in Viennese banks during the war—money isn't safe in every bank. The bridge tilted farther; it sounded like the gates of a decrepit old mansion being opened rustily after a century of disuse. Frobisher went flat on his face. Soldiers try to bury themselves in Mother Earth when the artillery barrage starts up; and I saw Frobisher trying to bury himself doomfully in the floor of the sagging bridge. . . .

He got up when the movement had finished. The splintery creaking continued; I pictured in my macabre way a techy old man in a rotted coffin twisting about to adjust himself. Frobisher shuffled on and reached the other side. He looked small and lost to us in the moonlight. He shouted across the gorge, "I'm over."

'You're going to be lonely over there,' I thought. Suicide is for adults, not for children. I looked at the drunkenly inclined bridge; the heat oozed out of the charred wood as tangibly as water; the smoldering struts were running again with secret little worms of flame.

234

I was probably only half listening when Charlie said to Father Doonan, "I think we could hold it up." The statement didn't register—I imagine if Samson had said to me in Gaza, "With these bare arms I am going to pull down the temple," it wouldn't have registered, either. The mind rebels against the absurd. Then I caught Charlie's throaty murmur, "Make a pad for my back." He seemed to accept the rôle of Samson—he was built for it (short of the piety: I remembered his careless "I wouldn't say I believe in God"). Father Doonan evidently understood him. I watched them hastily making a thick pad of the blankets. . . . I watched with incredulity as Father Doonan laid them across Charlie's shoulders. . . . I watched, cringing mentally, as Charlie slid under the yielding struts and shoved his protected back against the glowing embers, settling his thick toes in the earth for purchase.

He had been perspiring amply—the sweat leaped out on his heavy wooden face as he thrust hard against the struts, opposing the tilt of the bridge, scrabbling at the loose soil for grip, listening with a blind anxiety for the creak of the relieved wood. And then Father Doonan fell into place with him, as naturally as a pair of wily football forwards who have agreed on a preconceived plan. He bent underneath Charlie. The Negro placed his hands on the priest's stooped back, levering himself upward—I heard wood groan faintly, I didn't see the bridge slope back: men aren't bulldozers; but when Father Doonan muttered something urgently the Matron put her foot on the bridge, walked a few feet suicidally farther, and the structure seemed to have stopped its sag.

I have never seen a woman so petrified in my life—she grinned back at me frozenly. I should have offered to go, it would have been a gallant instinct, but I have always thought gallantry is for young men who are fond of *panache*. The Nazis in Vienna spoiled me for *panache*. I

didn't look at her—I made the busy useless gesture of trying to beat out the sneaking flames that were nibbling at
the wood. Then the Matron stared at Charlie and Father
Doonan, crouched like horse and rider under the bridge—
they couldn't hold together for long, wrenching their guts
in that inconceivable posture. . . .

I had to burst out, in sheer pity for them, "Hurry up.
Walk."

She began to walk. She went the way a mannequin goes
—stiff back, looking blankly ahead—impervious to the
audience, as if books are piled on the skull. Of course, she
was terrified of looking down. The bridge made its rebellious grunting noises, yielding wood chafing wood; she
reached the middle, a couple of distorted treads rattled
under her feet, then she was on the last span and her nerve
broke . . . she made a bitter sound and broke into a
panicky run. Harry Frobisher was waiting for her. She
fell into his arms ravenously on the other side.

I had just said to Father Doonan futilely, "Can I help?"
and his voice came bursting out of his chest—it was as
spasmodic and uncontrolled as the sweat gushing out of
his face——"Now the children. Hurry. Not too many at a
time."

I lined them up, smacking the sleepiest to rouse them.
Perhaps sleep was the kindliest kind of drug—they didn't
know where they were going; they were insensitive to fear.
I sent them off in pairs, one behind the other, and they
went trudging disinterestedly into the moonlight. The
bridge, I swear, was human: the sounds its wooden throat
made were vindictive: it *threatened* us. I kept the corner
of my eye on the main struts, charred to the core; I saw
them flaking, but the bodies, the flesh and bone of Charlie
and Father Doonan, were reinforcing them. I was more
aghast . . . infinitely more, as the pattering feet of the
children echoed hollowly across the bridge, losing them-

236

selves in the moonlight . . . to smell wool burning.

I looked at Charlie's face: his mouth was wide; it was the featureless face of an animal. The hot embers were eating into the blankets, into the skin of his back—I didn't know which I smelled chiefly, the sour stench of burning wool or flesh.

I said to him painfully (who was it who was suffering the pain?), "Let me pad it again——" It wouldn't have helped much, the wood glowed too redly. And he looked at me blindly. A face out of the Inquisition, out of the Gestapo torture chambers . . . it was reeking flesh I smelled.

He gasped, "No," then again, spitting out the words like barbs, "No, get it over—quick—get it over." The first two pairs of children were across. They weren't much—skin, rickety bone. I sent them scurrying over four at a time. I said to them, making it more melodramatic than was necessary—they were all in a stupor—but I couldn't help it, "Run, run, in the name of God, run."

They scampered. The bridge creaked its resentment: the little bodies flew into the darkness, so that you couldn't pick out black skin against the massif of the gorge. I didn't want to set too many of them going. The whole structure looked so precarious.

Frobisher, by some kind of sensitive understanding, was priming me from the other side. As fast as they arrived he called out, "Next, next. Keep them going . . ." as if we had an endless supply of children to be piped across. There were twelve of them over now; and the next quartet already scuttling out along the grating wood. I heard Charlie make a thick beastly sound; I didn't dare look at the anguished face. I fumbled with my bottle for water to douse his back, but it was empty; and all the time the abominable smell of scorching flesh dragged at my nose. I shook as if in a fever. It was insupportable to the spectator—what must it have been like to him? I was crying out to the children as they fled from me across the gorge, "Be quick, be quick . . ." I meant, be quick to run from death, for I could see the gutted foundations giving, charcoal cracking, the mass of the bridge beginning to lean.

I looked at Father Doonan. He was crouched under Charlie like a fetus—he bore the thrust of the black man on his back in that dark womb under the bridge. I saw his feet digging convulsively into the soil, hands shoving at his knees. Atlas bearing more than his share of the world . . .

Then the last two pairs of children were on their way; I beckoned to Sonia (she had just been sick, I suppose the reek of burning flesh is the most nauseating of all smells) to get ready. She picked up one of the cripples. I whispered to Camille: she picked up another of the helpless children. It was the greatest risk of all, to send them across together, but the blind girl had to be guided; and when Harry Frobisher's voice called out urgently from his dark haven I said to them, "Go now, walk gently. Don't stop, don't look down."

I was giving orders like a general sending intrepid soldiers into battle—a general who hadn't yet tasted combat, whose bowels were beginning to loosen because his share of it was soon to come. The two girls walked across the bridge, carrying the cripples. I lost sight of them. The bridge made its treacherous machine-gun creaks. I thought, 'Count twenty, no more, and the whole carbonized structure'll be gone.'

I heard Charlie's horrid whisper: it pulled my eyes to his face, to his rolled eyeballs. Father Doonan must have heard the sound and I think he was moaning sympathetically. The Negro's back was raw with glowing wool, the blankets were charred, sticking gluily to the rawly blistered flesh. Then . . .

Harry Frobisher's voice sounded triumphantly, "All across." He was waiting for me. I picked up the last of the crippled children—it happened to be Marcel's tiny jockey; I knew that as long as it lived I would in some way always think of it as Marcel's flesh. And I willed my feet on to the first treads of the bridge. I had the dour feeling as I went that I was walking on the tortured backs of Charlie and Father Doonan; and I thought strangely, as if it had only just occurred to me (it hadn't), 'Who holds the bridge up for *them* to come across?' But when you have a cracking foundation under your feet—and below that a black windy gorge—you have the kind of spur that keeps you moving, that banishes all thought.

I felt the crunching sideways sway of the bridge, I heard the rasping timber mutter . . . the sensation was dreadful: eyes and stomach combined against me, the bowels joined the conspiracy, I wanted to stop and get my balance, to clutch something despairingly for support. There were the side rails—on a slant—but I was afraid to touch them; I knew that if once I grabbed them for relief I would never let go of them, I would freeze to them helplessly.

And I did the unforgivable thing: I looked down.

It was the hollow murmurous vault of Tophet . . . I think I was behaving like a baby, swaying foolishly with the slip of the bridge, crying demeaningly. I looked into the confused face of Marcel's jockey. The baboon eyes were screwed up in bewilderment. I had brought recognizable fear for the first time into a child's life.

I passed the loose treads; the fire that Frobisher had put out; the last span approached. I walked with a stiff unbuckled movement, then I saw Frobisher's face coming out of the moonlight. I did what the Matron did, I ran to him.

He seized me. I felt his hands yank at my shoulder. The child was out of my arms and I was sitting on loose soil, shivering, wanting to vomit, a salvaged general who had won a personal battle but lost a war . . .

That was when I heard Frobisher's cheated cry. He had just made a spasmodic movement—shoving past me—he was three, four insane steps across the bridge, yelling. I heard wood rending like the Eiffel Tower coming down . . . the earth thudded as the struts on our side snapped; there was dust and exploding soil, and then Frobisher was staggering back—dragged back, I think, by the Matron— as the arch of the bridge fell from beneath him. The strange hollow sound from the gusty blackness, the distant wooden hammer like someone knocking on an empty tub, confused me . . . for a moment I didn't realize that it was the great timbers of the bridge clattering into the gorge.

Frobisher lay on me, clutching my shoulder madly. He was shouting, as if I had duped him, "We've left them, left them . . ." and I wanted to shout back, 'What's your brain been doing with itself these last few minutes, didn't you know that some of us would have to be left? That the noose would have to be put voluntarily around somebody's neck?' I didn't say it—I didn't say anything—I felt too much like Judas; the betrayal had been accomplished, we had the children's lives, our thirty pieces of silver.

I just shoved him off and said feebly, "You're hurting me."

Harry Frobisher started shouting across the gorge. There was no answer—at first, no recognizable answer— then the sounds I wanted to hear least: Charlie's puppy-like whimper, then the soft whisper of Father Doonan trying to console him. I could see Charlie lying on the ground, cradled in the priest's arms, the black face turned up in anguish, in accusation of the God he didn't believe in . . .

Harry Frobisher yelled, "Charlie!"

Father Doonan said quietly, "Go."

"Go? What do you . . . ?"

Then the voices, echoing from each side of the gorge, started conflicting—Father Doonan's was too soft, too lost; Frobisher's shouts simply didn't make sense, he was half incoherent. I shook him irritably. The instant he shut up it let us catch Father Doonan's resigned murmur:

"We're all right, don't worry. Hurry now. Go on, see to them, take them down."

"What the hell are you talking about? What about you?"

"Don't worry about us, I told you. We're going to be all right."

"For Christ's sake. Do you expect us to just . . . ?"

Father Doonan's voice rose, belligerently Irish, "Of course we expect it. What are we doing here? Why else did we come? Go on down—quick—see to the children. You mustn't waste time." And as the wordy battle went on, the frantic useless phrases tossed in the cold disinterested moonlight across the gorge, Frobisher leaning on his staff, gaunt with idiocy, yelling confusedly, Father Doonan made himself heard—even Frobisher had to be quiet. "Don't betray us. It mustn't be for nothing. Go—go—go," the bodiless voice insisted harshly . . . for the moon had slipped behind a cloud and I couldn't see the priest any more.

But finally I heard him. We were all so quiet—straining nervously to hear:

"We'll get together with you again. You'll see. We're just going a little ahead of you, that's all. We all have to meet sometime . . ." and I thought cynically, 'Where: in heaven? The membership qualifications could be a little difficult for some people, maybe not all of us are going to get into the club.' But do you know what moved me most terribly? The secret chuckle, that wild exaltation—the ripe assurance—in Father Doonan's voice. It started Frobisher off again . . . it was almost impossible to get that distracted creature to subside. The rest was lost in the jabbering echoes, the place was a vast sound box. The last words I caught from the other side, trying to reassure Frobisher, were, "God bless . . ." and then nothing. The Matron grabbed hold of Frobisher's arm.

She wasn't callous; she was the only one among us who was able to put first things first. She said to him, "We have to go."

Frobisher said, "What?" vaguely; he didn't move. I looked timidly at the raw edge of light beginning raggedly to compete with the stars. Dawn wouldn't hold off forever. I saw Frobisher looking at it, too. He shouted over for the last time, "Wait . . ." as if the pair on the other side might take it into their heads to stray foolishly and get lost. He stumbled round on us and we all went scampering down the slope.

I was the hindmost. For an instant—unnecessarily, as usual—I looked back.

The moon had slipped out again, slanting full on the two men across the gorge. It was the kind of intimate picture you get sometimes when a train slides unexpectedly by a nakedly lighted bedroom window: it gives you the queerest thrill because you know you're not supposed to look. I saw Father Doonan whispering to Charlie. He was holding him up, caressing him, trying to relieve his burned back. I wondered curiously what he was saying to him. Perhaps it was just the abandoned posture of the two men? I don't want you to think me blasphemous, but it reminded me of something, those ultimate words of comfort—you know where they come from, who it was said them to that other malefactor—"Today shalt thou be with me in paradise" . . . then the train slid past the window, taking me with it.

The children, insensitive to sacrifice like all children,

were departing quickly, leaving their saviors to their inescapable paradise.

I thought shakenly, 'That'll finally cure you of looking back.'

It took us an hour and a half to get down to the outskirts of the town. By then the sky was almost gray with light. We only broke the descent once—to give the torpid, succumbing children a breathing space—then we shoved them on unfeelingly. Father Doonan had said it would be easy all the way now. And it was. . . . He'd said, with that naïve inflexible assurance of his, "The Norwegian Captain's a good man. He promised; of course he'll be there." Well, he was.

Frobisher was the first to see the schooner; he stood, swaying on his crutch, pointing to the apparition of the spindle masts, a pair of dark matchsticks just outside the reef. We went on like maniacs. We were shouting, shouting frenziedly (where did we get the breath from? I don't know)—we were afraid they'd never hear us, so we lit some pine branches, waving the torches like crazed Walpurgisnight revelers as we rushed down into the town.

The place was a forsaken shambles. The last eruption had demolished it like an executioner working his will on a corpse. A few shops burned raggedly; except for that empty crackle there was the silence of death in the rubbled streets. A ghost town . . . nothing moving in it but a dog. It came yapping wildly out of a gutted cottage, attaching itself to us.

It could never have expected its providential survival. The mongrel lives on here in Tahiti—one of the restaurants has it—like us, maybe, a monument to the astonishing tenacity of life.

And so we came in a final excruciating stagger to the

wharf. They'd seen us; a boat was pulling round the reef to pick us up. The Norwegian Captain must have given up hope that his charitable vigil would pay off; in fact he was watching us with incredulity from the deck. He told me later that in four and a half minutes (the dead time of sunup) he would have made off with all sail from that fissionable slag heap of an island; he hadn't slept a wink for two nights, just watching the glaring disintegrated crater. He said it was like standing helplessly in a zoo while a dangerous beast got ready to break out of its cage.

Very simply, like an undecorated veteran, "We smelled its breath," I said.

So we sprawled there in the gray light—a litter of human refuse—waiting on the edge of the wharf. And then Harry Frobisher came up to me, tugging at my arm. He had left Camille; she was dozing numbly on the jetty. He looked at her nervously, drawing me aside.

"Tell her something for me, will you?" he muttered, and I knew then that he was in a terrible state: that we could expect something unpredictably emotional from him.

But I couldn't unglue my eyelids. I was dying to snatch a few moments of sleep while the boat approached. I said petulantly, "She's here, isn't she? Why don't you tell her yourself?"

He shrank back. "No, I couldn't bear to talk to her. You could put it into words for me. Tell her I'll see her sometime, you'll know what to say."

I was still two-thirds drowned by sleep and I said, "I don't know what you mean."

"I have to go back."

That woke me up. "Go back?" I stared at him. "What are you talking about, go back?"

His voice began to rise, "We can't just leave them up there by themselves, can we? Somebody has to be with them."

"But there isn't anything you can do for them."

"That isn't the point, is it?"

"What *is* the point? What good could it do?"

He repeated angrily, as if I had no feelings, "Somebody has to be with them. Just sit with them, talk with them. They mustn't be there by themselves."

"It would be utterly senseless."

He said sullenly, "That's my affair."

The Matron was listening with stupefaction; she couldn't believe her ears. She cried, "How could it help them? They are lost."

"Worse than that," Frobisher said to her strangely. "They're alone."

He was still looking at Camille: from that moment until he disappeared finally I don't think he took his eyes off her.

The Matron shouted, "You are mad." She turned on me furiously, as if by sheer neglect I was letting something dreadful happen, "Talk to him."

"Listen," I said persuasively, seizing Frobisher's arm. "Wait a minute. Let's talk it over . . ." But he shook me off, backing away, as if afraid he might be talked out of it, adjusting himself on that pathetically rudimentary crutch.

"You tell her," he said obstinately, nodding over towards the sleeping Camille.

He stood a few feet distant—half a ghost already—almost as unsubstantial as his comrades up there on the other side of the gorge. The red flush from the crater made the whole scene unreal; perhaps that was why I felt so helpless? Everything about it was unbelievable. . . . He was arguing feebly, "It's no good, it just wouldn't be any good. We've been together too long, me and Charlie and Marcel, it's been like three men standing on one pair of legs. His, too, lately," he muttered, looking up, and I knew that the one he meant was Father Doonan. What an odd picture it gave me—three men united hopelessly on one pair of legs, a sad indivisible abortion—with Father Doonan propping them up.

And all the time Frobisher was moving away from me. He just wouldn't let me approach.

I think I know what had happened to him. Men can suddenly take a long look at themselves: they stop seeing the stranger they have created for their private vanity; for the first time they see a friend with whom they can share bad news. I wanted to stop him. I said again—I could hardly see him now, he simply wouldn't let me get near him—"Wait, wait . . ."

I heard his faint murmur, "How could I be the only one to come out? I'd be lost, I couldn't live with myself. I knew the minute I had to shove Marcel under . . ." but I never found out what he really knew: there was no face to peer into, to reason with, he was a hobbling withdrawing shadow.

The Matron shouted after him passionately, "You'll miss the boat."

He was at the far end of the jetty now. I heard his dim sardonic chuckle ". . . I missed that a long time ago."

"He can't be allowed to," the Matron said to me. "Stop him, quickly, before it's too late."

"What are you going to do?" I cried out. I took a few abortive steps after him. I couldn't see him any more.

There was no answer. I ran to the end of the jetty. I strained to listen for the tap-tap of his crutch, but the grumble of the mountain killed it. I thought for a moment I saw something retreating quickly along the burning street—but the shadows were jumping fitfully, I don't know if it was him I saw in the distance. I stood there guiltily, shouting out, "Frobisher, Frobisher!" Still no answer. I knew he was gone.

Then I heard the Matron calling out to me. The boat had arrived. It was no use waiting. I walked back, knowing that the Matron would look at me accusingly, strick-enly, for somebody would have to be blamed; that we would now have to explain it to Camille; that, sooner or later, I would have to start explaining it to my conscience. And however would I do that?

We were some miles off the island in the schooner when the business of dawn was finally done. The hot ball of the sun was moving zestfully over the horizon, but the sea had a still maidenly pallor—a cool expectant silence, as if the whole serious ritual of sunup had to be respectfully observed. The island lay, barely visible, a smoky smudge on the rim of the ocean; something red twinkled on its summit. It might have lighted a beacon to say farewell.

The pilgrimage was over; we were safe, and I couldn't get used to the sensation of safety. It seemed to be a wholly unnatural state.

The children were heaped all over the deck—small blown candles—finally submerged in sleep. The Matron was huddled like a felled pugilist with the nurses. I won-dered if she had told Camille: the girl lay inertly with her head on the Matron's lap. I was too exhausted to sleep—my nerves too vibrant—but I knew that in a little while fatigue would start to possess me, and I stood solitarily at the rail, watching the island fall over the horizon, like a man who has swallowed a barbiturate waiting patiently for it to take effect. . . .

. . . The shadows of dawn disappeared suddenly in a photographic glare; a rival to the sun boiled into the sky; in that vast yellow flush the ocean glittered as nakedly as a woman caught in her bath. For a measurable time the dazzle hung there, effervescent, the glowing froth rolling up into that uncomfortably familiar mushroom lid. The island had blown itself out of the sea.

I had been staring straight at it: it seared my eyeballs. I had been thinking loosely of the men who hadn't come away with us, and in the instant of that hurtful dazzle—before even the thunderclap of the explosion reached us—I thought vacantly: 'Where are they now? Part of that Biblically theatrical vapor rushing up into the sky . . . ?'

Maybe it was just that I was emotionally triggered for it: but I saw them all in a kind of queer processional intimacy—almost nudging my elbow—against that brief religious flash. Charlie, the heavy black face glimmering at me blandly, "You're telling yourself bad fairy tales, you'll frighten yourself to death . . ." Marcel sampling the Matron's buttocks wickedly, "No Frenchman can resist a fine female bottom. This one was made to be pinched . . ." Harry Frobisher, propped on his staff, peering at me amusedly because suddenly I needed his help, "You'll live to buy me a drink . . ." And Father Doonan—assuring me fervently, "We have to show them that we have faith in them, it's their only salvation, don't you see . . . ?"

And then the bang of the explosion flitted across the sea, erasing them. I felt the blast hotly—a belch from the pit. Everybody became insanely busy about the deck. The Captain was shouting something about the tidal wave, they were rushing to batten down hatches, but I didn't wait for it. The barbiturate of exhaustion was finally working. I went stumbling below.

They tell me that the tidal wave was something to see. That it came flooding spectacularly out of the gassy hole in the ocean. But I didn't see anything of it, not even a ripple. I was asleep the instant I fell into the bunk.

I slept like a stupefied dog half the way to Tahiti. Hamlet—it was Hamlet, wasn't it?—said, "What a piece of work is a man!" When I woke up it was out of my system. I was ravenously hungry. I never felt better in my life.